THE CURE FOR LOVE

AND OTHER TALES OF THE BIOTECH REVOLUTION

by

Brian Stableford

The Borgo Press
An Imprint of Wildside Press

MMVII

CONTENTS

Introduction..5
About the Author 6

The Cure for Love...7
Ashes and Tombstones...29
Slumming in Voodooland 46
The Color of Envy..66
The Lady-Killer, as Observed from a Safe Distance 93
Busy Dying 114
The Man Who Invented Good Taste....................................139
The Road to Hell 156
The Scream..179

ABOUT THE AUTHOR

BRIAN STABLEFORD was born in Yorkshire in 1948. He taught at the University of Reading for several years, but is now a full-time writer. He has written many science fiction and fantasy novels, including: *The Empire of Fear*, *The Werewolves of London*, *Year Zero*, *The Curse of the Coral Bride*, and *The Stones of Camelot*. Collections of his short stories include: *Sexual Chemistry: Sardonic Tales of the Genetic Revolution*, *Designer Genes: Tales of the Biotech Revolution*, and *Sheena and Other Gothic Tales*. He has written numerous nonfiction books, including *Scientific Romance in Britain, 1890-1950*, *Glorious Perversity: The Decline and Fall of Literary Decadence*, and *Science Fact and Science Fiction: An Encyclopedia*. He has contributed hundreds of biographical and critical entries to reference books, including both editions of *The Encyclopedia of Science Fiction* and several editions of the library guide, *Anatomy of Wonder*. He has also translated numerous novels from the French language, including several by the feuilletonist Paul Féval.

INTRODUCTION

The nine stories in this collection belong to a loosely-knit series tracking the potential effects of possible developments in biotechnology on the evolution of global society. Most involve relatively moderate variations of the future history sketched out in a series of novels comprising *Inherit the Earth* (1998), *Architects of Emortality* (1999), *The Fountains of Youth* (2000), *The Cassandra Complex* (2001), *Dark Ararat* (2002) and *The Omega Expedition* (2002), all published by Tor, which was itself a modified version of a future history mapped in *The Third Millennium: A History of the World 200-3000 A.D.* (Sidgwick & Jackson 1985, written in collaboration with David Langford).

The broad sweep of this future history envisages a large-scale economic and ecological collapse in the twenty-first century brought about by global warming and other factors, followed by the emergence of a global society designed to accommodate human longevity (although that is not necessarily obvious in stories set in advance of the Crash). Other stories of a similar stripe can be found in two earlier collections, *Sexual Chemistry: Sardonic Tales of the Genetic Revolution* (Simon & Schuster U.K. 1991) and *Designer Genes: Tales of the Biotech Revolution* (Five Star, 2004), and in two companion collections from Borgo: *The Tree of Life and Other Tales of the Biotech Revolution* and *In the Flesh and Other Tales of the Biotech Revolution* (both 2007).

Four of the stories first appeared in *Isaac Asimov's Science Fiction*: "The Cure for Love" in the mid-December 1993 issue, "The Scream" in the July 1994 issue, "The Ladykiller, as Observed from a Safe Distance" in the August 2000 issue, and "The Color of Envy" in the May 2001 issue.

5

THE CURE FOR LOVE, BY BRIAN STABLEFORD

"The Man Who Invented Good Taste" and "The Road to Hell" first appeared in *Interzone* in issues #45 (March 1991) and #97 (July 1995), respectively. "Slumming in Voo-dooland" first appeared as *Pulphouse Short Story Paperback* #26 (1991). "Busy Dying" first appeared in the February 1994 issue of *The Magazine of Fantasy & Science Fiction.* "Ashes and Tombstones" first appeared in *Moon Shots* (DAW 1999), edited by Peter Crowther.

—Brian Stableford
April 2007

THE CURE FOR LOVE

It was the expression on the man's face that caught her gaze and made her stop to take a longer look at him. He was standing on the pavement that skirted the open space in front of the King's Manor, staring at Bootham Bar and the Theatre Royal in the bemused manner of one struggling to reconcile old memories with changed appearances, mesmerized by the combination of the new and the half-familiar. It was only because she guessed *what* he was—a native of the town who had been away for a long time—that she was able to take the further step of realizing *who* he was.

He was Don Sherrington, and she had been at school with him for five years, before she left to have the baby. She had last seen him three years after that, before he and Di left the city for good.

She walked towards him, but before she spoke she hesitated, wondering if, after all, she might be mistaken—and wondering too, whether there was any point in saying anything to him even if she were not. Had it happened six months before, she might have smiled to herself and walked on, but she was more vulnerable to impulse nowadays, and she stopped, then moved to stand beside him and said: "Excuse me, but aren't you Don Sherrington?"

He turned his pale blue eyes on her, without any particular expression on his face. She saw him squint slightly through his spectacles as he brought her face into focus and tried to place it. It would have been nice if he had recognized her at once, but he couldn't.

"I'm Catherine Tyldesley—Catherine Grant when you first knew me."

For a second or two he was still struggling, but then the memory clicked into place and he blinked. "Carrie Grant!" he said, smiling faintly at the stale old joke, its comicality renewed by a combination of long disuse and nostalgia.

"That's right," she said. "Carrie. It must be twelve or fourteen years since...."

"It must have been 1991," he said. "The summer of 1991."

How typical of him, she thought, to be able to remember the date as soon as the name clicked. He always had a memory like a computer. But then she realized that it must be easy enough for him to remember the year when he left to go south on the big adventure. He probably didn't remember the last time he had seen her at all.

"We were at school together until '88," she told him, to demonstrate that she too had a head for dates, even though she was only subtracting three from 1991. You stayed on when I left. You and Di."

"Yes," he said. "You had to get married." As he said it he must have realized how it sounded, because he suddenly blushed and looked uncomfortable. The blush brought on a sudden fit of nostalgia, because she remembered that they had both blushed that same way—he and Di—when they were kids. Their complexions were so pale that their blushes always stood out like traffic lights.

"It's all right," she said, quickly. "It's true. Pregnant at fifteen, married at sixteen, divorced at twenty-three, dead on my feet at thirty-one. I bet your life's been much more interesting. I read something about you in the paper, you know—must have been about five or six years ago. Said you were in...I'm not sure—something to do with viruses."

"Virus engineering," he said.

"What brings you back here?" she asked.

"I'm running away," he said, so soberly that for a moment she had the bizarre idea that he was on the run from the police. But then he pinked again and flashed her a half-embarrassed smile, and she knew that he only meant that he had come back up north to get away from London for a while. A sentimental journey, no doubt. But then the smile died and the sobriety came back, and she realized that the carelessness of his earlier remark had been born of a genuine preoccupation. His smiles were more than slightly forced. He was distracted; maybe he had come away to give himself a chance to think.

She took her courage in both hands, surprised to discover how much courage she actually needed in order to ask, and said: "I can give you somewhere to hide for a while, if you like. My flat's only ten minutes away, out towards the football ground. It'd be nice to talk about old times."

His embarrassment was suddenly increased again, and he looked down at the bag which he was carrying in his right hand. It was one of those many-zipped contraptions carefully designed to the maximum dimensions that airlines allowed as hand-baggage, and it seemed to be full.

"I'm not sure I have time," he said. "I haven't found a hotel yet...I just wanted to walk around a bit while the sun's still shining."

"It's only four o'clock," she said, defensively. Her heart sank at the thought of her invitation being turned down, after she'd risked so much in asking. "The tourist season never really ends these days, but it is November—you won't have any trouble getting a room. Just a cup of coffee."

She saw his eyes change again as he caught on to the fact that she wasn't just being polite—that she actually wanted him to come.

"All right," he said. "That's very kind."

She turned away, and he fell into step with her.

"How's Di?" she asked, when it became clear that he couldn't find anything to say. "Do you see much of her these days?"

"She's dead," he said, so simply and so brutally that she was stabbed by shock. She felt tears well up in her eyes, though she knew how silly that was, given that she hadn't seen Di Sherrington in thirteen years, and hadn't been particularly friendly even when they were girls together at school.

"Oh!" she said, when she had taken control of herself. "I'm sorry, Don...I didn't know. What...when...?"

"Five years ago," he said, dully. She expected him to elaborate, but he didn't. Suddenly, the cup of coffee and the cozy chat about old times didn't seem like such a good idea. If Di was dead, how could they possibly laugh together about the times they'd had at school? Whatever they remembered, Di would be center-stage. Di had always been center-stage.

In fact, Carrie realized that she couldn't remember Don apart from Di at all. He had always been in her shadow. Everyone had always thought of Di as Don's "big sister," although they were twins. Di had only been an inch or so taller but she had been much more full of life, much more self-confident, much more grown-up. Girls matured so much faster than boys that a teenage girl was always likely to outgrow a twin brother, but there had been more to it than that. Di had been much more lively than Don, much more sociable, much more popular. Everybody had loved Di.

Carrie remembered that she had been a little bit stuck on Don at one time—when they were twelve, or maybe thirteen—because he was so frail and serious and *pretty*. But when she'd got a little bit older she'd started to look for more masculine and masterful traits in her boyfriends, and had come to think of prettiness as an unfortunate attribute in a boy, suggestive of wimpishness or queerness. God, what a fool she had been! If only she had had the sense to stick with the wimps! But it wouldn't have done her any good to stay stuck on Don Sherrington, she knew. He had been too shy to be lured out of his shell; too nervous and inarticulate—in spite of his unusual cleverness—ever to get into a relationship with anyone who didn't happen to have been born his twin.

But Di was dead! Dead at twenty-six!

Carrie didn't have the nerve to probe for more details. If he was going to tell her what had happened, he would have to tell her in his own time and in his own way. But she couldn't think of any other way of re-opening the conversation. How could she switch from the news that Di was dead to some by-the-way enquiry about how the virus engineering was going, or how long he planned to stay, or whereabouts he was living down in the capital city? All she needed to make the disaster complete was for Don to take it into his head to ask about Malcolm—but mercifully, he didn't. He probably couldn't remember Malcolm's name, if he had ever heard it.

She was glad when they reached the flat, so that she could tell him to sit down and hang up his coat for him and ask him how he took his coffee. By the time she had boiled the kettle and made the coffee and poured it into mugs she had decided how best to carry on.

"I've been living here for fifteen years," she told him. "Stuck in a time warp. My mother still lives two streets away. She's divorced too, now—got out just after me. Only time in my life I ever set anyone a good example."

"I don't remember your husband very well," said Don, warily.

"Gavin Tyldesley," she said. "He was two years ahead of us at the comp. You wouldn't have known him, unless you were one of the smaller boys he bullied."

Don winced slightly at that, and dropped his eyes to stare into his coffee cup. "I didn't get bullied much," he said. "They were all afraid of Di, I think. Even if they weren't scared that she'd hit them, they all wanted her to like them."

"I could have done with some protection myself," said Carrie, trying to sound flippant but not succeeding. "If I'd only kept an aspirin between my knees I wouldn't have needed so many later to stop my head ringing." She was surprised—not by her bitterness but by the fact that she felt free to let it out to someone she hadn't seen for so long, and hadn't really known that well. She could see that he was surprised too, but he was less embarrassed now. He was beginning to relax—but not because he felt at ease...more as if he were being claimed by some awful tiredness.

"He used to hit you?" he said, but not as though he thought the idea was unduly shocking or horrible.

"Only when he was drunk. He had fits of thinking that I'd ruined his life by tying him down when he was only eighteen. When he was sober he knew how useless he was, but when he was half-cut he began to get delusions of lost opportunity. Not that he thought he could have gone to university, of course, but he did think that he could have gone to London and *made it*."

"Made what?"

11

"I don't know. He never said. Become a yuppie, I guess—we had yuppies in those days, didn't we?"

"Yes," said Don, with a faraway look in his eye which suggested that he was remembering. "We certainly did. I guess I was one."

"No you weren't," she told him. "You got a degree, and went into something worthwhile. Yuppies were parasites, but virus engineers are conquering disease and making the world a better place. If they get rich, they deserve it."

"Maybe," he said, quietly. "Not that I *am* rich. And not everyone thinks virus engineers are so wonderful, even if we did manage to cure the common cold. Some people find the whole idea frightening."

"I may have left school early," she said, "but I'm not a moron. I've been going to night classes for four years, and I've just started an Open University degree. I know that virus engineering isn't a matter of inventing new plagues, and that it goes a long way beyond trying to cure the plagues we already live with."

He blushed again. "I'm sorry," he said. "I really didn't mean...."

"No," she said, "of course you didn't. God, isn't this difficult? Here we are, both in our thirties, remembering each other as silly school kids. No wonder we're dying of embarrassment! But I liked you when we were little—I really did. I fancied you when I was twelve." She hadn't meant to say that, even though it was true enough, but it had slipped out as she tried to rescue the conversation from terminal awfulness, and now she had to worry about whether it had made things even worse.

His reaction to the revelation was odd. Instead of reddening again and looking down at the mug which he was cradling defensively in his hands he looked her straight in the eye, with an authority and confidence of which she had judged him incapable, and in a tone replete with honest puzzlement, he said: "Did you?"

It was her turn to blush. "Yes," she said. "Quite a few of us did, on the quiet. But you didn't notice us at all."

He continued looking at her for three seconds, then dropped his gaze. "I never knew that," he said. "I thought nobody liked me. I thought everybody liked Di."

"Everybody did," said Carrie. "But you were her twin brother. Why shouldn't they like you too?"

"We weren't identical twins," he said, matter-of-factly. "In fact, there were never two siblings less alike."

"That's not true," she told him. "Your faces were very similar, and you had the same blond hair. Maybe the look suited a girl rather better than a boy, and the specs didn't do you any favors, but..."

"That's not what I meant," he interrupted. "I meant *temperamentally*."

"Oh," said Carrie. "Well, maybe. But there's nothing wrong with being quiet and shy...." She stopped when she saw the way he was looking at her. It was all bullshit, she knew. When kids were that age, there was a lot wrong with being quiet and shy. That was why she had grown out of her slightly sentimental attitude to Don Sherrington, and started wiggling her stupid fanny at the likes of Gavin Tyldesley, because he was older, and didn't give a damn about the teachers, and acted as though he could hand out a licking to the whole bloody world.

In fact, of course, the only thing Gavin could consistently hand out a licking to was her—and it had been quiet little Don Sherrington, always hiding behind his sister's skirts, who had really had it in him to get to grips with the world and play his part in changing the course of history. Carrie looked at him now, still pale and apparently ineffectual, and wished that she had had the sense to love him, and let him get her up the stick.

She wondered, recklessly brazen in the privacy of her own thoughts, whether she could do it now. Could she keep him here all night, instead of letting him go forth in search of a hotel? Could she make up, even if it were just for one night, for nineteen years of folly? It had been a long time since she had let a man fuck her, and she hadn't missed it at all—but she missed, or thought she did if her memory wasn't playing tricks with her—the way she had felt about Don Sherrington when she had been twelve years old.

That's sick! she suddenly thought, disgusted with herself. *Jesus, have I done so little with my life that I can go gaga about a kid I once simpered at in the back row of Mrs. Hatton's class, before I even started having periods?*

But she couldn't drown the chain of thought in the acid of self-loathing, because the very next thought that came into her head was more shameful still. *At least*, she thought, *I've got him on his own. I don't have to compete with Di. She's dead and buried.*

That really pricked her conscience, and made her say: "I'm very sorry about Di. I really am. I hope I didn't hurt you by asking about her. It must have been terrible, with your being so close—although I suppose you drifted apart in time. Was she married? Are you?"

She had to close here mouth firmly to stop the babble and give him a chance to respond.

"No," he said, calmly enough. "We hadn't drifted apart. We were still sharing a place when she died. Neither of us married. But you mustn't feel bad about asking. To save further blushes, I suppose I'd better say now that she died of AIDS. It was the mutated C-7 strain—we caught up with it soon after, of course, but not quickly enough to save her."

That stopped her train of dirty fantasies all right. She could see the tragedy in what he was saying only too clearly. He was a virus engineer, but his twin sister had been killed by a virus, just before the virus engineers had finally figured out how to stop it spreading. A real sickener.

So they had still been living under the same roof! She remembered the dirty jokes the kids had used to make about Don loving his sister and her loving him. Nasty jokes, born as often as not of fierce jealousy. All the boys had wanted to get into Di's knickers. Some of them had, too—but only some. Di had been no slag, although she had had an awkward habit of falling in love, too deeply and too often.

Didn't we all? Carrie thought, just before she began to wonder—because she couldn't help it—whether Don Sherrington might possibly have AIDS, and where he might have caught it from. She wished momentarily that she hadn't invited him back—not because he might have AIDS, but because his presence was making her think things she didn't much like herself for thinking.

"You're quite safe," he said, awkwardly, making her scream inwardly at the thought that he might have read her mind.

But he hadn't. "We're very careful at the labs," he went on. "We're in contact with nasty bugs all the time, but we take great care not to let them out. I know people get worried about what virus engineers might have caught at work, but...it's...." He trailed off, as though he had lost himself in mid-sentence.

"I'm not scared," she said, a fraction sharply.

He set his mug down suddenly. It still had an inch of coffee in it. "I shouldn't have come in," he said. "I'm sorry. It was thoughtless of me. I'd better go and find a...."

She cut him off before he spoke the final word. "Please," she said. "Don't go. I know I'm being stupid, but don't go. Of course I know you're not bringing any vile germs into my flat, and I really never meant to imply that you might be. I know it's embarrassing because I didn't know about Di, and asked about her in the wrong way, but I really would like you to stay for a while and talk to me because I'm lonely and because it really is nice to be reminded of a time before my life got into such a mess. I want you to stay, and I want us both to pull ourselves together and start being pleasant and civilized, and if you can't stand to stay I shall be very disappointed. Please."

She said it all quickly, not knowing whether it was sensible or stupid or whether it could possibly paper over the cracks or make things ten times worse. But she did want him to stay, for all the reasons she had cited as well as the unmentionable ones.

He hadn't managed to stand up yet, but he didn't look as if he intended to stay sitting down.

"I'm afraid you don't understand," he said. "I lied to you a few moments ago. You see, I really shouldn't have come into your home, because I *am* carrying a virus. You're quite safe, even though I've drunk out of your mug, because it would require prolonged intimate contact to infect you, and it's nothing anywhere near as bad as AIDS, but even so, I don't really have the right to come in here...or any-where...without telling people. I don't even have the right to be running away...not really."

He stopped, just as she had, because he didn't know whether he had said far too much, and made things ten times worse.

She stared at him. She wasn't in the least scared. In fact, she was glad. She was glad because she thought there was just a possibility that he might tell her the big secret whose existence he had just revealed to her. He, Don Sherrington, might tell her, Carrie Tyldesley, a secret! If only it could be something really awful—something which would bind them together in a conspiracy of shared silence! If only....

"I meant it," she said. "I really did like you a lot. I really wish I had told you. It would have been nice."

That threw him off balance, and made him hesitate. Good!

"No it wouldn't," he said, warily. "Twelve year old boys can't handle that kind of confession from twelve year old girls. I'd probably have been terribly rude to you, and I would have regretted it so much when I remembered it when you spoke to me out there in the square that...."

"But you can handle it now," she said. "And I want you to stay. Why should I care what kind of a virus you've got, if I can't catch it?"

She thought she had lost when he stood up, and said: "It's impossible. We don't even know one another. I'm sorry, but...." But then he sat down again, and finished the sentence with different words than those he'd started out to say. "...I'm being very rude, aren't I? And we do know one another, don't we? In fact, I probably know you at least as well as anyone I've met since I went away, even though we were never particular friends."

She knew then that he was going to tell her. Not right away, but eventually. She knew, too, that she was going to be able to hang on to him, at least for one night. He didn't really want to go to a hotel. Maybe he didn't really want to be anywhere, but now he was somewhere, he would cling to it at least for a little while.

He's going to tell me everything, she thought, trium-phantly. *Everything.*

And she was right.

* * * * * * *

"It's a long story," he warned her, when the time finally came. It was late; they had eaten dinner, and he had drunk enough wine to loosen his tongue, knowing full well that that was what it would do.

"I don't mind," she said, awarding herself full marks for understatement.

"It's all to do with Di."

"I guessed."

He nodded, slowly. "I didn't call her Di, you know—not in private. Our parents gave us the same initials—I suppose it's the kind of silly thing you do when you suddenly become the parents of twins. I was Donald James and she was Diana Josephine. To Mum, Dad and the world we were Don and Di, but as soon as we were old enough to think it was a neat idea we decided that to one another, we'd always be Jay and Jo. We could see that other people thought that our relation-ship was special, and we wanted it to be extra-special. I guess it's a natural hazard of being twins, even if you're non-identical.

"We were always very close—you probably thought we were close at school, but you didn't see what we were like at home. We were very different, though. She used to say that I was the brains and she was the brawn, but that we were just two halves of the same person. Jay and Jo; day and night; introvert and extravert; yin and yang. Never alike at all, ex-cept in looks, but always tightly together. Unhealthy, I guess, in more ways than one—but it was unbreakable. However different the things were that we did when we were apart, they never affected the way we were together.

"Maybe it would have changed if Mum and Dad hadn't been killed in the plane crash, but that drove us more closely together, and whatever possibility there might have been of Jo staying up north while I went to university in London vanished completely. We had enough when the estate was settled to buy a nice flat, and that's what we did. I studied, got my degree, went on to do research, joined the Institute. Di worked as a temp—here, there, everywhere.

"We didn't necessarily see one another, even in the evenings. Di went out a lot, had lots of boyfriends. When she was working a long way from home she often went out of the flat before I got up, and didn't come back until I was in bed asleep. Sometimes she didn't come home at all, and sometimes she brought her boyfriends back to her own bed. We weren't living in one another's pockets, but we were always, in some special sense, together. If she'd ever actually moved out...but it never came to that. She could never stay infatuated long enough to set up home with anyone else, in spite of the fact that she could become utterly and completely besotted with the men she took up with. Do you remember what she used to be like when she fell in love?"

"Do I?" said Carrie. "We were all awful about it, but she was the worst. Really lovesick. Moony, hyperactive, anxious, ecstatic...the lot. Maybe she could have done as well as you did, if she'd ever been able to keep her mind on lessons instead of boys. Surely it was just a phase, though?"

"No," he said. "With Jo—Di, that is—it wasn't a phase. She joked about it, of course. She could see how ridiculous it was, and she'd have given it up if she only could. She got very embarrassed about it. 'The only good thing you can say about love,' she'd say, 'is that it doesn't last any longer than the common cold.' It was truer than she realized—because, you see, love really did hit Di with symptoms uncannily akin to some kind of virus attack. She would be literally feverish, always hyped up while she waited for the phone to ring, tearful if anything went wrong. And it really did hurt—quite literally. I didn't understand, for a long time, because I didn't see how it could. But it really was painful for her. Her infatuations disrupted her body chemistry in a big way. I guess it takes a lot of other people the same way, though not so extremely."

"It does," said Carrie, softly, remembering. She also remembered the other kind of hurt, which came along when love had turned to marriage and marriage to divorce, and babies into serpents' teeth. Bruises and anguish...bruises and

18

anguish. Malcolm had disrupted her body chemistry far more than Gavin ever had—and they called that love, too, didn't they?

"But I was very different," said Don, reflectively. "I was very calm, very placid. Jo used to say that I was lucky, because I never fell in love at all, and maybe she was right. But maybe she wasn't, because...."

He paused, but didn't meet Carrie's eye.

"Because you were in love with her," she prompted, remembering the dirty jokes but not meaning to imply anything sordid.

"Because I was in love with her," he echoed. Then, for the first time, he managed to surprise her. "I'd had sex with her, you know, long before we went to London. She lost her virginity when she was fifteen, long before...well, in the end, she said she'd show me how...teach me. So she did. She was very nice about it, and she stopped when she decided I'd got the hang of it, and wouldn't be too nervous with another girl...and I never asked her to do it again, or said that I wanted to, or anything. And I really didn't want to, much. She decided that she'd finished what she set out to do, and that was it. I didn't feel desperate about it, or even jealous of all the other boys she did it with...but I didn't feel, after I'd done it with Jo, that I wanted to do it with anyone else, either.

"I was at the opposite extreme, you see—my body chemistry didn't give me any trouble at all; it was always perfectly well-behaved. I was in love with her—completely, I suppose...but also quietly. Quite platonically, really, in spite of our brief interlude when we were seventeen.

"I coped with the ups and downs of her love life reasonably well, I think. I didn't try to calm her down when she was as high as a kite on her own hormones, but I was always ready with hot chocolate and sympathy when she came down again. Hot chocolate was our private ritual; we used to joke about its therapeutic value. It was the only medicine that really seemed to help.

"I was the one who fended off the aggrieved boyfriends when she got bored and couldn't face them any more, and I was the one who got soaked by tears when she sobbed her heart out because her passion of the month was unrequited or had led to disappointment. She asked me often enough what was wrong with her, and why she had to feel and behave the way she did, and at first I simply told her that it was just the way of things...but when things did go wrong I could hardly help thinking about it, and wishing I could do something to ease her grief and her turmoil...and eventually I realized that, just because it was just the way of things, it didn't mean that nothing could be done about it. So I set out to find a cure."

"A cure for love-sickness?" said Carrie—not because she was amazed, but because he had paused, and seemed to need a cue to carry on.

"That's right," he said. "It really was a kind of *sickness*. The fact that it wasn't caused by a virus or a bacterium was really secondary. It was a sickness whose effects—once you isolated the physical from the mental—were in many ways very like the effects of some virus-infections, and that made me think of treating it in the same way. Do you know what an antivirus is?"

"Vaguely," Carrie told him, hoping that she did know, because she didn't want him to think that she was too stupid to understand. "It's a new way of treating diseases—a new way of making people immune. The old way—the injections we all had when we were kids—worked on the body's immune system, making it produce antibodies that would kill the disease germs without it actually having to go through all the symptoms. Antiviruses bring a whole new defense-system into the body...I don't know the technical details. You'll have to explain that."

"It's not so very complicated," he said. "Viruses are lumps of DNA wrapped in protein coats. They can't survive long outside a living cell and they can only reproduce themselves by hijacking the apparatus that a host cell has for producing its own proteins and reproducing its own nucleic acids. They're an unfortunate byproduct of evolution—they probably originate as fragments of the chromosomes of complex organisms.

"The immune system of a particular host eventually produces antibodies that attack the protein coat of a virus, preventing it from spreading any further, internally or externally. Because of this, the survival of viruses depends on their being able to induce certain symptoms in their hosts, which allow them to infect further hosts before the current one stops them in their tracks. Coughs and sniffles are the commonest, because they're the most effective—when you have a cold you're forever getting virus particles on your hands, which you're then likely to pass on to everyone else you touch. The viruses which do best are the ones that regularly change their protein coats by mutation, so that the old antibodies no longer recognize them—they can circulate in the same population more-or-less indefinitely.

"The old method of treating virus diseases, as you say, was to find some way of making an immune system produce antibodies without the person actually catching the disease. Usually this involved producing a virus-substitute with the right protein coat but without the vicious DNA—but the fast-mutating viruses were always one step ahead of the immunizers, and even slow-mutating ones could occasionally throw up a new mutant.

"One of the great achievements of virus engineering has been the production of antiviruses, which defend against the effects of hostile DNA rather than against protein coats. They take up residence in exactly the same cells that a virus affects in order to make a body more infectious—the epithelial cells of the nose and the throat, and so on—and they prevent those cells from being disrupted by other incoming DNA. They don't prevent a virus invasion, but they prevent the *symptoms* of a virus attack from becoming manifest, and they make it very difficult for the virus to be passed on from one host to another.

"The effects of antiviruses are usually short-term ones, because we design most antiviruses with that aim in mind, but a prophylactic dose of anti-coryza will make sure that you can't catch a cold for a fortnight, and if you take a dose as soon as you do catch a cold, it wipes out the symptoms in a matter of minutes. You know how easy it is to take—you just get a fresh cell-culture from the chemist and pop it on your tongue. Magic!

"Once we began working with that strategy, the common cold and flu were as good as dead. It's extinction time for the vast majority of viruses—not just human ones, but plant and animal viruses too. You've already lived through the first wave of successes. Within five years the only viruses still able to give us trouble will be the sexually-transmitted ones. In another ten years' time, they'll be finished too—even the ingenious AIDS gang. The only viruses left will be the benign ones that we use as vectors in genetic engineering, which we'll be very careful to preserve. Then we'll get busy on the symptoms of non-virus diseases: the stress-related syndromes, the menstrual problems. Anti-viruses can take care of the lot, given time for us to design them right."

He paused, to check that Carrie was still following the argument. She nodded, to say that she was.

"The point is," said Don, "that even though Di's symptoms were purely psychosomatic, not caused by a virus at all, they could be attacked in exactly the same way. We were already trying to produce antiviruses to counter most of the symptoms that she had. In time, you see, she'd have been cured anyhow—as a by-product of cures issued for diseases with the same symptoms. It was just a matter of making up the right cocktail, and smuggling a dose out of the lab every time the symptoms began to show. I figured that two or three doses would be enough to break the bad biochemical habits that her body had formed, so that she'd be able to be sexually attracted to men without her whole system going haywire."

"Did it work?" asked Carrie, when he paused again.

"Yes and no," said Don. The words, spoken in a different way, might have been funny, or at least ironic—but there was nothing funny about the way he said them.

"What went wrong?"

"Nothing," he said. "The symptoms disappeared. There were one or two minor side-effects, but nothing damaging. The biochemical habits that she'd somehow formed were well and truly broken. It's surprising how tenacious quirks of that kind can be—it's very easy to pick up idiosyncratic associations from one's earliest sexual experiences, which get built into behavior as obsessive fetishisms, but when you attack them at the root, they can be exorcised.

22

"Think about that for a moment, Carrie. All the hang-ups people have—ranging from the most innocent ones to the nastiest—can be unwound using antiviruses, provided that the person affected wants to be rid of them, and is willing to take an appropriately-tailored antivirus whenever his or her particular symptoms develop. That's the future, Carrie—we'll be able to take control of our emotions, if only we want to do it badly enough.

"The trouble is, we might miss them once they're gone. Di did. When we'd abolished the symptoms, it felt to her as if we'd also abolished the emotion. What I tried to do was to transform her particular kind of love into something gentler and more reasonable—something more like mine. Maybe I really did do that...but she couldn't recognize what she had left as love. It seemed to her like something else entirely: something arid, and numb, and not worth having.

"I thought it was just a matter of getting used to it...I thought that, with time, she'd adapt, and come to realize that what she had was a better kind of love than she'd had before. But she didn't have time. Her immune system was already failing, and the cancers were already spreading. One of the less fortunate corollaries of the great success of antiviruses is that it's become harder to pick up early warnings that the immune system is in trouble.

"Everything has its price, you see....

"Jo died thinking that she'd lost an important kind of love, Carrie. She died thinking that she was incomplete. She never blamed me, and the one kind of love she was still sure she had was the kind she had for me. It was just that she thought she ought to have a different kind of love on top of that, for men who weren't her brother. I didn't see things the same way—but then, I never had a different kind of love for women who weren't my sister. Not then."

He looked so very sad that Carrie wanted to put her arms around him and hug him. It was a reaction which she knew only too well. She couldn't bear to see people hurt—especially people who bore their hurt with such ostentatious dignity and fortitude. Sympathy always flowed out of her. Gavin had used that response of hers to make her forgive him again and again. Malcolm seemed to have learned it

23

even before he could talk, and had always used it, over and over and over....

She wanted to hug Don Sherrington. She also wanted him to hug her. She wanted them both to remember how full of promise the world had been when they were twelve years old and innocent. And she wanted...more.

But all she could find to say was: "What do you mean, *not then?*"

He studied her with his pale blue eyes, though the concave lenses of his spectacles. "The technique works either way," he said. "It's as easy to attach physical symptoms *to* emotions as it is to detach symptoms *from* emotions. That's how we get our hang-ups in the first place. I'd always assumed, you see, that my way of being was better than hers—that Jay's way was right and Jo's way was wrong. But I'd never tried any other way than my own.

"It's been five years since she died. I've tried three different cocktails since then. Three different sets of physical symptoms. It's very difficult to make the conditioning take—I guess people of our age are far less vulnerable to hang-up formation than teenagers are—but it can be done if you work at it. Science is never easy for pioneers, and aphrodisiac technology is only in its infancy.

"In twenty or thirty or forty years time it will all be as simple as falling off a log, but for the time being...it's not. Even so, I've managed to do it, if only for short periods. I've experienced something like the kind of free-falling love that Di was stuck with, and a couple of others. How many more kinds there are, I don't know. I haven't even begun to figure out how much meaning there is in people's attempts to distinguish between the kinds of love they can feel naturally. Everyone I ask seems to have a different answer, although most people say that parent-love is very different from spouse-love, and sibling-love is different again....

"You probably know more about that than I do. I'm pretty much a newcomer to the riot of different kinds of love, but you've probably been juggling half a dozen sets of symptoms all your life."

The import of what he was saying slowly sank in while he was saying it. She didn't know quite how to react to it—

or whether the reaction which she felt ought to be discounted as just another set of symptoms.

"You've made viruses that make people fall in love?" she said, not quite sure that she had understood properly.

"No," he replied, patiently. "I've made viruses that can alter the biochemical corollaries of sexual arousal. The whole point is, you see, that there's no such thing as a pure emotion. Everybody experiences their emotions in a different way, because the feedback loops between sensory perception and biochemical response, mediated by consciousness, depend on haphazard intersections of genetic priming and particular experience, which can send them in lots of different directions. In technical terms, you see, it's a chaotic system...."

He had lost her, and must have been able to see that in her expression.

"My viruses can't make people fall in love," he said, returning to the basics. "They can only alter the *kind* of loving feelings that people have. But that's not a trivial alteration, Carrie. It can make more difference than you might think."

She already knew that her question had been wrongly-phrased, and she couldn't blame him for thinking she was dumb. But she wasn't. She really did see what he was getting at. She understood what he had tried to do for Di, and why the result hadn't been as obviously good as they might have wished. And she understood, too, how the implications of what he was saying affected her own predicament—her own particular sickness of the soul.

"What, exactly," she asked, more starkly than she had intended, "is this virus that you say you're carrying?"

"It's not infectious," he said, quickly. "It's not like a cold that you could catch from a touch. The only way you could possibly become infected would be...."

He trailed off in embarrassment, and she realized that it had crossed *his* mind too—not as an intention, but as a fantasy. He was lonely too; he too had lost his one true love...but that was getting silly.

"That's not what I asked," she pointed out. "Just suppose, for the sake of argument, that I did manage to pick it up. What, exactly, would it do to me?"

"It would make you feel slightly different," he said. "Not really ill...just different. But the effect would be intensified if you were then—in the brief period before you formed antibodies to combat the virus—to experience sexual arousal. It's tailored, you see, to affect the kinds of cells that are activated in particular ways by arousal. It's impossible to predict whether you'd think the altered sensations were better, or worse. That's largely a subjective thing. But they'd be different."

"And it wouldn't affect me otherwise?" she queried.

"Not as much," he said. "But other forms of arousal have biochemical correlates that overlap sexual arousal. The quality of any strong emotion—anger, grief, elation—would be altered."

"Less intense or more intense?" she asked.

He blushed again, as though the question were too personal to be asked; as, in a way, it was.

"Less," he said. "You see...I really didn't like Jo's kind of love. I really didn't like it at all. But at least I tried it—and when I had, I didn't stop trying. I'm not complacent—not at all. I'm morally certain that I can improve on what nature and accident provided, if I keep experimenting. What I find will be an answer just for me, but in time—in twenty or thirty or forty years—everyone will be able to follow in my footsteps, looking for their own personal ideal state of mind.

"I want that, Carrie. I want that...for Jo's sake. I failed her...but I can make up for it, if I do the job properly."

Carrie looked at him long and hard. His face was still flushed; the last blush hadn't entirely faded away. The wine had helped to heighten his color a little. She saw his gaze settle to the face of the clock, and she saw him start with surprise as he realized how late it was.

"You don't have to go," she said, quickly. "You can stay in Malcolm's room."

"Malcolm?" he said, in a puzzled tone. Then he remembered. "Oh—your son. What is he now, fifteen or sixteen? But he'll need the room himself, won't he?" He pronounced the last question haltingly, obviously realizing that the answer might well be no.

26

"He's gone," said Carrie, softly. "Gone to London, to stay with Gavin. To live with Gavin. They're both trying to make it, you see, whatever *it* is. Without me to hold them back. He's sixteen—in theory, I still have custody, but in practice...there's nothing I can do. He said that he hated living here. He said that he hated me. He said...well, you know how kids are. I remember what I was like, when I was that age...maybe you do too."

He looked at her hard, and she knew that he could see the tears which had formed in the corners of her eyes, threatening to fall if she could not control herself.

In the end, she had to lift a hand to wipe them away. "Only symptoms," she said. "That's all it is—only lovesick symptoms."

He didn't say anything. He was beset by confusions, and possibilities, and maybe even regrets about the way he had blurted it all out, explanations and all.

Suddenly there was born in her a conviction that she was in control of this situation—that she could decide what would happen, and what would happen next...and how the future might now take shape. What Don Sherrington had told her he had told her because she had known him long ago, and had known Di too, and because that knowledge meant that, even though she had not seen him for thirteen years, still she knew him better than anyone else, still they had the makings of an understanding.

She knew that what he'd told her wasn't really that big a secret. It was the kind of gosh-wow possibility you could read about every week in *The Guardian*. It wasn't truly awful. It certainly wasn't enough to bind them together in a conspiracy of silence for the rest of their lives, even though it was the kind of news that might put the wind up all the people who thought virus engineering was a truly dangerous art....

But he had told it to her. He had shared it with her. He had trusted her, because he remembered what she had been before her life had got out of hand.

"I'm sorry," he said, lamely, when he could bear the silence no longer. "I didn't mean...."

She knew that. She knew what he didn't mean.

"There's no need to be sorry," she said, wishing she had the courage to go to him right now and take his hand, and hoping that she could find it soon enough. "One way or another, we get over these things, don't we? In twenty or thirty or forty years time it might be easier, but it's not impossible even now. And if I were to make a fool of myself over you, Don Sherrington, it wouldn't be because I wanted to catch your virus, or get a head start on the rest of the world in playing your wonderful new games. It would be because the past always has to end somewhere, and the future always has to begin, and now is always the best time."

She was proud of that speech, when she'd finished it. Intensely proud. And although she still had to wipe another pair of tears away from her eyes, and sniff to get rid of the others that were clogging up her nose, she didn't feel nearly as bad about it as she might have done. And she waited, very politely in spite of her anxiety, to hear what he might find to say in reply.

What he said was: "Have you got any hot chocolate?"

And when she said "yes," and he said "I'll make some," she felt reasonably certain that it was going to be all right, at least for tonight and tomorrow, and that it might just prove, in the end, to be the cure that she was looking for.

ASHES AND TOMBSTONES

I was following Voltaire's good advice and working in my garden when the young man from the New European Space Agency came to call. I was enjoying my work; my new limb-bones were the best yet and my refurbished retinas had restored my eyesight to perfection—and I was still only 40% synthetic by mass, 38% by volume.

I liked to think of the garden as my own tiny contribution to the Biodiversity Project, not so much because of the plants, whose seeds were all on deposit in half a dozen Arks, but because of the insects for which the plants provided food. More than half of the local insects were the neospecific produce of the Trojan Cockroach Project, and my salads were a key element in their selective regime. The cockroaches living in my kitchen had long since reverted to type but I hadn't even thought of trying to clear them out; I knew the extent of the debt that my multitudinous several-times-great-grand-children owed their even-more-multitudinous many-times-great-grandparents.

When I first caught sight of him over the hedge, I thought the young man from NESA might be one of my descendants come to pay a courtesy call on the Old Survivor, but I knew as soon as he said "Professor Neal?" that he must be an authentic stranger. I was Grandfather Paul to all my Repopulation Kin.

The stranger was thirty meters away but his voice carried easily enough; the Berkshire Downs are very quiet nowadays, and my hearing was razor-sharp, even though the electronic feed was thirty years old and technically obsolete.

"Never heard of him," I said. "No professors hereabouts. Oxford's forty miles thataway." I pointed vaguely north-westwards.

"The Paul Neal I'm looking for isn't a professor any more," the young man admitted, letting himself in through the garden gate as if he'd been invited. "Technically, he ceased to be a professor when he was seconded to the Theseus Programme in Martinique in 2080, during the first phase of the Crash." He stood on the path hopefully, waiting for me to join him and usher him in through the door to my home, which stood ajar. His face was fresh, although there wasn't the least hint of synthetic tissue in its contours. "I'm Dennis Mountjoy," he added, as an afterthought. "I've left messages by the dozen, but it finally became obvious that the only way to get a response was to turn up in person."

Montjoie St. Denis! had been the war-cry of the French, in days of old. This Dennis Mountjoy was a mongrel European, who probably thought of war as a primitive custom banished from the world forever. It wasn't easy to judge his age, given that his flesh must have been somatically tuned-up, even though it hadn't yet become necessary to paper over any cracks, but I guessed that he was less than forty: a young man in a young world. To him, I was a relic of another era, practically a dinosaur—which was, of course, exactly why he was interested in me. NESA intended to put a man on the moon in June 2269, to mark the three-hundredth anniversary of the first landing and the dawn of the New Space Age. They had hunted high and low for survivors of the last space program, because they wanted at least one to be there to bear witness to their achievement, to forge a living link with history. It didn't matter to them that the Theseus Project had not put a single man into space, nor directed a single officially-sanctioned shot at the moon.

"What makes you think that you'll get any more response in person than you did by machine?" I asked the young man, sourly. I drew myself erect, feeling a slight twinge in my spine in spite of all the nanomech reinforcements, and removed my sunhat so that I could wipe the sweat from my forehead.

30

"Electronic communication isn't very private," Mount-joy observed. "There are things that it wouldn't have been diplomatic to say over the phone."

My heart sank. I'd so far outlived my past that I'd almost come to believe that I'd escaped, but I hadn't forgotten. I was surprised that my inner response wasn't stronger, but the more synthetic flesh you take aboard the less capacity you have for violent emotion, and my heart was pure android. Time was when I'd have come on like the minotaur if anyone had penetrated to the core of my private maze, but all the bull had leached out of my head a hundred years ago.

"Go away and leave me alone," I said, wearily. "I wish you well, but I don't want any part of your so-called Great Adventure. Is that diplomatic enough for you?"

"There were things that it wouldn't have been diplomatic for *me* to say," he said, politely pretending that he thought I'd misunderstood him.

"Don't say them, then," I advised him.

"Ashes and tombstones," he recited, determinedly ignoring my advice. "Endymion. Astolpho."

There were supposed to be no records—but in a crisis, everybody cheats. Everybody keeps secrets, especially from the people they're supposed to be working for.

"Mr. Mountjoy," I said, wearily. "It's 2268. I'm two hundred and eighteen years old. Everyone else who worked on Theseus is dead, along with ninety percent of the people who were alive in 2080. Ninety percent of the people alive today are under forty. Who do you think is going to give a damn about a couple of itty-bitty rockets that went up with the wrong payloads to the wrong destination. It's not as if the Chaos Patrol was left a sentry short, is it? Everything that was supposed to go up did go up."

"But that's why you don't want to come back to Martinique, isn't it?" Mountjoy said, still standing on the path, half way between the gate and the door. "That's why you don't want to be there when the Adventure starts again. We know that the funds were channeled through your account. We know that you were the paymaster for the crazy shots. You probably didn't plan them and you certainly didn't execute them, but you were the pivot of the seesaw."

I put my hat back on and adjusted the rim. The ozone layer was supposed to be back in place but old habits die hard.

"Come over here," I said. "Watch where you put your feet."

He looked down at the variously-shaped blocks of salad greens. He had no difficulty following the dirt path that I'd carefully laid out so that I could pass among them, patiently plying my hoe.

"You don't actually eat this stuff, do you?" he said, as he came to stand before me, looking down from his embryonically-enhanced two-meter height at my nanomech-conserved one-eighty.

"Mainly I grow it for the beetles and the worms," I told him. "They leave me a little for my own plate. In essence, I'm a sharecropper for the biosphere. Repopulation's put *Homo sapiens* back in place, but the little guys still have a way to go. You really ought to wear a hat on days like this."

"It's not necessary in these latitudes," he assured me, missing the point again. "You're right, of course. Nobody cares about the extra launches. Nobody will mention it, least of all when you're on view. All we're interested in is selling the Adventure. We believe you can help us with that. No matter how small a cog you were, you were in the engine. You're the last man alive who took part in the pre-Crash space program. You're the world's last link to Theseus, Ariane, Apollo, and Mercury. That's all we're interested in, all we care about. The last thing anyone wants to do is to embarrass you, because embarrassing you would also be embarrassing us. We're on your side, Professor Neal—and if you're worried about the glare of publicity encouraging others to dig, there's no need. We have control, Professor Neal—and we're sending our heroes to the Sea of Tranquility, half a world away from Endymion. The only relics we'll be looking for are the ones Apollo 11 left. We're not interested in ashes or tombstones."

I knelt down, gesturing to indicate that he should follow suit. He hesitated, but he obeyed the instruction eventually. His suitskin was easily capable of digesting any dirt that got on to its knees, and would probably be grateful for the piquancy.

"Do you know what this is?" I asked, fondling a crinkled leaf.

"Not exactly," he replied. "Some kind of engineered hybrid, mid-twenty-first-cee vintage, probably disembArked fifty or sixty years ago. The bit you eat is underground, right? Carrot, potato—something of that general sort—presumably gee-ee augmented as a whole-diet crop."

He was smarter than he looked. "Not exactly whole-diet," I corrected. "The manna-potato never really took off. Even when the weather went seriously bad you could still grow manna-wheat in England thanks to megabubbles and microwave boosters. This is head stuff. Ecstasy cocktail. Its remotest ancestor produced the finest mélange of euphorics and discreet hallucinogens ever devised—but that was a hundred generations of mutation and insect-led natural selection ago. You crush the juice from the tubers and refine it by fractional distillation and freeze-drying—if you can keep the larvae away long enough for them to grow to maturity."

"So what?" he said, unimpressed. "You can buy designer stuff straight from the synthesizer, purity guaranteed. Growing your own is even more pointless than growing lettuces and courgettes."

"It's an adventure," I told him. "It's *my* adventure. It's the only kind I'm interested in, now."

"Sure," he said. "We'll be careful not to take you away for too long. But we still need you, Professor Neal, and *our* Adventure is the one that matters to us. I came here to make a deal. Whatever it takes. Can we go inside now?"

I could see that he wasn't to be dissuaded. The young can be very persistent, when they want to be.

I sighed, and surrendered. "You can come in," I conceded, "but you can't talk me round, by flattery or blackmail or salesmanship. At the end of the day, I don't have to do it if I don't want to." I knew it was hopeless, but I couldn't just give in. I had to make him do the work.

"You'll want to," he said, with serene overconfidence.

* * * * * * *

The aim of the project on which we were supposed to be working, way back in the twenty-first, was to place a ring of satellites in orbit between Earth and Mars to keep watch for stray asteroids and comets that might pose a danger to the Earth. The Americans had done the donkey-work on the payloads before the plague wars had rendered Canaveral redundant. The transfer brought the European Space Program back from the dead, although not everyone thought that was a good thing. "Why waste money protecting the world from asteroids," some said, "when we've all but destroyed it ourselves?" They had a point. Once the plague wars had set the dominoes falling, the Crash was inevitable; anyone who hoped that ten percent of the population would make it through was considered a wild-eyed optimist in 2080.

The age of manned spaceflight had been over before I was born. It didn't make economic sense to send up human beings, with the incredibly elaborate miniature ecospheres required for their support, when any job that needed doing outside the Earth could be done much better by compact clever machinery. Nobody had sent up a payload bigger than a dustbin for over half a century, and nobody was about to start. We'd sent probes to the outer system, the Oort Cloud and a dozen neighboring star-systems, but they were all machines that thrived on hard vacuum, hard radiation and eternal loneliness. To us, there was no Great Adventure; the Theseus project was just business—and whatever Astolpho was, it certainly wasn't an Adventure. It was just business of a subtly different kind.

Despite the superficial similarity in their names, there was nothing in our minds to connect Astolpho with Apollo. Apollo was the glorious god of the sun, the father of prophecy, the patron of all the Arts. Astolpho was a character in one of the satirical passages of the *Orlando Furioso*, who journeyed to the moon and found it a treasure house of everything wasted on Earth: misspent time, ill-spent wealth, broken promises, unanswered prayers, fruitless tears, unfulfilled desires, failed quests, hopeless ambitions, aborted plans, and fruitless intentions. Each of these residues had its proper place: hung on hooks, stored in bellows, packed in trunks,

34

and so on. Wasted talent was kept in vases, like the urns in which the ashes of the dead were sometimes stored in the Golden Age of Crematoria. It only takes a little leap of the imagination to think of a crater as a kind of vase.

The target picked out by the clandestine Project Astolpho was Endymion, named for the youth beloved of the moon goddess Selene, whose reward for her divine devotion was to live forever in dream-filled sleep.

Even in the days of Apollo—or shortly thereafter, at any rate—there had been people who liked the idea of burial in space. Even in the profligate twentieth, there had been dying men who did not want their ashes to be scattered upon the Earth, but wanted them blasted into space instead, where they would last *much* longer.

By 2080, when the Earth itself was dying, in critical condition at best, those who had tried hardest to save it—at least in their own estimation—became determined to save some tiny fraction of themselves from perishing with it. They did not want the relics of their flesh to be recycled into bacterial goo that would have to wait for millions of years before it essayed a new ascent towards complexity and intellect. They did not want their ashes to be consumed and recycled by the cockroaches which were every bookmaker's favorites to be the most sophisticated survivors of the ecoholocaust.

They knew, of course, that Project Astolpho was a colossal waste of money, but they also knew that *all* money would become worthless if it were not spent soon, and there was no salvation to be bought. Who could blame them for spending what might well have proved to be the last money in the world on ashes and tombstones?

Were they wrong? Would they have regretted what they had done, if they had known that the human race would survive its self-inflicted wounds? I don't know. Not one member of the aristocracy of wealth that I could put a name to came through the worst. Perhaps their servants and their mistresses came through, and perhaps not—but they themselves went down with the Ship of Fools they had commissioned, captained and navigated. All that remains of them now is their legacies, among which the payloads deposited by illicit

Theseus launches in Endymion might easily be reckoned the least—and perhaps not the worst.

Dennis Mountjoy was right to describe me as a very small cog in the Engine of Fate. I did not plan Astolpho and I did not carry it out, but I did distribute the bribes. I was the bagman, the calculator, the fixer. Mathematics is a versatile art; it can be applied to widely different purposes. Math has no morality; it does not care what it counts or what it proves. Somewhere on Astolpho's moon, although Ariosto did not record that he ever found it, there must have been a hall of failed proofs, mistaken sums, illicit theorems and follies of infinity, all neatly bound in webs of tenuous logic.

Had I not had the modest wealth I took as my commission on the extra Theseus shots, of course, I could not have been one of the survivors of the Crash. Had it not been for my brokerage of Project Astolpho, I could not have been, by the time that Dennis Mountjoy came to call, one of the oldest men in the world: the founder of a prolific dynasty. I too would have been nothing but ash, without even a tombstone, when the New Apollonians decided that it was time to reassert the glory and the godhood of the human race by duplicating its most magnificent folly: the Great Adventure.

I had never had any part in the first Adventure, and I wanted no part in the second. I had worked alongside men who had launched rockets into outer space, but the only things I ever helped to land on the moon were the cargoes provided by the Pharaohs of Capitalism: the twenty-first century's answer to the Pyramids.

I was companion to Astolpho, not Apollo: whenever I raised my eyes to the night sky I saw nothing in the face of the moon but the wastes of Earthly dreams and Earthly dreamers.

* * * * * * *

"None of that is relevant," Dennis Mountjoy told me, when I had explained it to him—or had tried to (the account just now set down has, of course, taken full advantage of *l'esprit de l'escalier*). He sat in an armchair waving his hands in the air. I had almost begun to wish that I'd offered him a cup of tea and a slice of cake, so that at least a few of his gestures would have been stifled.

"It's relevant to me," I told him, although I was fully cognizant by then of the fact that he had not the least interest in what was relevant to me.

"None of it's ever going to come out," he assured me. "You can forget it. You may be two hundred and some years old, but that doesn't mean that you have to live in the past. We have to think of the future now. You should try to forget. That's what a good memory is, when all's said and done: one that can forget all the things it doesn't need to retain. There's no need for you to be hung up on the differences between Apollo and Astolpho in a world that can no longer tell them apart. As you said yourself, ninety percent of the people alive today are under forty. To them, it's all ancient history, and the names are just sounds. Apollo, Ariane, Theseus—it's all merged into a single mythical mishmash, including all the sidelines, official and unofficial. From the point of view of the people who believe in the New Adventure, and the people who *will* believe, once we've captured their imagination, it's all part of the same story, the one we're starting over. Your presence at the launch will confirm that. All that anyone will see when they look at you is a miracle: the last survivor of Project Theseus; the envoy of the First Space Age, extending his blessing to the Second."

"Do you know why Project Theseus was called by that name?" I asked him.

"Of course I do," he replied. "I know my history, even though I refuse to be bogged down by it. Ariane was the rocket used in the first European Space Program, named for the French version of Ariadne, daughter of Minos of Crete. Theseus was one of seven young men delivered to Minos as a tribute by the Athenians, along with seven young women; they were to be sacrificed to the minotaur—a monster that lived in the heart of a maze called the labyrinth. Ariadne fell in love with Theseus and gave him a skein of thread, which allowed him to keep track of his route through the maze. When he had killed the minotaur, he was able to find his way out again. Theseus was the name give to Ariane's successor in order to signify that it was the heroic project that would secure humankind's escape from the minotaur in the maze: the killer asteroid that might one day wipe out civilization."

"That's the official decoding," I admitted. "But Theseus was also the betrayer of Ariadne. He abandoned her. According to some sources, she committed suicide or died of grief—but others suggested that she was saved by Dionysus, the antithesis of Apollo."

"So what?" said Mountjoy, making yet another expansive gesture. "Whatever you and your crazy pals might have read into that back in 2080, it doesn't matter now."

"Crazy pals?" I queried, remembering his earlier reference to the Astolpho launches as "crazy shots." Now I was beginning to wish that I had a cup of tea; my own hands were beginning to stir, as if in answer to his.

"The guys who gave you the money to shoot their ashes to the moon," the young man said. "The Syndicate. The Captains of Industry. The Hardinist Cartel. Pick your cliché. They *were* crazy, weren't they? Paying you to drop those payloads in Endymion was only the tip of the iceberg. I mean, they were the people with the power—the people who had steered the world straight into the Crash. That has to be reckoned as causing death by dangerous driving—manslaughter on a massive scale. Mad, bad and dangerous to know, wouldn't you say?"

"They didn't see it that way themselves," I pointed out, mildly.

"They certainly didn't," he agreed. "But you're older and wiser, and you have the aid of hindsight too. So give me your considered judgment, Professor Neal. Were they or were they not prime candidates for the straitjacket?"

I granted him a small laugh, but kept my hands still. "Maybe so," I said. "Maybe so. Can I get you a drink, by the way?"

He beamed, thinking that he'd won. One crack in the facade was all it needed to convince him.

"No thanks. We know how bad things were back then, and we don't blame you at all for what you did. The world is new again, and its newness is something for us all to celebrate. I understand why you've tried so hard to hide yourself away, and why you've built a maze of disinformation around your past. I understand how the thought of coming out of your shell after all these years must terrify you—but we *will* look after you. We need you, Professor Neal, to play Theseus in our own heroic drama. We need you to play the part of the man who slew the minotaur of despair and found the way out of the maze of human misery. I understand that you don't see yourself that way, that you don't *feel* like that kind of a hero, but in our eyes, that's what you are. In our eyes, and in the eyes of the world, you're the last living representative of early humanity's greatest adventure—the Adventure we're now taking up. We need you at the launch. We really can't do without you. Anything you want, just ask—but I'm here to make a deal, and I have to make it. No threats, of course, just honest persuasion—but I really do have to persuade you. You'll be in the news whether you like it or not—why not let us doctor the spin for you? If you're aboard, you have input; if not...you might end up with all the shit and none of the roses."

No threats, he'd said. Funnily enough, he meant it. He wouldn't breathe a word to a living soul—but if he'd found out about Astolpho, others could, and once the Great Adventure was all over the news the incentive to dig would be there. Expert web-walkers researching Theseus would be bound to stumble over Astolpho eventually. The only smoke-screen I could put up now was the smokescreen he was offering to lend me. If I didn't take it, I hadn't a hope of keeping the secret within the secret.

"Are you sure you wouldn't like something to drink?" I asked, tiredly. His semaphoring arms had begun to make my newly-reconditioned eyes feel dizzy.

He beamed again and almost said "Perhaps I will"—but then his eyes narrowed slightly. "What kind of drink?" he said.

"I make it myself," I told him, teasingly.

"That's what I'm afraid of," he said. "I've nothing against happy juice, but this isn't the time or the place—not for me. And to be perfectly honest, I'm not sure I could trust that home-grown stuff. You said yourself that it's been subject to generations of mutation and selection, and you know how delicate hybrid gentemplates are. Meaning no offence, but that garden is *infested*—and not everything that came out of Cade Maclaine's souped-up Trojan Cockroaches was a pretty pollen-carrier."

"Why should I help out in your Adventure," I asked him, lightly, "if you won't help out in mine?"

He looked at me long and hard. It didn't need a trained mathematician to see the calculations clicking over in his mind. Whatever it took, he'd said. Anything I wanted, just ask.

"Well," he said, finally, "I take your point. Are we talking about a deal here, or what? Are we talking about coming to an understanding? Sealing a compact?"

"Just the launch," I said. "One day only. You can make as much noise as you like—the more the merrier—but I only come out for one day. And everything you put out is Theseus, Theseus and more Theseus. What's lost stays lost, from here to eternity."

"If that's what you want," he said. "One day only—and we'll give them so much Theseus they'll drown in it. Astolpho stays under wraps—nobody says a word about it. Not now, not ever. The records are ours, and we have no interest in letting the cat escape the bag. If we thought anyone would blow the whistle, we wouldn't want you waving us off. This is the Adventure, after all: the greatest moment so far in the history of the new human race. So far as we're concerned, the ashes of Endymion can stay buried for another two hundred years—or another two million. It doesn't matter; come the day when somebody stumbles over the tombstones, they'll just be an archaeological find: a nine day wonder. By then, we'll be out among the stars. Earth will be just our cradle."

I had thought when he first confronted me that he didn't have anything I wanted, just something he could threaten me with. I realized now that he had both—but he didn't know it. He and his crazy pals thought that they needed me at their launch, to give the blessing of the old human race to the new, and I needed them to be perfectly content with what they thought they had, to dig just so far and no further. It had been foolish of me to refuse to return his calls, without even knowing what he had to say, and exactly how much he might have discovered.

"All right," I said, with all the fake weariness that a 40% synthetic man of two hundred and eighteen can muster. "You've worn me down. I give in. I do the launch, and the rest is silence. I appear, smile, disappear. Remembered for one brief moment, forgotten forever. Once I'm out of the way, your guys are the only heroes. Okay?"

"There might be other enquiries from TV," he said, guardedly, "but as far as we're concerned, it's just the one symbolic gesture. That's all we need. I can't imagine that there'll be anything else that you can't reasonably turn down. You're two hundred and eighteen years old, after all. Nobody will get suspicious if you plead exhaustion."

"If you're so utterly convinced that you need it," I said, "who am I to deny you? And you're right—whatever other calls come in, I can be forgiven for refusing to answer on the grounds of creeping senility. I'll program my answer-phone to imply that I really couldn't be trusted not to wet myself if I were face-to-face with a famous chat show host. *Now* do you want a drink? Nothing home-made, if you insist—for you I'll make an exception. I'll even break the seal in front of you, if you like."

"There's no need," he said, with an airy wave of his right hand. His voice was redolent with relief and triumph. "I trust you."

* * * * * * *

Theseus betrayed Ariadne; of that much the voice of myth is as certain as the voice of myth can ever be. If she did not die, she was thrust into the arms of Dionysus, the god of intoxication. If grief did not kill her, she gave herself over to the mind-blowing passion of the Bacchae.

"Ashes and tombstones" were the names that the Pharaohs of Capitalism gave to the payloads they paid my associates to deposit in Endymion, near the north pole of the moon. Ashes to ashes, dust to dust...but the remnants of their flesh that they sent to Endymion, actual vases to be placed within a symbolic vase, were not the remains of their dead. The "ashes" were actually frozen embryos: not their dead, but their multitudinous unborn children.

The "tombstones" carried aloft by valiant Astolpho were not inscribed with their epitaphs but with instructions for the resurrection of the human species, so deeply and so cleverly ingrained that they might still be deciphered after a million or a billion years, even by members of a species that had evolved a million or a billion light-years away and had formulated a very different language.

Like the Pharaohs of old, the Pharaohs of the End Time fully intended to rise again; their pyramids were not built as futile monuments but as fortresses to secure themselves against disaster.

Against all disaster, that is.

My "crazy pals" had believed that the world was doomed, and humankind with it. There was nothing remotely crazy in that belief, in 2080. The Earth was dying, and nothing short of a concatenation of miracles could have saved it. Perhaps the Pharaohs of Capitalism had been crazy to have let the world get into such a state, but they were not miracle-workers themselves; they were only men. They thought that the only hope for humankind was to slumber for a million or a billion years in the bosom of the moon, until someone might come who would recognize the Earth for the grave it was, and would search for relics of the race whose grave it was in the one place where such relics might have survived the ravages of decay: hard vacuum.

The disaster they had feared so much had not, in the end, been absolute. The human race had come through the crisis. Cade Maclaine's cockroach-borne omnispores and the underground Arks had enabled them to resuscitate the ecosphere and massage the fluttering rhythm of its heart back to steadiness.

By now, of course, the game had changed. The Repopulation was almost complete, and the Adventure had begun again. The New Human Race believed that its future was secure, and that the tricentennial launch of the mission to the Era of Tranquility would help to make it secure.

Well, perhaps.

And perhaps not.

I knew that if the new Adventurers found the vases of Endymion, they would be reckoned merely one more Ark: one more seed-deposit, to be drawn on as and when convenient. The children of the Pharaohs would be disembArked at the whim and convenience of men like Dennis Mountjoy, who believed with all his heart that the minotaur at the heart of the labyrinth of fate was dead and gone, and every ancient nightmare with him.

That, to the crazy men who had paid my prices in order to deposit their heritage in Endymion, would almost certainly have seemed to be a disaster as great as the one that had been avoided. The Pharaohs had not handed down fortunes so that their offspring could be reabsorbed into the teeming millions of the New Human Race, but in order that they should become *the* human race: a unique marvel in their own right.

Perhaps they were crazy to want that, but that is what they wanted. "Ashes and tombstones" was a smokescreen, intended to conceal a bid for resurrection, immortality and the privilege of uniqueness in a universe where humankind was utterly forgotten—and nothing less.

My motives were somewhat different, of course, but I wanted the same result.

At two hundred and eighteen years of age, and having lived through the Crash, I could never convince myself that it could not happen again—but even if it never did, I wanted the vases of Endymion to rest in peace, not for a hundred years or a thousand, but for a million or a billion, as their deliverers had intended.

I did not want the "ashes and tombstones" to become an archaeological find and a nine day wonder. I wanted them to remain where they were until they were found by those who had been intended to find them: unhuman beings, for whom the task of disembArkation would be an act of recreation. It did not matter to me whether they were the spawn of another star or the remotest descendants of the ecosphere of Earth, remade by countless generations of mutation and selection into something far stranger than the New Human Race—but I too wanted to leave my mark on the face of eternity. I too wanted to have gouged out a scratch on the infinite wall of

43

the future, to have played a part in making something that would last, not for seventy years or two hundred, or even two thousand—which is as long as any man might reasonably expect to live, aided by our superbly clever and monstrously chimerical technologies of self-repair—but for two million or two billion.

All I had done was to calculate the price, but without me, none of it would have happened. The moon would have been exactly as Astolpho found it: a treasury of the lost and the wasted, the futile and the functionless.

Thanks to me, it is more than that. In a million or a billion years time, the time will come for the resurrection, and the new life. I do not want it to be soon: the longer, the better.

* * * * * *

I thoroughly enjoyed the launch. I enjoyed it so tremendously, in fact, that I was glad I had allowed myself to be persuaded to take my place among its architects, to give their bold endeavor the blessing of all the billions of people who had died while I was young.

I was unworthy, of course. Who among us is not? Nor can I believe, even now, that Dennis Mountjoy was correct in thinking that his heroes needed me to set the seal of history on their endeavor—but the sight of that rocket riding its pillar of fire into the deep blue of the sky brought back so many memories, so many echoes of a self long-buried and half-forgot, that I almost broke down and wept.

"I'd forgotten what a sight it was," I admitted to the young man, "and I thought that I'd lost the capacity to feel such deep emotions, along with the fleshy tables of my first heart."

He did not recognize the quotation, which came from Paul's second epistle to the Corinthians: an epistle, according to the text, "written not with ink but with the Spirit of the living God; not in tables of stone, but in fleshy tables of the heart." All he had to say in reply was: "I told you that you'd want to be here. This is Apollo reborn, Theseus reborn. This is what all the heroes of the race were made to accomplish.

This time, we'll go all the way to the stars, whatever it costs."

Astolpho, your creator had not the least idea what truth he served when he sent you to the moon, to discern its real nature and its real purpose.

SLUMMING IN VOODOOLAND

It's only when you hit the open road, Benny thought, as he gunned the engine of the Thunderbug, taking them out towards the old city limits, *that you realize what a shithouse the Uplands really is*.

It had always seemed to Benny that the air in the Uplands Estate was as stale as the people—or, if not quite *always*, for as long as he could remember. He had certainly been of that opinion long before he'd scraped up the enough credit to buy the Thunderbug—in the teeth of parental opposition, of course—and had first tasted the delights of slumming. The Estate straights said that it was the suburban swamplands that stank, but Benny didn't think that way at all. Maybe his nose had been wired up wrongly, or maybe it was the elixir which turned his sensations around, but to Benny, the neotropic wetlands nourished by the Greenhouse Effect possessed a heady sweetness that was the very essence of zooming.

"Zooming" was the cutting edge of experience, the chain of impacts that his atom of consciousness made as it crashed into new territory, leaving the familiar behind. It was Benny's own word, invented to describe his own private feelings, because none of the words which already existed had seemed sufficient to that purpose. All his friends had picked it up from him—Mikey and Delilah used it all the time, and even Fay had recently condescended to adopt it—but he doubted whether they meant the same thing by it, and whether they ever experienced the sensation that had compelled him to invent it. They were straighter than he was—richer too, despite that he was the one who owned the Thunderbug—and they all belonged to the Estate in a way he didn't.

Once, the Thunderbug itself had been all that Benny needed in order to zoom, but those days were gone. Nowadays, the vehicle was simply a set of wheels and a suit of armor—a means of getting there and back again, in one piece. It wasn't particularly fast and it wasn't particularly roomy—the back seat had just enough space for him to lay his hat and a few special friends—but it served its purpose. It was the ideal slummer's car, sufficiently well-defended to be difficult to steal and unsexy enough not to be too tempting regardless. Not that it was safe to get out and leave it, of course—but Benny didn't need to get out in order to get his kicks. All he had to do was let a little of that sweet neotropic air in, and head for whichever drive-in took his fancy.

Old Suburbia had all kinds of drive-ins. Drive-ins were the economic lifeblood of the suburbs. Every one of them offered something a little bit special—something that the uptight citizens of the Estates were determined to keep out; something dangerous. Benny liked the kind of danger in which the drive-ins traded: the danger of ideas. Physical danger he could live without—he was no motorpsycho, ambitious to take off into the wildlands; he was strictly a Thunderbug man—but dangerous ideas were something else. He liked his pornypops spicy, and he liked to dally with the demons of exotic desire. Tonight, he hoped, the four of them would take in the most dangerous drive-in of them all—the only one that dared not settle on a permanent site for fear of being raided.

"Go, go, go!" chanted Mikey from the back seat, as the last lingering trace of the Estate's lights faded into the western horizon and left them to a world of rapidly-deepening shadows.

"Zoom, zoom," said Delilah, hitching up her skirt so Mikey could paw her. "Voodooland here we come."

Fay, who was in the front seat with Benny, didn't say anything. She was busy checking her face while there were still a few streetlights around. It would be pretty dark out in the wasteland, despite the fact that the patch for which they were headed would become a theatre for the night. In any case, nobody would be looking at her while the show was on. But Fay was a perfectionist. Daddy hadn't paid for all that epidermal recrafting so that she could get sloppy. She was always ready, just in case a beam of light should briefly illuminate her luscious lips.

Fay was far to good for Benny, lookswise and cashwise, but the real Uplands élite didn't have to buy Thunderbugs in order to go slumming—all they had to do was take the lift from the penthouse to the thirtieth floor. Fay had taken up with Benny mainly because her father had expressed the opinion that he was a total loser; if she hadn't been so fastidious she would have found someone even more appalling to screw. So far, Benny had been content to play along, being exactly as loathsome or amiable as Fay wanted him to be in any particular situation, but he was beginning to get tired of it. Going with Fay had been a real zoom in the beginning, but she was one of those girls who *endured* being screwed rather than trying to enjoy it, and Benny was starting to regret that he had so expeditiously handed Delilah on to Mikey when Fay came along. He had a sneaking suspicion that Fay was beginning to tire of him too.

"It's great to be out!" sang Mikey. "Armor-plated in a wild, wild world."

"Go, go, go," said Delilah, lasciviously. Benny knew that she would be clenching her thighs about Mikey's hand, and he felt a pang of regretful jealousy.

"Are you *sure* you know where this thing's going to happen tonight?" asked Fay, putting her mirror away now that she could no longer see her face in it. "It won't be much fun if Froglet fed you the wrong information."

"It'll be there," said Benny, insistently. "Froglet knows that I'd break him in two if he conned me out of fifty with dirty data. Hell, it may be secret, but they have to get customers, don't they?"

"If it cost you fifty to find out where it is," she went on, "how much is it going to cost us to get in?"

"Two hundred," Benny told her, through pursed lips. "I got it—don't ask me how, but I got it. Okay?"

Fay was close enough to him that he could feel the shrug of her shoulders.

"How far is it?" asked Mikey.

"*All the way*," giggled Delilah

"It's not so far," said Benny, grimly. "It started way out in the swamp, but it got too popular."

"It'll be on TV soon, I guess," said Fay, rather more dismissively than Benny liked. She could have tried to be grateful for the trouble he was taking. Two hundred was two hundred when all said and done—not much to Fay but a hell of a lot to Benny.

"No chance," he told her. "Not even that high-powered pay-TV you cultured folks watch in order to avoid the ads on the networks. This whole thing is so illegal and outrageous that the City Fathers have been talking about sending the boys out to bust it up and run Papa Ogo clean out of the state. Besides, Papa Ogo don't like cameras—he reckons they steal the soul away, even from the risen dead. Put his babies on the screen, he says, and they'd be just as dull as all the live actors."

"He's right, boy," said Mikey, raising his voice to be heard over Delilah's cooing and gurgling. "Ain't much soul in the soaps, an' even less in the ads."

"Whatever his feelings about cameras," said Fay, "it's difficult to believe that Papa Ogo's puppets could have anything to lose. He's putting out bullshit to justify the price of admission. Or maybe he's just afraid that close-ups would blow the lid off his scam."

"It ain't a scam, Fay," said Benny, steering the Thunderbug round a huge pothole left by a recent roadmine. "It's the real thing. They ain't puppets and they ain't people in fancy make-up. They're authentic zombies."

"Made according to the authentic voodoo magic, no doubt," she countered.

"That's right," said Benny, doggedly. "Papa Ogo says that the secret was in his family a long time, and goes all the way back to the days before the slaves were brought over from Africa. But even if that ain't entirely true—even if it's something he worked up himself—it's still the same thing: reanimation of the dead; zombies."

"If people could really reanimate the dead," said Fay, "they wouldn't make a theatrical performance out of it. If it wasn't a scam, it wouldn't be on the stage at some sleazy drive-in."

"It ain't just in the theatre," said Delilah, between her breathless giggles. "According to my dad, we got zombies in Congress and zombies in the Supreme Court. The japs have got whole factories staffed by zombies, and there's a whole tribe of rogue zombies living in the sewers under the Estate. Half the bike gangs in the mid-West are zombies but...ouch! I'm gonna chew your balls for that, Mikey darling—just you wait."

Benny felt that the discussion was getting a little out of control. He had heard enthusiastic reports of Papa Ogo's *Grand Guignol*, and he didn't want it to be a scam. For two hundred he wanted it to be real. For two hundred he wanted it to *zoom*. And now he'd committed himself by promising the others that it *was* real, he stood to lose face if it wasn't. It shouldn't be like that, because they were his guests in his Thunderbug, and they ought to be grateful for the chance of driving anywhere that wasn't an Estate playground for straights and busted flushes, but it *was* like that, and there was no denying it.

"Wait and see," he said, ducking reflexively as a couple of six-year-old dirtboys threw something disgusting at the windscreen. "This is going to be *really special*. It'll knock your eyes out, Miss False-Face."

He didn't have to look sideways to know that Fay was giving him the kind of look she'd have given to whatever the dirtboys had thrown if it had landed in her lap, but he wasn't particularly worried about that. A little bit of judicious insult helped to make him interesting to her. He was only worried that Papa Ogo's show might not live up to his promises.

"Break out the cans," said Mikey, from the back seat. "I think I'm going to get *hot and thirsty*."

"Go, go, go," purred Delilah. "All the way to lovely voodooland!"

* * * * * * *

Benny heaved a secret sigh of relief when his information turned out to be good. He hadn't really doubted it, but it would have been such a bummer if Froglet had made a fool of him that he couldn't entirely suppress his anxiety.

They had tried to be early for the performance, but they weren't early enough to get a position close to the stage. There were a hundred vehicles in already. The stewards were bikers, wearing the colors of Satan's Stormtroopers.

The dog-and-burger stand was surrounded by swamprats who jeered when Benny rolled down his window, and told him loudly that an Uplander could easily lose his arm that way. One volunteered to climb in and help him with Fay, but didn't attempt to follow up the threat. It was par for the course, and Benny got the window up again without admitting anything more sinister than a stray mosquito.

"Oh shit," said Delilah, when they were stowed in their slot. "We ain't going to see much from here—that ain't no sixty-foot screen up there, y'know."

She was right—the elevated stage was made out of loose planks balanced on rusty scaffolding. Benny figured that Papa Ogo and the Stormtroopers would clear forty grand on tonight's admissions, with junk profits on top, but they obviously didn't like to lay out too much on overheads.

"It's okay," said Mikey, soothingly. "I brought a set of glasses."

"I should have brought a camera with a zoom lens," said Fay, sarcastically. "That way I could have stolen a few souls without anybody noticing."

"Zoom lens," echoed Delilah, with the usual giggle. "You ever look through one of those, Benny?"

"The only zoom lens I got," Benny told her, "is in my naked eye. Maybe you need your eyes testing, Lila—they say too much of it makes you go blind."

"You're just jealous," said Mikey—but shut up quickly when Fay turned around to fix him with a deadly stare. Benny grinned. He and Mikey both knew that Fay was one girl Benny wouldn't be passing down the line to his old pal. Mikey might be the junior partner now, because Benny was older and tougher, but Mikey wasn't yet doomed to be a long-term loser the way Benny was—his father had connections. There was just a slim chance that, after Benny, Fay's

Daddy would *approve* of Mikey. He was no good to her, and so she was free to despise him the way she despised Delilah.

Oddly enough, both Mikey and Delilah put up with being despised by Fay, and seemed to expect no better. Maybe it was because she was so rich, or so calculatedly beautiful—or maybe because, whenever the four of them went out together, they were soon too stoned to care. The beer in the cans was saturated with Benny's special elixir of ecstasy, fraction-distilled with his own fair hands. Organic chemistry was his hobby and his living.

"We could start a collection of zombie souls," said Fay, obstinately carrying on her own line of facetious argument, "if only we could figure out some way to display them. Or maybe we could put them to work, if we could only figure out what work a zombie's soul might do."

"We could sell 'em to the Devil for three wishes each," suggested Mikey. "But I already had one of *mine*."

"I'll take that one," said Delilah. "Three wouldn't be *nearly* enough for me. I could use up a *lot* of wishes."

"It's yours, kid," said Mikey. "And you can take the other two with it. All I need is you."

Maybe that was all I needed, too, thought Benny, as he wiped his greasy hands on his jeans. *Maybe I need Frigid Fay like a hole in the head*. But he couldn't fool himself. Whether he needed Fay for herself or not, he certainly needed her good opinion now. He needed Papa Ogo's act to be a real ace, even at this distance. He needed the walking dead to strut some pretty fancy stuff.

"Hey," he said, as the lamps in the makeshift auditorium were snuffed out and a spotlight picked out a single figure center-stage. "Let's cut the shit and watch, okay—it's beginning."

* * * * * * *

Blacks stripped to the waist moved up the steps in pairs, each pair carrying a coffin between them. They moved in single file, matching their steps to the beating of half a dozen hidden drums. They were barely visible in the faint radiance which scattered from the spotlight, and there was something undeniably creepy about the way they emerged from total darkness into the shadowy half-light.

The guy in the spot was only an MC. He was dressed all in black but he had shiny black sequins sewn to his tux so that he could glitter in the light. He had no mike, but he had a big booming voice and there was no difficulty in hearing him above the softened murmur of the drums.

His spiel was all hype. He began by saying what a hell of a magician Papa Ogo was, and how he was the greatest master of voodoo witchcraft left in all the world, and how certain Fundamentalist bigots had got so panicked by his power to deal with the dead that they had put a huge price on his head. Then he went on to proclaim that Papa Ogo had a mission—that the Last Days of the World were now approaching, and that it was necessary for all men to be certain that death was not the end. Faith, said the MC, wasn't enough in the twentieth century: men needed the evidence of their own eyes before they could believe in something. Papa Ogo could provide that evidence, and tonight he was going to prove beyond the shadow of a doubt that dead men still had souls inhabiting their corpses, ready for that great day when all must rise from their graves and march to face their maker.

"Bullshit," muttered Fay, before taking another swig from her can. But her voice was less steady now and Benny smiled. Once the burger got her digestive system into gear the elixir would send her up like a rocket and blow her bad mood to smithereens. Then, she'd be *ready*. She wasn't so tough once her nerves started jangling.

The spot winked out for a moment. It was barely a flicker, but when it came back on the MC was gone and there, in his place, was Papa Ogo. Delilah gasped, but whether it was because she'd been fooled by the quick change or simply because of the way the voodoo-man looked Benny couldn't tell.

The guy was certainly strange: his face was flat and lavishly decorated with swirling designs—not just colored tattoos but sculpted ridges and circles. The whites of his eyes were visible all around the rim of his near-black irises, and there were small bones knitted into his bushy hair to form a mock-crown. He was dressed in a loose black robe, with not the slightest trace of a sequin, and he carried a long feathered wand with a phallic bulge at the end.

The drums were louder now, and had increased their beat somewhat, but Papa Ogo's voice—although it was very different in timbre from the MC's—could easily be heard. It was a high-pitched voice, which babbled away in some foreign tongue, its cadences rising and falling as Papa Ogo swayed from side to side. Once the audience had taken a good long look at his monstrous face, though, he turned away to the rank of coffins—abandoned now by their porters—which stood behind him on the stage. There were ten in all.

Papa Ogo pointed the wand at the first of the coffins and raised his eerie voice once, twice, thrice...and a new spotlight showed that the lid of the coffin was slowly pushed up.

Mikey balanced his field-glasses on Benny's shoulder, and Benny could feel the boy's hot breath on the back of his neck.

The thing that rose from the box was no disappointment. Benny had been anxious that it might after all be a living man in make-up, playing a part, but all such fears were laid immediately to rest. This was the real thing. The guy had been a black man but he wasn't black any more; he had faded to grey. He was stark naked, and he looked as if he had been dead for weeks. He was thin to the point of emaciation, and the meager flesh had begun to split and come apart while it stretched upon the bones.

"Holy shit!" said Mikey, refusing to surrender the glasses when Delilah made a grab for them.

Benny had not the slightest doubt that the guy was dead—and yet, having lifted the lid of his own coffin, the zombie slowly came erect, raising himself to his feet. Then, very carefully, he stepped out of his coffin. Absurdly, he raised his bony arms above his head, as though he were a victorious boxer acknowledging the cheers of the crowd.

Benny could see that the flesh had peeled back from the tips of the zombie's fingers, and that some of the phalanges had already been disconnected.

Another spotlight came on, revealing that the second lid was already being raised, and the first dead man patiently stood still while the attention of the crowd shifted to his neighbor. Benny had not thought that anyone could be more obviously dead than the first performer, but he had not reckoned with the extent of possible evidence. This man also had been black when he was alive, but he too was a rather different color now. His flesh was not shriveled but bloated; the processes of putrefaction were puffing him up in a hideous manner which Benny had not imagined possible. Whether the guy had been drowned or exotically poisoned Benny did not dare to guess, but that he was authentically and horribly dead no one could doubt.

Fay was silent, tautly holding her breath.

Like the first, this dead man moved slowly, as though he had to take great pains to ensure that his much-abused frame did not simply fall apart. He did not raise his arms above his head, but he took a bow. If anyone was actually applauding, they could not be heard—Benny did not suppose that anyone was.

The third corpse was a white man, in a much better state of preservation than the other two—except that he had three bullet-holes in his chest. They didn't look so bad, and it seemed just conceivable that they might have been painted on—until the corpse did a slow pirouette, which showed off the exit wounds where the bullets had come out again. The three huge gaping holes—two of them overlapping—allowed a perfectly clear view of minced organs and splattered bones.

The fourth corpse was a woman. She had a machete embedded in her torso; it had been driven in to the hilt and the point projected from her back.

Mikey finally surrendered the binoculars to Delilah, and their dead weight was shifted from Benny's shoulder, though he could still feel Mikey's breath.

The spotlights kept coming on, gradually flooding the stage with weak light. After the fifth corpse—a woman who had been burned to death—had taken her bow Benny was sure that there could be no more surprises, and he began to breathe a little easier as the earlier motifs began to repeat—but Papa Ogo had saved a punchline for the end.

As the parade of the shrivelled, the bloated and the mutilated reached its terminus there was just a moment's pause before the last coffin, whose lid was more slowly raised. When the lid had been tipped back there was another interval, as though the zombie might have exhausted itself and could not stand up like his fellows. But then he began to rise from his confinement.

At first, Benny thought that the corpse was simply headless, but then he realized that this was the oldest melodramatic joke in the world.

The guy had been beheaded, but he still had his head. It was carefully and reverently cradled in his two hands, held in front of his broad and hairy chest.

"Sweet Jesus," whispered Fay, forced at last to speak.

"Zoom," whispered Benny, with utter satisfaction. "Zoom, zoom, *zoom*."

* * * * * *

The show went on.

Papa Ogo swayed and spewed out his nonsensical chant, while the drums beat time, seventy-six beats to the minute. The corpses wouldn't give way to the rhythm; they stood up straight. Then they turned left, like a squad of ill-trained army recruits, and they began to march, led by the guy who was little more than a skeleton. They marched in a lurching and uncomfortable fashion, but they kept in step.

They turned when they neared the edge of the platform and then turned again, so that they came back in the other direction behind the rank of coffins. They went round and round and round...

If they'd been living men it would have been as exciting as watching paint dry, but they weren't, and it was riveting.

"The Grand Old Duke of N'yawk," Delilah improvised, gloating over her own cleverness, "he had ten zombie men; he marched them right across the stage, and he marched them back again."

She passed the binoculars forward, and Benny took them—Fay didn't try to snatch them before he could get to them. Benny focused the lenses, and trained the glasses on the faces of the walking dead: on their unseeing eyes and their rigid lips, on the skin that the worms had already begun to eat. The only face he couldn't see was the face of the man who carried his head in his hands, but he knew that it wouldn't be any different.

The marching stopped, and the zombies resumed their single file at the front of the stage. Papa Ogo swayed and keened.

The zombies turned sideways again, but not all the same way; they turned so that there were five pairs facing one another. Only three of the pairs included a woman, but there didn't seem to be any particular incongruity in that.

Benny thought that they were going to dance, and he wondered how the guy who had his head in his hands was going to take hold of his partner—but they didn't dance. They didn't even jig about the way Papa Ogo was jigging about. Instead, all but one of them reached out with their ragged hands, and began to stroke one another's faces.

The beheaded man was the only one who could not return the caress—but he was also the only one who was able to push his face forward to meet his partner's hands half way.

Slowly, like pairs of entranced lovers, the corpses began to move closer to their partners.

Benny passed the field-glasses to Fay. She accepted them, but didn't immediately put them to her eyes.

"The grave's a fine and private place," said Delilah, quite carried away by her own poetic flair, "but none I think do there embrace. But what the fuck do *you* know, smartass?"

There was a moment of suspended disbelief in which Benny thought that the zombies might actually be going to *do it*, but then he gathered his wits about him and took the trouble to notice that the corpses were hardly touching one another at all. They were making only the lightest of contacts, as if they were afraid that any real friction would do too much damage. The caresses were only apparent; the zombies were only pretending.

The man with the portable head had lifted it almost all the way to his partner's lifeless lips, as though the two of them were about to exchange a bizarre kiss—but they weren't. It was just a tease. Papa Ogo was quite a showman, and he knew how to string an audience out.

Benny wound down the window just a little, to let some air in through a slender crack. It wasn't that he wanted to smell the ordinary sweetness of the swampland air—he was curious to know whether the stink of corruption was drifting from the stage through the still night air. But any such scent was drowned by the reek of the dog-and-burger stand: cooked meat, fried onion, and spices.

Benny's head was singing; the elixir was making free with all the neurons in his brain, sending electrical energy zooming hither and yon, from thought to desire to instinct to the dark subconscious, and back again.

Much the same, he figured, must be happening up on the stage. The zombies were dead, but somehow the vital energies had been made to flow in them again. Their stalled brains had been crudely restarted, but the example of the headless man proved that a brain wasn't actually necessary to control these kinds of motor impulses. The headless zombie was animated by his spinal cord alone, cruising on his autonomics.

But can they think? Benny asked himself, silently. *When their brains were switched back on, did their identities come on too? Do they know who they are? Do they know* what *they are?*

"If I strangled you now," said Mikey to Delilah, in a sepulchral voice, "you could go up on stage and join in the act. This could be your big break in show business."

Mikey was undoubtedly hoping that Delilah would be overwhelmed with horror by the suggestion, but she was made of sterner stuff. "What would be the use of that," she asked, scornfully, "if I couldn't get into TV?"

If anyone was freaked out with the horror of it all, Benny realized, it was Fay. Frigid Fay, freaked by fear. Maybe, he thought, the six-sevenths of her icebound emotions that had always been submerged in the lower depths of her being were rising to the surface for once...as slowly and awkwardly as a zombie from its coffin.

Fay had the binoculars to her eyes now, and she was watching the zombies pretend that they really liked one another, and really cared. She didn't say a word.

"Can't take one home, honey," said Benny, lazily. "Daddy wouldn't approve."

"Shut your mouth," she said, tautly—scoring a point off Mikey for him. "Just shut your fucking mujo mouth, okay?"

"Okay," said Benny.

Up on the stage, the zombies lowered their hands again, and moved back to stand in line.

What next? thought Benny, rapt with anticipation. *What next?*

He didn't have to wait long for an answer to his question. Within two seconds the whole sky was ablaze with brilliant white light. It seemed to his astonished brain that all hell had been abruptly let loose upon the earth, and that the Day of Judgment promised by the sequined MC was already here.

* * * * * * *

Even the zombies turned their sightless eyes Heavenward, as though it might be given to them by some miracle that they could behold the glory of the coming of the Lord.

But it wasn't the Lord's angels that were descending in that blaze of light; it was Estate paycops in a squadron of whirlybirds. As the copters floated down from the clouded sky the incredibly vivid beams of their searchlights separated and became countable.

There were six birds in all, and although the thrumming of their rotor blades seemed thunderous, the voice that bellowed from their loudspeakers came through strong and clear.

"This is a police action," it declared. "Everybody please stay perfectly still. This is a police action. Members of the public are in no danger—repeat, *no danger*. This is a police action whose only purpose is to apprehend Edward Ojeki, *alias* Juju Jake, *alias* Papa Ogo, on charges of industrial espionage, grand larceny and illicit use of patented biotechnologies. Please stay where you are, and no one will be hurt."

It wasn't like the paycops to say "please," but they must have been in an ironic mood. They surely knew full well that it wouldn't do any good. There were a good many people in the crowd—tourists as well as ganglanders—whose first instinct on being told to stay put was to run like hell. There were a good many more whose first instinct was to start shooting, and *then* to run like hell.

Satan's Stormtroopers belonged to the latter camp. Benny had heard a rumor that they had some beef against the Uplands Estate anyhow, because of some unfortunate incident at a roadhouse way out west, but they weren't the kind to need a special excuse. All of a sudden there were half a dozen shotguns banging away, backed up by the rattle of pistol-fire. But what went up was nothing compared to what came down. The birdmen had machine-guns, and the troopers suddenly found that it was raining death.

The voice of the loudspeaker was still gibbering away, trying desperately to explain that the only purpose of the raid was to grab Papa Ogo, but it was blotted out now by the general pandemonium.

Up on the stage, Papa Ogo had produced an absurdly tiny handgun from the voluminous folds of his black cloak, and he was firing up at the bellies of the descending helicopters. Benny was too surprised to laugh, but his eyes fixed themselves upon the spitting barrel of the pistol, and he didn't immediately notice that Fay had grabbed his arm and was shaking him violently.

"Benneeee...!" she was shrieking.

Even Mikey was yelling: "Get us the hell outta here!"

Benny didn't bother to shout back, although he tried to thrust Fay's urgent hands away. He fired up the motor of the Thunderbug, but he didn't put her into gear.

There was no point, because there was absolutely nowhere to go. They were hemmed in on all four sides.

Benny knew, at the level of conscious thought, that the danger wasn't extreme. The cops were using heavy metal, but they weren't dropping bombs—they were picking their targets and they were all skilled shooters. The stormtroopers were being massacred, but nobody was aiming at the slummers' vehicles. If the tourists stayed put, as they'd been told to do, they'd be okay—probably. But the level of conscious thought wasn't the only level at which Benny was functioning. He was as high as a kite and his guts had ideas of their own. The excitement that only a few moments before had seemed to be a kind of ecstasy was now coming through as pure terror.

"Go, go, go," crooned Delilah, not meaning what she normally meant at all. Benny would have done it if he could, but there was no empty space to aim for, and all he could do was clench his fingers about the wheel and pray for the cage to open up. His staring eyes felt hot and hard, and he could see from his ghostly reflection in the windscreen that the whites were visible all around the irises, just like Papa Ogo's.

Cheat! he howled, silently. It was all too obvious now that Papa Ogo's secrets hadn't been handed down from African antiquity at all. Voodoo they might be, but they were biotech voodoo straight out of some corp's busy research labs. Real—oh, very real—but still a lousy scam, still a stupid show...just one more way to rustle cattle.

Papa Ogo had gone from the platform now, and was doing his level best to dodge the searchlights and disappear into the trees behind the stage. But the zombies were still up there, still standing patiently to attention, heads tilted back as though in bewilderment. Even the guy who held his head in his hands was tilting it, to point its useless eyes at the fire-filled sky.

Then, while Benny was still watching them and cursing them for not being quite what they were supposed to be, the scaffolding began to crumple, and the planks comprising the stage began to come apart. The zombies fell, one by one, like rag dolls tumbled from their stations.

The party of the two parts was the last to go, and before he went he dropped his head.

"Move!" screamed Fay, scrabbling at him again with her neatly-manicured fingernails. "Get me out the hell of here!"

At last, a gap was opening up. The driver in front had been waiting with his foot on the pedal, just like Benny had, and when the gap came for him he went through it like a bat out of hell. Benny didn't hesitate—he slammed his foot down and followed, hoping that the other guy wouldn't hit anything, and wouldn't have to brake. The cars to either side were still stuck fast, making a steel corridor; Benny knew full well that any one of them would swing out in front of him, if he gave the driver half a chance, so he didn't. Let them get on his tail, if they could!

The corridor wasn't long, and beyond its end there was an open space—but they couldn't keep going forwards because of the tangled wreckage of the scaffolding that had supported the stage. The car in front turned left, in the direction of the Uplands, and Benny followed him—-the last thing he wanted was to find himself charging straight into some other bastard's headlights, and most of the shooting was coming from the other side, where the troopers had parked their bikes and their armory.

The other car swerved left to go round something, but, as it skewed away, the beams of its headlights showed Benny that there wasn't enough room for the swerve, because there were other vehicles trying to come out. The other driver braked, but they were almost past the wrecked stage by now, so Benny swerved around him on his right-hand side.

The Thunderbug bucked and bumped as it ran over a couple of pieces of scaffolding, but it didn't stop, and they were free and clear—or so it seemed, until something hit the hood with a sickening thud.

Even then, they didn't stop, because they hadn't hit anything solid enough to stop them. What they'd hit was a human body, which was still on the hood, with its face pressed up against the windscreen on the passenger side. If the body had been alive when they hit it, the impact would almost certainly have killed it, but it hadn't. It had been dead for a long time.

Benny recognized the guy immediately. It was number two—the bloated one. His swollen face was like one great big ugly bruise, with the whites of his eyes seeming almost to glow against the dark background. His mouth was open, so that his lips formed a perfect letter O, in the center of which was his inflated tongue, like a black balloon.

Fay screamed.

The zombie's face was no more than a couple of feet away from hers. In the field of her vision it must have displaced her own lovely reflection, superimposing its nightmare gaze upon the placid perfection of her sky-blue eyes. Benny had only the slightest notion of what that vision might mean to Fay, but he knew one thing that must be relevant: he knew that the beauty which she wore was not her natural heritage; it was a present from Daddy, the best that cosmetic biotech could offer.

She screamed again.

The show was over and the zombie was finished, but Papa Ogo's spell was not completely broken. The dead man's body was still capable of movement, and his decaying hands were groping at the windscreen, as if trying to find a hold upon its treacherously smooth surface. Whether he was truly capable of wanting anything or not, there was some reflex working within him, which aimed at keeping him where he was.

The reflex had no chance; the zombie couldn't cling on. Benny wrenched the wheel to take the Thunderbug back towards the road, and the zombie slid away, lost in the gathering gloom.

But it wasn't quite over—as they passed across the fringe of the arbitrary auditorium they came into a region where fire was still being exchanged between earth and sky. There was a sudden pitter-patter of metallic raindrops along the offside wing, and Benny jumped with alarm, but the bullets bounced off the armor-plate like so many dried peas. If the point of impact had been a foot higher they'd have spangled the window, but as things were Benny knew they'd only make dents—and there was nothing like a few modest battle scars to add a touch of class to a slummer's Thunderbug.

"Holy shit!" whispered Mikey, reverently. "We did it. We fucking did it."

"Easy," said Benny, as evenly as he could. "Easy, easy, easy."

"Go, go, go," sang Delilah, giggling like a maniac again.

Fay said nothing, but only trembled. Benny could feel the tremor in her body, and knew that it was a one-hundred-per-cent all-over fleshquake. That wasn't all, either—but

Benny was far too much of a gentleman ever to mention that his best girl-friend had suddenly begun to stink.

* * * * * * *

About three hours later they checked back into the Estate. The cop who checked them in ran an appraising eye over the fresh bullet-scars, and he grinned.

"Hi Benny," he said, amiably. "You kids had a good time?"

"Sure," said Benny. "We were really zooming tonight, sir. Really zooming."

"Heard a newsflash on the TV," said the cop, who was in no hurry to return their ID. "Seems there was some action east of the city tonight. Our boys chased down some rogue tech who'd borrowed some illicit machinery so he could set hisself up as some kind of voodoo hoodoo man. You kids see anything of that?"

"Nope," said Benny, laconically. "We just went out to get a little fresh air, that's all."

"Is that right?" said the cop, with a chuckle.

"That's right," said Benny. "But we were really zooming, weren't we guys?"

"Zooming," said Mikey and Delilah, in unison.

"Zooming," echoed Fay, just half a syllable behind. Her voice had a kind of hollow ring to it—but funnily enough, Benny was sure that, for the first time ever, Fay was using the word correctly; she had finally discovered what it meant. He had the feeling, nevertheless, that she wouldn't be going slumming with him again. In fact, he had a sneaking suspicion that she wouldn't be going slumming with anyone for quite some time. She would be staying home in the Uplands Ark, trying to forget about the wild, sweet world of the Greenhouse.

She couldn't take it. She'd broken, while Benny was still intact. He realized that ever since he'd first set his admiring eyes on Fay's neatly-sculpted face he'd been trying to prove something to her, but he had only just discovered what it was.

Straights and busted flushes, he said to himself, as he pulled away from the gate. *Stupes and skirts and stay-at-homes. That's what they are, the Uplanders. Peel away the polished skin and they're all the same underneath. They think they own the world, but they just can't stand the heat.*

Bloated with satisfaction, he swung the Thunderbug into the dark maw of the garage beneath the air-conditioned cap-stack where they all lived, and wondered again what it might feel like to be raised from the dead.

THE COLOR OF ENVY

"And why do you want to take part in this particular program, Miss Eliot?" asked Mrs. Parkinson, the lady from the Ethics Committee. It was the sort of question that people from Ethics Committees always asked, although Tess couldn't see that her motivation had anything to do with the moral justifiability of the experiment. So what if her interest *was* in the money that was on offer? What difference did it make?

She decided to lie anyway, carefully marshalling her armory of clichés. "I think it's something of real benefit," she said. "I know that human somatic engineering is considered to be rather risky, because of all the unknowns involved, but it's an important new method of tackling all kinds of medical problems. Generally speaking, it's the way forward—the cutting edge of progress. I suppose this particular experiment seems a little weird, but I've read the prospectus carefully and I think there's a lot to be learned from it. As Dr. Coghlan says, we've become so hung up on pill-popping that we don't realize how important the skin is to our general health, or the subtle opportunities it offers for improvement of the human condition."

Tess saw Dr. Coghlan grinning contentedly as his words were repeated in the tone of innocent credulity she had cultivated for such occasions as this. Dr. Hubbard's smile was slightly ironic, but it was a smile of approval nevertheless, nicely lit by the sunlight streaming through the ample windows of the hospital's plush Committee Room.

Tess had never volunteered for actual somatic engineering before, although she had rented out portions of her skin for several contact tests, and still had a couple of scars to prove it. She'd popped her fair share of pills and had become more intimately acquainted with powderject systems than she'd ever wanted to, but the main problem with those kinds of gigs were that she usually had to report to the labs on a daily basis for tests. Coghlan and Hubbard's experiment wasn't just better paid; it only called for once-weekly monitoring. Given that she was supposed to be writing her dissertation, Tess didn't want to be overcommitted to any kind of routine drudgery.

"You've done rather a lot of this kind of work during the last four years," Mrs. Parkinson observed, putting on a show of being worried that Tess might be becoming a guinea-pig junkie ripe for full-blown Munchhausen's Syndrome. Tess was an old enough hand by now to know that a good guinea-pig must never seem guilty of self-neglect, let alone self-abuse.

"Tuition fees have to be paid," Tess observed. A little bit of honesty couldn't hurt, provided that she used it as the prelude to something more grandiose. "I couldn't have stayed on to do the MA if the volunteer work as an undergrad hadn't demonstrated that there was a decent and bearable way to pay for it. I suppose I could have done bar-work or lap-dancing, but I like myself too much to put myself through it. I figure that if I'm going to end up tired and nauseous I'd rather do it for some higher cause than the gluttony and lust of middle-aged men still mourning the demise of *Loaded*."

Even the lady from the Ethics Committee smiled at that one. Not all feminists were ethicists, but all ethicists were feminists. "Won't your boyfriend object to the discoloration?" she asked. It was the ultimate trick question; good guinea-pigs were single, free of dependants and unlikely to drop out because of intimate peer pressure, but they were also normal, average and representative.

"I don't have a steady boyfriend at present," Tess told her. "The MA's only a one-year course and it's important that I do well. The job market's very competitive. I find that it's best, for the time being, to go out with a crowd—to enjoy myself without anything getting too intense. I expect I'll get teased, but it isn't going to cause any problems."

Mrs. Parkinson nodded approvingly. If she suspected that Tess was bullshitting she certainly wasn't going to say so. At the end of the day, she had as much interest as Drs. Coghlan and Hubbard in making up the sample number. "Okay," the ethicist said. "I don't see any problem here. Is Miss Eliot acceptable to you, doctors?"

Tess was, of course, acceptable to the doctors. Researchers in genetic engineering might not think of themselves as being in mourning for *Loaded*, but they were mostly nerdy middle-aged males, and Coghlan and Hubbard were no exception to that generalization. Twenty-one-year-old females were their favorite kind of experimental subject, even when they were awkwardly tall and not very pretty.

Sometimes, Tess reflected, guinea-pigging wasn't all that much different from lap-dancing—but even when you set aside the bullshit, it really did serve a higher cause. She knew that she might have to get used to being the butt of an awful lot of jokes while her arms and legs were green, but she figured that it would be worth it, in more ways than one. As well as clearing the last vestiges of her student loan, the pay-off would actually leave her in credit, and the experiment itself would be interesting. There was bound to be a certain cachet in being one of the first human beings ever to be equipped with chloroplasts. If things went well—or even if they went badly in an interesting kind of way—she might be able to dine out on the story for the rest of her life.

* * * * * * *

Because Tess's degree was in Media Studies, Drs Coghlan and Hubbard took it for granted that she wouldn't be able to understand the finer details of what they planned to do to her, but the Principle of Informed Consent required them to make the best effort they could. They were still making the effort when they got things under way in the basement lab, while Tess lay on an operating-table under the merciless glare of the striplights.

"The artificial chloroplasts are different in several significant ways from the ones that occur naturally in the leaves of plants," Dr. Coghlan told her, as he prepared to slap the first generous helpings of the pale green goo on to her more-than-ample arms and thighs. "The ones in plants are adapted to function within a specific biochemical context, and animal cells don't come equipped with the same kind of support structures. We've had to add a couple of extra twists to ensure that the carbohydrates synthesized by our babies can actually be used within the cells. There's a slim possibility that the add-ons won't work as well *in vivo* as they did *in vitro*, thus resulting in an unexpected build-up, but we don't think the surplus carbohydrate would do any harm if that happened. There are several kinds of protozoans that can function either as proto-plants or proto-animals, depending on the presence or absence of chloroplasts, *Euglena* being the best-known example, and we suspect that human cells are just as clever. The preliminary tissue-cultures suggest that skin cells are more adaptable than nature usually requires them to be."

"The one thing we can't expect, of course," Dr. Hubbard put in, as he hurriedly pulled on his own sterile gloves, determined not to miss out on the thigh-slapping fun, "is that the chloroplasts will be able to play a significant nutritive role. You'll probably get sick and tired of people asking you whether you can give up eating now that you can fix solar energy just like a tree, but we want you to carry on eating normally. We don't expect any significant diminution of your appetite. Humans are much more active than trees, you see. They need a great deal more energy, not just for locomotion but to maintain a stable internal temperature. The point of our experiment isn't to relieve you of the necessity to eat, even partially."

The goo felt cold as the two experimenters spread it over Tess's limbs, but it was a warm day and the coldness was refreshing, almost like taking a dip in a swimming-pool. The texture was more discomfiting; although the carrier was the color of mushy peas it felt more like treacle.

"I understand that," Tess assured Dr. Hubbard. "I've read the proposal. The technical stuff is mostly Greek to me, of course, but I get the general drift. The skin already plays a slight nutritional role, not in terms of basic carbohydrate building-blocks but in stimulating the synthesis of the odd vitamin or two. Ever since the backlash against the skin-cancer scare of the 1990s people have been hunting for all kinds of evidence that exposure to sun can actually do us good, by helping the skin to repair itself, reducing wrinkling and so on. What you're trying to do, basically, is to give those processes of repair and self-improvement an extra boost." *Purely in the interests of good health, of course*, she added, silently. *Perish the thought that either of you might be looking to bale out of biomedicine by selling out to the cosmetics industry.*

"That's right," said Dr. Coghlan enthusiastically. "We're hoping the weather holds throughout the eight-week run, so that you can spend as much time in a bikini as you can—while keeping up your academic work, of course. Your skin is renewing itself continuously as the top layer of epidermal cells dies and the cells are sloughed, so the chloroplasts will work their way out of your system naturally. If the preliminary experiment is a success, we might actually have a product on the market before you're thirty—long before you need to worry about wrinkles."

The researcher's reference to bikinis was entirely gratuitous; Tess's belly—like her face—would remain off-white throughout, and she would be able to expose the treated surfaces perfectly adequately while wearing shorts and a T-shirt. At present, she was wearing a modest one-piece bathing suit, and she felt a trifle over-conspicuous even in that.

"Well," Tess said, deciding as she turned from a supine position to lie prone that the ignominy of her situation licensed a little cynical humor, "I guess I won't qualify for the *real* test. By the time I have to make the big decision, the PR people will either have on the war or lost it."

"How do you mean?" said Dr. Hubbard, who tended to be somewhat less articulate when he was forced to abandon his prepared scripts. "What *real test*?"

"The test that will determine whether middle-aged women will be prepared to turn their faces green if that's the price they have to pay for not getting wrinkly. I can imagine the slogans and headlines already, can't you? BETTER GREEN THAN HAS-BEEN. GREEN IS THE COLOR OF

ENVY. A FINAL FAREWELL TO FRAIL FAWN FLESH."

"Now, Tess," said Dr. Coghlan, censoriously, "if you've read the proposal, you know there's far more at stake here than mere matters of vanity. Lie still now—we have to give the vector virus-coats a chance to get the chloroplasts across the cell-membrane. I see from your record that you're familiar with the uses of DMSO as well as powderjects, but this is more complicated. If you'll forgive the mildly pornographic comparison, it's more like sperm-cells fertilizing ova. Perfectly harmless, of course—we'll scrub you down with sterilizing fluid in half an hour or so, when the chloroplasts have had a chance to sink in."

"No problem," said Tess. "You couldn't possibly let me have a pair of those gloves, could you? This stuff is too sticky to stay exactly where it's put, and it would probably help to cut down on the silly jokes if I didn't actually have green fingers when I walk out of here."

"Of course," said Dr. Hubbard. "We should have thought of that. Just keep as still as possible while I find one of the lab assistants to put them on for you."

"You'd better make sure you keep your own hands away from your faces," Tess advised the experimenters, more out of mischief than altruism. "You could end up with some embarrassing spots."

* * * * * * *

Fortunately, Tess's skin didn't end up the same virulent shade as the goo from which the artificial chloroplasts had been absorbed. The transferred greenness was distinct enough, but it was a pleasant pastel shade. *I'm not as green as I'm cabbage-looking*, Tess thought, remembering something her maternal grandmother used to say. Her grandmother's maiden name had been Green, and she'd taken a certain amount of teasing because of it when she was a child. What she'd have said about Tess's latest project could only be imagined, because Tess had not the slightest intention of telling any of her relatives exactly how she was paying her way through university.

For the first few days there were no other symptoms to accompany the change of color. It was as if she'd been given a light coat of intangible paint. She presumed that Drs. Coghlan and Hubbard would be able to detect some changes at the physiological level when she returned to the hospital on the following Monday for her weekly check-up, but the early indications were that this would be the easiest money Tess had ever earned.

At first she was a little wary about sitting outdoors in the full glare of the summer sun, and not just because she was bound to attract attention, but when no itches developed she grew bolder. She had no more classes to attend, and the research for her dissertation on "The Image of Biotechnology in Popular Journalism" involved several routine tasks—reading tabloid newspapers, for example—that could as easily be carried out on the lawns outside the Hall of Residence as anywhere else.

Oddly enough, her neighbors didn't hurl nearly as many feeble jokes in her direction as she'd expected. In fact, the almost-unanimous reaction of people who knew her name was alarm bordering on horror. The most oft-repeated comment was the distinctly humorless: "It's not catching, is it?"

"You're completely mad, you know," said Sheila, the English Ph.D. student who lived in the room next door and qualified as Tess's only real friend. "I thought the business with the blisters had taught you a lesson. Suppose that stuff doesn't come off—you could be stuck like that forever."

"Only if the wind changes," Tess told her—but the irony was lost.

"It's dangerous, Tess," Sheila insisted. "It's genetic engineering, for God's sake."

"I know all about the risks," Tess assured her. "Once you get past the yuck factor, it's no big deal."

"Well, it's no wonder you can't get a boyfriend. You've no chance now. Who'd want to be hugged by green arms?"

That, of course, was totally uncalled for. "The reason I don't have a boyfriend," Tess retorted, frostily, "is that they're a waste of time and space even when they don't expect you to do their washing for them. If I did have one, he wouldn't be in the least put off by the fact that my arms and

72

legs will be a discreet shade of green for a couple of months."

"You have no idea what it's doing to you," Sheila insisted. "While normal people are still trying to keep GM soya and peanut-oil out of the supermarkets, you're actually letting those Frankensteins modify you. Crazy."

"I'm not going to metamorphose into a triffid," Tess assured her, figuring that she might as well supply the jokes if no one else would. "I don't even feel any insidious urge to join Greenpeace, or pose for Tretchikoff."

"So how *do* you feel?" the ever-curious Sheila wanted to know—and when she didn't get the answer she was looking for on Wednesday, she asked again on Thursday, and yet again on Friday—by which time the pedestrian traffic on the path through the lawns seemed to Tess's slightly anxious eye to have increased considerably. She told herself sternly that it was ridiculous to suspect that people who had no real reason for walking past the Hall were taking detours, so that they could catch a discreet glimpse of the notorious girl with green limbs, but she couldn't quite convince herself. Having green arms and legs for a couple of months had seemed like a minor inconvenience when contemplated in the abstract, even when the researchers had told her that she had to give the treated surfaces as much exposure to the sun as she could contrive, but Sheila's comments only served to emphasize her own growing sense of embarrassment and unease.

She had to fight back, of course. The last thing she wanted to do was let anyone else see her discomfort or share her distress. The first couple of times, Tess answered Sheila's question as to how she felt by simply saying: "Fine." On Friday, however, she made it: "Better than fine. Pretty good, in fact."

"I don't believe you," was Sheila's blunt retort. "You can't tell me that you really are getting energy out of the sunlight!"

"But I *am*," Tess insisted. "That's the whole point of the experiment. The chloroplasts are producing glucose and half a dozen other beneficial compounds, and the glucose is being metabolized right there in my skin cells. I really do feel a sort of *healthy glow*."

"Green glows aren't healthy," Sheila said, unhesitatingly. The confident generalization was presumably based on a more careful study of bad science fiction movies than Tess, even as a Media Studies student, had ever felt compelled to make.

"It's not a glow in the sense that you *see* it," Tess said, with a sigh. "*Glow*, in this context, is a kind of warm feeling. Well, not exactly warm, more...." She was forced to tail off at this point, because she hadn't thought the story through any further. It occurred to her, too, that while she'd been so busy worrying about what she must look like she hadn't actually tried to interrogate her real feelings. It hadn't seemed necessary, until the challenge was formally issued—but now it had been issued, she felt obliged to meet it squarely. "I *do* feel that my skin is enjoying its exposure to the sun," she went on, after a pause, trying not to sound too surprised, "but that's not all. There's a certain almost erogenous superficial excitement, but there's also something deeper, something that touches my fundamental being-in-the-world."

"You Media Studies people are so full of existentialist and deconstructionist bullshit," was Sheila's inevitable response. "You'll be telling me next that you feel a new kinship with the trees and the grass—that you'd only have to roll naked on the lawn to have multiple orgasms. *Almost erogenous superficial excitement!* You don't listen to yourself, do you?"

The truth of the matter, however, was that Tess had only just begun to listen to herself, and to wonder how accurately she was describing her sensations. She wasn't sure that she was making sense, but she was trying. Was it possible, she wondered, that her green skin really *had* become more sensitive to trivial sensations—not just external sensations like the pressure of the wind but internal sensations too. Was it possible that she was more aware of *herself* in consequence—or, if not more aware, at least differently aware.

Tess was still thinking about these possibilities when the sun went down and she returned to her room. She was not normally one for looking at herself in a mirror, but she did so now, wondering if her undiscolored face had changed somehow in response to what the chloroplasts had done for her inner being.

"It's bullshit," she murmured. "It's all in the mind." But *what* was in her mind, exactly? And how had it got there?

She decided, on due consideration, that her new self-awareness wasn't at all unpleasant—nothing like an itch or the "restless legs" she sometimes got if she had to take anti-histamines for hay fever—even though the mere fact of it was slightly worrying. On the other hand, what Sheila had said about rolling around on the lawn didn't seem quite as absurd as she had intended. Tess did feel a certain inchoate desire for contact with other living things, so that her tempo-rarily-green flesh might be touched by its natural counter-parts. It wasn't a sexual desire—not, at least, in the familiar terms of human sexuality—but it was a temptation of sorts, which might even qualify as an appetite.

Maybe I am crazy! Tess thought. *I'm certainly going to sound crazy if I lay this on Cocky and Hub—unless, of course, they've already heard it from the other boys and girls.*

For a moment or two she wondered whether it would be too heinous a crime to break protocol and confer with the other subjects. She didn't know any of their names, of course, but they presumably lived within a few miles of the hospital, and they could hardly make themselves inconspicu-ous. She decided against it, though; quite apart from risking her pay-check, it would be wrong to prejudice the experi-mental findings.

Better wait and see, she thought. *It's probably just my imagination playing up.*

* * * * * * *

Tess didn't dare say too much to Drs. Coghlan and Hub-bard in case she came across as the kind of person who could develop all manner of imaginary symptoms just by reading a medical textbook, but she did drop heavy hints to the effect that she was feeling different. She knew that she couldn't have been the only subject to do that because the first thing Coghlan asked her was whether she'd talked to any of the others. "Of course not," she replied, virtuously. "I know the rules. What have they said?"

"If you know the rules," Dr. Coghlan riposted, "you'll know why I can't tell you that. I suppose you considered the possibility that these strange sensations are purely psychosomatic?"

"Of course I have," Tess told him. "I'm an old hand at guinea-pigging, remember. I know all about the hazards of suggestibility and the methodological curse of the placebo effect. Isn't there a danger of going to the opposite extreme, though? It *might* be real."

"It is possible that there's some extra stimulation of the nerve-endings," Dr. Hubbard put in, pensively. He was talking to his colleague rather than Tess, and he shouldn't have been doing it in front of her in case it put ideas into her head, but Tess was too interested to let it pass.

"I thought of that," she said. "When I told one of my friends that it was a sort of glow I had to start asking myself what I meant by it. I wondered whether I might simply be feeling the warmth of the sunlight more intensely, but I don't think that's it. I know that what we lump together as the single sense of touch actually involves several different types of nerve receptors—pressure, pain, heat and so on—but I don't think it's any of those kinds of stimuli. It's more diffuse, more rarefied. You might think this is silly, but the fact that plants don't have nervous systems doesn't mean that they're insensitive, does it? They react to their environment—and most of all, they react to light. Their chloroplasts must be involved in whatever kind of chain-reaction is going on. You said yourselves that protozoan cells can accommodate chloroplasts or not, and that human skin cells are more adaptable than might be expected. I can't help wondering whether your artificial chloroplasts have awakened some kind of sensory mechanism that's been lying dormant in *all* animal cells for billions of years."

Dr. Coghlan stared at her, wearing a stern frown. "It's not good for experimental subjects to do so much *thinking*," he said. "The principle of informed consent may be ethically necessary, but it does carry methodological risks. The process of observation always affects the properties of whatever's being observed, but we have to try to keep that kind of effect to a minimum."

"Easy enough with tissue-cultures," Tess told him, offended by his lack of appreciation. "When you use real human subjects, you get a real human response. Isn't that the point?"

"The point Dr. Coghlan is trying to make," Dr. Hubbard put in, soothingly, "is that it might be better if you were to try to make an objective record of your sensations rather than trying so hard to interpret them theoretically."

"There's no such thing as an objective record of sensations," Tess came back. "Sensations have to be interpreted, whether you use theoretical jargon or not. If we were used to the kinds of sensations I'm now experiencing the language would already be equipped with commonplace descriptive terms, but we aren't and it isn't, so I'm doing my best to make up for the lack, okay?"

"Okay," said Dr. Hubbard, hurriedly. "We do appreciate it—but it's not exactly what we're looking for. Our interest is primarily physiological."

"Well," said Tess, "I dare say that I can leave measuring the wrinkles and tracking the carbohydrate levels to you. If there are any undesirable physiological side-effects, I'm sure that you'll be on to them like a flash—but we guinea-pigs can hardly ignore psychological side-effects, can we? And if we don't try to compile a sensible account of them, you'll miss them altogether, won't you? The PR department will have to deal with them someday. Admen aren't going to be able to invite the women of the future to GIVE YOURSELF THE GREEN LIGHT TO LOOK YOUNGER if the psychological side-effects of the treatment outweigh the intended ones."

She could tell that she wasn't getting anywhere. They thought that it was all paranoia, and that it was getting in the way of the experiment—and she was horribly afraid that they might be right, and that she mightn't be such a good guinea-pig as she'd hoped. She didn't like to think that of herself. She might not be able to compete with girls like Sheila on looks and charm, but she'd always hoped to make up for it with intelligence and integrity. The best thing, she figured, was to make light of it—at least for the present.

"But hey!" she went on, languidly waving one of her long green arms. "Let's look on the bright side. I don't feel bad. In, fact, I feel good in a way I never even knew I *could* feel good. Maybe chloroplasts will turn out better than you ever imagined. Think how much money you could make if they turn out to be marketable as the new Prozac as well as one more small step on the long and winding road to the Fountain of Youth!"

The two researchers should have scolded her for impugning their motives, but her less-than-reverent manner reassured them and they were glad of the opportunity to smile.

"Thank you, Tess," said Dr. Coghlan, tolerantly. "I think that's all for now—we'll see you next week. Please try to keep your imagination within reasonable bounds in the meantime."

"You've got a green spot on your right cheek, Dr. Coghlan," Tess said, by way of reprisal. "I told you to be careful about touching your face while you had those gloves on, didn't I?"

* * * * * * *

A ridge of high pressure sat above the southern counties for the entirety of the following week. There was hardly a cloud to be seen in the sky and Tess took full advantage of the sun's uninterrupted glare. Although she was careful to take her books and newspapers with her, so that she could maintain the pretence of working on her dissertation, she was far more concerned with her introspective analysis of the existential effects of being equipped with chloroplasts. She'd decided to take the view that even if it turned out to be a fantasy, at least it was an *interesting* fantasy.

The initial exhilaration that she had described, rather inaptly, as a warm glow soon faded away. It was not that she had ceased to feel good, she told herself—merely that she had begun to take the goodness of it for granted. There was no need to be dismayed by this. Now that she had got past the mere goodness of the effect, she might be able to find more exact and delicate metaphors with which to capture its essence.

She felt energized, but not in the vulgar sense that she wanted to take exercise. As the two researchers had pointed out, the extra nutrition she was receiving by virtue of the chloroplasts' activity was negligible. She wasn't putting on weight, thank God. Her energization was of a different kind, and she couldn't help recalling the words that had sprung to her mind when she had groped for a way to explain to Sheila how she felt. "Almost erogenous" was as near as she could get even after ten days of further cogitation. It wasn't lust that was energizing her, she decided, but it was something conceptually akin to sexuality. She felt *fertile*, in some admittedly perverse way that had absolutely nothing to do with ovulation.

In fact, Tess eventually conceded, Sheila had got nearer to the mark than she could possibly have supposed when she had referred scornfully to feeling a new kinship with trees and the orgasmic possibilities of rolling around in the grass. Tess *did* feel a new sense of belonging to the natural world, and a curious sense of participation in its collective activity.

Better not say that to Sheila, though, she thought, *or to Cocky and Hub. One or other of them would be bound to start talking contemptuously about Gaia, and that's not it at all.*

But why wasn't that it?

Tess decided, after further reflection, that there was nothing in what she felt that could be likened to a sense of the supposed balance of nature—quite the reverse, in fact. The energization she felt had far more conflict in it than harmony, far more assertiveness than homeostasis. The pseudo-kinship she felt with the vegetal kingdom wasn't reflected in her own passivity but in a new sense of the activity and virility of flowering plants. Like her, they might appear to be passive and motionless as they soaked up the sunlight, but they weren't. All kinds of physiological processes were going on within them, and the protoplasm within their cells was just as active, in a biochemical sense, as the protoplasm of animal cells. After their own fashion, plants were *busy*, and in spring and early summer they were as actively engaged in the business of reproduction as the birds and the bees. They couldn't experience lust in an animal fashion, but that didn't mean they were insensitive to the vagaries of the season.

What, Tess wondered, did plants have instead of the pornographic imagination? What passed for romantic fantasy within the turgid flesh of stem and flower? The colors and scents of flowers were, of course, the pornography that plants manufactured to attract and nourish the insects on which they relied for pollination—but what was its echo in the plant's own inner being? What answered the plucking fingers of the wind within the heart of a reed? How did a bush respond to the seizure of its luscious fruits by the birds that would carry its indigestible seeds to distant sites?

It was all imagination, of course, and theorized imagination to boot: exactly what Dr. Coghlan had warned her against. And yet, Tess was convinced that she *did* feel different. The artificial chloroplasts transplanted into the lower layers of her epidermis had changed her, and not for the worse. She felt that they had extended the range of her potential wisdom, perhaps far more than any mere BA or MA ever could.

But she knew that it wouldn't last.

Within six weeks the ceaseless processes of self-renewal that were at work within her skin would start killing off the cells that contained the chloroplasts, and the greenness of her skin would fade as the shriveled cells became sustenance for the legions of dust-mites infesting in the mattress on the bed that she only used for sleeping.

Well, she told herself, *at least it'll help me concentrate on my dissertation. And if I'm a really good girl, maybe I can get Cocky and Hub to take me on for some kind of long-term study.*

For the first half of the third week she stuck to the shorts and T-shirt that she had grown used to thinking of as her "working clothes," but as the weather became hotter and hotter she began to feel overdressed by comparison with the other people sunbathing on the lawns. She was a little worried about exposing the variegations of her skin-color to public view, but it became so uncomfortable wearing the shorts over her knickers that on Thursday she decided to take up Dr. Coghlan's lascivious suggestion and treat herself to her first ever bikini.

She needn't have worried about attracting sarcastic comments; with the exception of the still-censorious Sheila her neighbors seemed to have been driven by the yuck factor to extend an invisible *cordon sanitaire* around her customary station.

"You'd better put some sun block on that," Sheila said, when she observed the pale expanse extending extravagantly between the two halves of Tess's brand new bikini. "The green areas are only growing greener, but your lily-white belly will burn before it tans."

"I don't have any," Tess confessed.

"You can borrow some of mine," Sheila offered, generously. "I'll do your back if you'll do mine—provided that you're absolutely sure that it isn't catching."

"In science," Tess informed her, loftily, "nothing is ever absolutely sure. That's the beauty of it."

* * * * * * *

Tess decided not to mention the results of her experiments in introspection when she reported in to Drs. Coghlan and Hubbard for the third time. She contented herself with assuring them that she still felt fine, but that it didn't seem so startling any more. She didn't say in so many words that she'd made too much fuss the first time, but the two researchers clearly took that inference. Tess was longing to know what kinds of reports the other subjects were putting in—and, come to that, what the various clinical tests had so far revealed—but she knew there was no point in asking. The enquiry had passed the stage of informed consent and the ruling protocol now was the minimization of subject expectation.

Tess couldn't help noticing that the green spot on Dr. Coghlan's face seemed more noticeable than it had before, but she didn't comment on the fact. After all, she thought, a ruling protocol ought to cut both ways. There was no way an experiment of this kind could be provided with a proper double blind, but that didn't mean that she ought to disregard the influence of the experimenters' expectations.

She waited until the following Monday—by which time she had laid in her own supplies of low-factor sun block—to ask Sheila the question that had risen spontaneously to the forefront of her mind.

"When you said that the green areas were getting greener," she said, "did you mean it literally?"

"Of course," Sheila replied, feigning innocence. "Aren't they supposed to?"

"I'm serious," Tess said. "I've looked hard, but I can't see a difference."

"You've been looking at it every day," Sheila told her. "I haven't. It's a slight difference, but I think it's real. Didn't they say anything at the hospital? Surely they'd know if the green bugs were breeding."

"They're not bugs and they can't breed," Tess replied, reflexively. On the other hand, she thought, the tests that Coghlan and Hubbard had done would surely tell them if there were any increase in the population of chloroplasts. If there *were*....

Suddenly, the jokes that most of her acquaintances hadn't bothered to make but which Tess's fertile imagination had catalogued anyway didn't seem so funny. Sheila had been the only one who had dared to suggest, even in jest, that Tess might be stuck like his forever, but she couldn't have been the only one who'd thought of it.

"Well," said Sheila, "maybe your body has got hooked on your almost erogenous glow and it's started to make its own."

Tess didn't think that was any more likely than the chloroplasts having learned a way to reproduce themselves. On the other hand, she thought, neither possibility might be quite as absurd as she'd previously assumed. The vector that had ferried the chloroplasts across the membranes of her living skin-cells had been a protein virus-shell of the kind that acted like a microminiaturized hypodermic in certain kinds of infection. In the absence of any supportive DNA, the shells were supposed to be incapable of reproducing themselves, let alone the artificial chloroplasts, but Tess knew little or nothing about the process by which they were manufactured or the reliability of whatever trick was used to dispossess them of their native DNA.

She remembered, belatedly, something she had read in the *Guardian* science pages, in the course of researching her dissertation, about the reasons for the latest delay in finalizing the results of the Human Genome Project. There was, she recalled, a distinction to be made between the mapping of the genes on the various chromosomes and the sequencing of the DNA, and some dispute as to whether all the extra DNA revealed by the sequencing was just junk, or whether it contained "deactivated genes" that couldn't or needn't be mapped because they were unexpressed in all kinds of human cells. Suppose, she thought, the artificial chloroplasts and their associated paraphernalia had contrived to wake up some of the deactivated genes....

That night, Tess began a careful examination of the edges of the discoloration introduced into her flesh by the green goo.

It was very difficult to be certain, but she thought that she could already detect a slight expansion of the green area. There was no sign of greenness about her face, or the areas between the two parts of her bikini, but the white margins exposed by the skimpier costume did seem to be shrinking slightly.

Tess's first reaction was direly anxious—but her second thoughts swung like a pendulum to the other extreme. *If it's true,* she said to herself, *there's no way they can stop me being part of a long-term study, and they'll have to take the subjective feelings more seriously.* Then, of course, they swung right back again, as she realized that if green arms and legs were enough to make a pariah, green arms and legs that were growing greener by the week might well turn into a serious social handicap. It was one thing to put her love-life on hold while she was doing her MA—or, at least, telling herself that that was the reason—and quite another to blight its prospects indefinitely.

Oh shit! she thought. *I'm going to have to tell my parents!*

After a while, however, she calmed down sufficiently to take a more balanced view. *One way or another*, she told herself, carefully, *the chloroplasts really are multiplying— but that doesn't mean they can keep on multiplying indefinitely, or that they can migrate from one epidermal layer to the next. Even if Cocky and Hub really are the Frankenstein twins, that doesn't make me a monster.*

* * * * * * *

The next time Tess reported in for examination, she wasn't at all surprised to find Mrs. Parkinson in attendance. The slight worries she was still entertaining as to whether the expansion of her green areas might be an illusion vanished immediately. Researchers only recalled ethicists if their experiments had thrown up real ethical problems.

The first thing Tess said to Dr. Coghlan was: "I suppose you've noticed that the green spot on your cheek is getting bigger and brighter."

He didn't try to deny it. He nodded, and looked at her with wary eyes, wondering what she was going to say next.

"I expect you've been trying to get rid of it," Tess commented, keeping the tone of her voice scrupulously even. "No luck yet, I guess."

"Actually," Dr. Coghlan said, smugly. "We think we've already found the fix."

"But you decided to let it go on growing," Tess deduced. "That way, you can experience for yourself what I've been trying unsuccessfully to explain to you. Good for you. I suppose, all joking aside, that there really isn't any possibility that it's catching?"

Dr. Coghlan didn't rush to answer that. Dr. Hubbard opened his mouth as if to cover up the hesitation, but it was Mrs. Parkinson who got in first. "There's no need to worry unduly, Tess," she said. "The fact that the chloroplasts are multiplying within the skin of some of the subjects doesn't mean that they can be communicated to other people. Nor does it mean that you're stuck with them indefinitely. So far as we can tell, the chloroplasts can only spread to skin that's exposed to sunlight—and they don't persist for very long in skin that's permanently covered up. If you want to stop the coloration spreading, it seems that all you need to do is cover the relevant parts of your body—ditto if you want to be rid of the color you've already got. The Ethics Committee has decided, in view of the fact that the situation has changed materially, that you'll still be paid in full even if you decide that you'd rather do that, but we'd prefer it if you didn't."

Tess wasn't stupid enough to think that the offer to pay her even if she decided to try to get rid of her chloroplasts was a noble gesture. What Drs. Coghlan and Hubbard wanted now was a divided sample. They needed to be able to track the progress of one group whose members were resolved to get rid of their chloroplasts, and a second whose members were prepared not merely to hang on to them but to let the chloroplasts spread—if not to the face, at least to the rest of the body—and maybe a third whose chloroplasts were dying off anyway no matter what they wanted. The Ethics Committee wouldn't allow the experimenters to demand that any of their guinea-pigs do the kind of overtime that required them to stay green and become even greener, but they were prepared to send their own representative down to ask—maybe even to beg.

"Okay," said Tess, figuring that this was one occasion when she wouldn't have to put on an act. "You can count me in. I'll hang on to mine."

The way the two doctors perked up told her that she had just volunteered for the minority. That wasn't a surprise. Mrs. Parkinson had already let slip the fact that some of the subjects hadn't experienced any multiplication at all.

"Green is the color of envy," Tess said, glad of the opportunity to quote herself. "I guess I'm a sinner at heart, or maybe just a born copywriter. They say that seventy percent of advertising is aimed at people who already use the product, just to help them feel better about it. If the chloroplasts like me, I'm prepared to like them."

"Tess is a Media Studies graduate," Dr. Hubbard reminded Mrs. Parkinson.

"You do realize, Tess," said Dr. Coghlan, carefully, "that the reformulated study is going to last a lot longer than eight weeks? You will be paid commensurately, of course."

"Oddly enough, "Tess said, "it's not just the money that interests me. I want to understand what's happened to me, in every dimension. I think we're all on the same side—but I do want you to be on mine as well as me being on yours."

Perhaps because he was the one with the green blot on his facial landscape, it was Dr. Coghlan who nodded. "That's fine," he said. "If this *is* a whole new ball game, you'll have some say in the way it develops. Everyone who's still involved will have a voice."

Tess saw Dr. Hubbard frown at that, because it was blatantly bad methodology to let experimental subjects dictate the terms of the experiment, but Mrs. Parkinson seemed relieved that Tess wasn't making difficulties of a different sort. As a Media Studies graduate, Tess understood just how close the screwed-up experiment had come to being exactly the kind of public relations disaster that could ruin the hospital and put back the cause of human somatic engineering by five or ten years. Right now, the fact that being green made at least some of the experimental subjects feel good—even if it *was* all in the mind—was the best thing Cocky and Hub had going for them.

* * * * * * *

By the time the green tinge finally made it to her fingertips, toes and throat, Tess had finished her dissertation and her course. The time had come to say her final goodbyes to the people who had been her neighbors in the Hall for the past year. Most of them politely refused to notice the fact that she was still getting greener, but Sheila had kept in close touch with the week-by-week progress of the experiment.

"Have your parents seen it yet?" she asked.

"Not yet," Tess confessed. "I had to tell them, but they won't actually see it until next week. Even then, it'll just be a flying visit. Dr. Coghlan's fixed up a flat for me. I'll be sharing with the other woman who decided to stay with the study, although I haven't actually met her yet. Next Monday will be the first time all five of us will be allowed to get together and compare notes—six if you count Dr. Coghlan."

"They're going to think it's some horrible disease, aren't they?" Sheila asked, refusing to be distracted from discussion of the likely views of Tess's nearest and dearest.

"Not once I've explained it to them," Tess said, without overmuch confidence. Although she'd made every effort to keep her friend in touch with developments, she knew that Sheila still thought that it *was* a horrible disease. "Once I've given them the good news," Tess plugged on, doggedly, "they'll hardly be able to wait for the chance to try it out themselves. That's what every sensible person will think."

"It'll never catch on, Tess," Sheila told her, firmly. "No matter how good the treatment is at fighting wrinkles, and no matter how hard people like you try to convince people that it can also give you a new a kind of high, nobody is going to use it—unless you can develop a suntan-colored version. Just because radical environmentalists say that green is good, it doesn't mean that people will ever be willing to have green arms and legs, let alone faces."

"Don't knock it until you've tried it," Tess advised her. "You'll be able to do that one day, you know. It's *not* catching, and you can get rid of it easily, any time you want to. That doesn't mean that it isn't going to change the world, but it does mean that the change will be gradual, and voluntary, and controlled: the best of all possible worlds. Believe me, Sheil, you'll be green all over before you're forty—and so will everybody else. I know I can't convince you of that now, but it doesn't matter. When you're ready, you'll convince yourself."

"Well, if it makes you feel better to believe that...."

"I don't have to believe anything to make me feel better," Tess told her, sternly.

"I *told* you that you'd be stuck like that," Sheila said, sticking to her own guns with equal determination.

"Yes, you did," Tess admitted. "But you thought it was a threat, and it wasn't. I'm happy to be stuck—more than happy."

"It's your decision," Sheila conceded, grudgingly, "but the sun won't always be shining. This is England, and winter's on its way—and you won't always be able to talk yourself into believing that it makes you feel great. I've known you long enough to know that you were desperate for something to make you feel better, even if you didn't know it."

Sheila wouldn't consent to be hugged before she went on her way, even though Tess had assured her that Dr. Coghlan was "ninety-nine percent certain" that the chloroplasts couldn't possibly be communicated from one person to another even by contacts far more intimate than a fully clothed hug.

* * * * * *

Although winter *was* on its way, it still seemed a fair way off to Tess, and the warm weather had already extended all the way through September. As soon as Sheila's taxi had departed Tess stripped down to her bikini and went back to her customary station on the lawn. She knew that she was going to miss Sheila, who had at least been willing and able to talk to Tess about what she was doing, but she felt that she had every right to hope and expect that life with her new flatmate would be frictionless.

As the sun began to play upon her skin Tess felt the familiar "glow" spread across all the affected areas of her body, and wished that she had the opportunity—or the courage—to expose all the remaining parts: the parts that she couldn't help thinking of, nowadays, as "etiolated." She wished that she'd been able to make Sheila understand that it wasn't a "new kind of high" at all, but a new kind of level: a new awareness of the fact of life. That was, admittedly, all that it was—the rest was just the free play of intelligence and imagination—but it was an awareness worth having for all that, and greenness was a price that Tess was more than willing to pay for it.

She knew that it wasn't going to be easy to be a pioneer, although it would be fun. The interviews she'd so far given to magazine and TV journalists had been filtered through the hospital's PR manager, and discretion had prevented any mention of her ambition to keep her chloroplasts indefinitely, but the journalists had already begun to speculate and pose more awkward and more interesting questions. Almost as soon as she had explained herself to her parents she was going to have to start explaining herself to the world—but she was prepared to meet the challenge, and looking forward to it. She had never expected to find such an easy route to celebrity—or, for that matter, to self-satisfaction.

The only thing worse than being talked about, she reminded herself, as she closed her eyes and stretched herself out to obtain the fullest benefit of the sun's rays, *is not being talked about*.

To begin with, of course, there would be a great many people who would not be able to envy her—but in time, and with the right encouragement, that would change. No matter how marginal the effect of Cocky and Hub's invention might be on the appearances of aging, it might well catch on among the young merely as a fashion. Tattoos and tongue-studs had come and gone, but greenness could be forever. Cleverly marketed, it could be as great a leap forward, in its way, as the invention of clothing. Properly managed, it could give the human race a new consciousness of self and environment, of life and light, of sensation and sensitivity....

Her reverie was interrupted by a polite cough. She opened her eyes to see a young man standing over her. He was dressed in shorts and a T-shirt, and his arms and legs were dappled with pale green patches.

Tess sat up abruptly.

"I'm Sam," he said. "Mine didn't take. I haven't tried to cover it up, but it's almost all gone anyway. Dr. Coghlan says that's good, because it allows him and Dr. Hubbard to make comparisons, to make a better start on figuring out the whys and wherefores—but I don't think so. You're Tess, right?"

Tess realized that he was looking for sympathy, and that he had sought her out in the expectation of getting it. He wasn't one of the lucky five—but he wished that he had been.

Suddenly, everything Tess had just been trying to tell herself seemed to click into place. It was as if it had all been in suspension, waiting for some crucial final endorsement—and here it was. Sam was short and spindly, not at all the kind of boy who would normally entertain the notion of chatting up someone as tall and solid as she was, but all normal prejudices were irrelevant to their present situation.

"Right," said Tess, belatedly. "I'm sorry, Sam. I can imagine what you're feeling."

"Sure," he said. "They'll have to let me have another crack, won't they? I've earned it, haven't I?" The point he was trying to put across, Tess realized, was that he had earned it no less than she, because he'd volunteered in exactly the same way.

"You'll be first in the queue," she said, as she came to her feet so she could look him in the eye. "Bound to be." As their stares locked she saw that there was admiration in his gaze. When she held out her hand he took it, not merely readily but avidly, as if he hoped that in spite of what Dr. Coghlan had concluded, it just might be catching.

"Hi," she said, unnecessarily.

"I expect we'll be seeing a more of each other," Sam said. "They're letting me stay on, as part of the control group. Compare and contrast—you know the sort of thing."

"I do," she said.

"There are five of you, not counting the doc," he observed, parroting the same information that Tess had earlier given Sheila. "Three green males, two green females. I'll be part of sample two—three males and two females who couldn't stay green even though they wanted to. Then there'll be the real weirdoes—the ones who've been green but want to be rid of it."

"It's okay," Tess assured him, with what she hoped was a winning smile. "I'm not prejudiced—against the ungreen, I mean."

"I am," Sam admitted, dolefully. "I didn't used to be, but I am now."

"Green is the color of envy," she quoted, hoping he hadn't heard it before—but it was far too obvious. He probably hung out with the kind of people who wouldn't let the unease of the yuck factor get in the way of their jokes and insults.

"If only envy were enough," he said, plaintively.

"Envy is what makes the world go round, Sam," she assured him, assuming that she was entitled to treat him with a measure of friendly condescension, given their different circumstances. "It's the motor of progress. You might be losing your first crop of chloroplasts, but we're both on the fast track to the future. For us, at least, envy will be enough. The hoi polloi will have to pay good money for what we'll get for free. So much for the cynics who never volunteer."

"I only did it for the money, to begin with," Sam confessed.

"I bet that's not what you told Mrs. Parkinson."

Sam grinned. "For her," he admitted, "I wanted to repay a little of the debt I owed for the wonderful inheritance of civilization. It wasn't exactly a lie—just a truth stretched to the limit."

"Altruism has its rewards," Tess observed. "I figure we're just as entitled to our share as anyone else. Cocky and Hub will have to do everything they can to keep us sweet. Once the journalists really get busy, we won't be experimental subjects any more—we'll be walking ads."

"You will," Sam said. "You're the one who's green *and* photogenic."

Tess accepted the compliment proudly. She wondered if it would be a good time to warn him that she didn't do anybody else's washing but her own, but she decided against it. If the occasion ever arose, he'd figure it out.

"It's a lovely day, isn't it," she said, stretching her limbs and neck to catch as much sun as she could.

"Lovely," he echoed. "How long do you think it will take?"

Tess didn't ask him what he meant. He was asking how long it would take Drs. Coghlan and Hubbard to sort themselves out well enough to be able to give him a community of chloroplasts that wouldn't perish so easily in his stubbornly unreceptive flesh. But what he was also asking, she figured—whether he knew it or not—was how long it would take to lead the hordes of the unenlightened to the Promised Land of eternal greenness and pleasantness.

"I don't know," she admitted. "The seeds of the future have to germinate and grow at their own pace, and the ground out there is stony in some parts and thorny in others—but life is stubborn. All the world was barren once, until the plants conspired to make it what it is today. We're the latest phase in the infinite plan—the journey-work of the stars. It might not be easy, but all it needs is patience."

THE LADY-KILLER, AS
OBSERVED FROM A SAFE DISTANCE

Stephanie was at her desk, catching up with what was still conventionally called "paperwork," when PC Courtland called from the front desk to say that a young man had walked in off the street wanting to talk to a detective about a murder.

"Whose murder?" Stephanie wanted to know.

Normally, she would have been delighted to be called away from her terminal to talk about a serious crime, but it was four o'clock in the morning, and her natural impetus was at its low ebb. If she hadn't cleared her backlog by the time the shift ended at six she would have to work on, looking like hell, while the valuable unmonitored space around her became crowded with the fresh faces of people who had actually managed to get some sleep. It seemed sensible to hesitate.

"Young woman named Lynne Wardle," Courtland reported. "DOA at the General two hours ago—cause of death yet to be ascertained, according to the notification. No signs of violence or other suspicious circumstances, according to the officer at the scene."

"Isn't DS Hammond on duty?" Stephanie procrastinated. She knew that if the man at the desk turned out to be anything but a compulsive confessor this might be a good opportunity to exercise her new-won authority to some effect, but she had to put on a show of being disinterested in case she was later held to account for her failure to complete her paperwork. In fact, she was definitely interested. Her curiosity was beginning to flow again; the only thing more calculated to excite it than a plain and simple murder was a murder mystery.

"He says he wants to see a senior officer," the PC told her. "He only agreed to settle for a DI when I told him that the DCI was away and couldn't be called in."

In Stephanie's experience, people who insisted on seeing senior officers were usually time-wasters, but she told herself that all allegations of murder had to be taken seriously in these days of rapidly-falling crime rates.

"What's his name?" she asked.

"Randolph Markham-James," the PC replied, lowering his tone slightly as he added: "No arrests, fines or convictions, but you definitely want to take a long look at what the ND has to say before you decide whether or not to talk to him."

Stephanie closed her own files and went into the National Database to see what its open section would tell anyone who cared to look about Randolph Markham-James. She could have obtained far more by accessing further stores to which the police had privileged access, but there was enough in the open record to let her see what PC Courtland meant.

Stephanie almost began to regret that the DCI was away, but she strangled the regret in its cradle. It was certainly arguable that the very last thing a recently-promoted DI ought to be doing at four o'clock in the morning was exercising her authority upon the uniquely precious scion of one of Britain's few super-rich families, but Mr. Markham-James would probably take it amiss if she declined to hear what he had to say. In any case, the flow of her curiosity had now become a tide. Had fate not cursed her with an insatiable appetite for arcane knowledge she would never have become a detective in the first place.

"Stick him in an interview room," she said, feigning a weariness that she no longer felt. "I'll be right down. Get on to the General and tell them we need everything they've got on Lynne Wardle, as and when it becomes available."

"Do you want me to call Markham-James Senior and tell him that his clone's here?" Courtland asked, in a conspiratorial whisper. That was, of course, the big question—

and there was no one to whom the buck could conveniently be passed.

"Not yet," Stephanie said, after taking a deep breath. "Let's hear what he has to say first. It's not as if we've arrested him, is it?"

* * * * * * *

The visitor looked exactly as Stephanie had expected him to look. His hair was blond and his eyes were blue. He wouldn't have been out of place at an audition to play the part of Dorian Gray. He seemed to be about twenty, but the flawlessness of his face made the seeming irrelevant. Given that the genetic engineers who had purged his skin of its vulnerability to mutational flaws had been the best that money could buy, there was no way to gauge his age by mere appearance. The open record had already informed her that he was twenty-two.

The fact that Randolph Markham-James did not look much like his sixty-five-year-old parent did not astonish Stephanie unduly, although it did make her wonder exactly what the point of producing a clone-son was, if he were then to be engineered in embryo in such a way as to obliterate the likeness.

The young man stood up politely as she entered the room.

"I'm Detective Inspector Greaves, Mr. Markham-James," she said. "Please sit down."

Stephanie had automatically adopted the even and scrupulously polite tone that was compulsory for all public servants in all monitored environments—which meant almost everywhere nowadays—but she knew that this particular interview would require all the extra vigilance she could muster. As she took the seat opposite the young man's she said: "I understand that you have some information about a death which took place early this morning."

Markham-James sat down again, but he was obviously uneasy. "This may seem absurdly twentieth century," he said, "but it might be better if I were to speak to a male officer." Not being a public servant, he didn't have to be careful about what he said, even in rooms where the walls had more than the usual quota of eyes and ears.

"You asked to see the senior detective on duty, Mr. Markham-James," Stephanie pointed out. "Would you prefer to talk to a female inspector or a male sergeant?"

The young man weighed up the two options carefully before saying: "I'm sorry. Yes, it's best that I talk to an inspector. The matter's delicate in more ways than one."

"Very well," Stephanie said, as gracefully as she could. "What is it that you want to tell me about Lynne Wardle's death?"

"I killed her," he said.

"Before you say any more, Mr. Markham-James, I must remind you that everything you say in this room is being recorded. If you intend to incriminate yourself, or even to risk self-incrimination, I strongly advise you to take legal advice before doing so. I hardly need to point out that a confession of murder is a very serious matter."

"I'm not the murderer," was all he said in reply. "I'm just the weapon. Not that you'll ever get him for murder, of course. Manslaughter is probably the best you can hope for. I'm no expert on the law."

Stephanie paused for a few moments before saying: "Who are you accusing, Mr. Markham-James? And of what, exactly, are you accusing him?" In an interview like this, even grammatical lapses might be reckoned unfortunate. Now that she had come so far there was no way back, but she had to do everything possible to make sure that she was safe from possible fallout.

"I'm accusing my so-called father, Sir Ronald Markham-James," the young man retorted—not altogether unexpectedly, in view of what Stephanie had read in the open record of Randolph Markham-James' *vita*. "I'm accusing him of making me what I am, and by so doing, causing the death of Lynne Wardle." He was mimicking her over-scrupulous manner of expression, although he didn't need to. He could say exactly what he wanted, any way he cared to phrase it.

Stephanie made herself pause again. It was the same hesitation, dragging on and on. In theory, there was only one law for the rich and poor alike, but that was in theory. She had the option of hearing what the young man had to say, so long as it was freely offered. She also had the option of calling a halt to the interview while she instructed Courtland to phone Sir Ronald Markham-James and inform him that his unnatural son had just made a serious allegation against him—and to suggest, in consequence, that he dispatch a squad of solicitors to take control of a situation which might get out of hand. The former option was the riskier as well as the more tempting alternative, but she figured, on due reflection, that she was brave enough to take it—and the curiosity visited upon her by her genes or early upbringing was urging her very powerfully to ignore the slight probability that she wasn't.

While she was putting on a show of deep thought for the cameras Stephanie reached out to the keyboard of the interview-room's terminal and summoned to the screen the information that PC Courtland had solicited from the General Hospital.

There had been no time, as yet, to carry out a full post-mortem but superficial inspection suggested that Lynne Wardle had died of anaphylactic shock, caused by an extreme allergic reaction. There was no external indication of the manner in which she had made contact with the allergen.

"Well?" said Randolph Markham-James. "Don't you want to know the full story?"

The bottom line, Stephanie decided, was that she did. Whatever the ultimate outcome might be, she wanted to hear the full story.

"I'll be happy to listen to anything you care to tell me, Mr. Markham-James" she assured him, "Although I must repeat my advice that you consult a solicitor before saying anything that might incriminate yourself." She could have added "or, for that matter, anyone else" but that would have been overdoing it, so she didn't.

"Good," he said, with a slight sigh.

Stephanie knew that he wouldn't really be talking to her at all. He would be talking to the cameras and the microphones; she was only there to act as a facilitator, for him as much as for the law. Even so, hers was the hot seat, and the only place for a real detective to be.

* * * * * * *

"You know what I am, of course," said Randolph Markham-James.

"I know that you're a clone, if that's what you mean," Stephanie admitted. "Given your age, you must have been one of the first dozen human clones produced in Britain in the wake of the House of Lords ruling."

One of the last acts of what the tabloid tapes called the Lords Rump, before the long-delayed final handover to the New Upper House, had been to rubber-stamp the Commons bill relating to the production of human clones. Any delay would probably have been a death-sentence, given the imminence and already-certain result of the 2027 General Election. Lord Westmoreland's speech on behalf of the already-beleaguered government of the day was still regarded as one of the more heroic *sorties* of the GM war. "The UN and European Charters of Human Rights forbid us to interfere with the right, which every human being has, to found a family," he had said. "How, then, can we possibly sustain a ban which refuses that right to people who have no other means of producing offspring but recourse to cloning technology. And if it is right for people who have no other means of founding a family to clone themselves, how can it be moral to deny other people the choice of so doing?" Stephanie knew that Ronald Markham-James was unlikely to have needed the final and most controversial phase of the noble lord's argument. It was probable that he, like so many men of his generation, had been rendered infertile by the pesticide plague, possessed of insufficient healthy spermatogonia to have any effective recourse even to the more ingenious varieties of IVF.

"But you also know, of course," the younger Markham-James added, "that I'm not exactly Daddy's identical twin."

"I understand that the stem cells taken from your father's bone-marrow were subjected to a certain amount of genetic repair," Stephanie conceded, carefully.

"And the rest," he said, bitterly. "It all depends, of course, what counts as *repair*—but the genetic engineers who had been tinkering with the embryos of sheep and cows for more than a generation were avid to try all their neatest tricks on human subjects. Applied homeotics at its most sophisticated, including a few judicious touches of stimulated allometry and a dash of enzymatic enhancement. Daddy didn't want his substitute self to be carrying any of his handicaps. He always took care to pose as an idealist—and I was just one more ideal."

"I'm sure that your father had the best of motives for asking the genetic engineers to make the modifications," Stephanie said, judiciously. Who was a mere public servant to say, or even to think, that narcissism might not be the best of all possible motives?

"He even called me Randolph because he thought it sounded so much classier than Ronald," said the younger Markham-James. "All his life he'd wanted to be a Randy instead of a mere Ron, in more ways than one. You know how he made his money, of course—or didn't your swift peek into the open files carry you that far?"

"Twenty years ago Ronald Markham-James was the administrator of one of the largest of the Amalgamated Pension Funds," Stephanie said, slightly hurt that he'd assumed she would have had to look it up. She'd only been in her teens back then, but she'd watched the TV news all the way through and she'd even clicked on to the economic add-ons during the big brouhaha. "As I remember it, his investment strategy was very successful—for which vast numbers of the nation's pensioners were duly grateful."

"*You* might have to put it like that," he said, perhaps intending to compliment her intelligence by giving her credit for meaning far more than she could safely say in a monitored environment, "but I don't. He threw in his lot with the Hardinist Cabal. Having learned at his own father's knee the lessons that the corporate raiders of the 1980s taught the old pension-fund managers, he set out to become one of the spurs urging a whole new generation of pirates to perfect the art of hostile takeovers and radical downsizing. He got right behind the men who cornered the future—and the rapidly-expanding ranks of Britain's new centenarians were behind him all the way, cheering every penny that he added to their annuities. It's ironic, don't you think, that the tab-tapes took to calling him one of the New Pharaohs of Capitalism?"

"Wasn't it one of the Pharaohs of the New Capitalism?" Stephanie asked, innocently. The reason that Randolph Markham-James thought it was ironic, whichever way round it might have been, was that common wisdom maintained that the Pharaohs of ancient Egypt had been in the habit of marrying their sisters to save their royal blood from dilution. Ronald Markham-James hadn't actually married his sister, but, when he had been required to find a surrogate mother to bear his clone-child, his medical advisors had urged him to recruit his sister, on the grounds that their fifty-per-cent genetic compatibility would work to the advantage of the child—or would, at least, avoid the slight hazards associated with genetically-incompatible surrogacy. Ronald Markham-James's sister—who was Randolph's aunt as well as his birth-mother—had been only too happy to oblige, in order to obtain Ronald's lavish financial assistance in the shaping of her own clone-child, who had every possible right to be reckoned Randolph's sister.

"Well, he wasn't quite a Pharaoh, either way," the young man said. "He might have backed the Cabal, but they wouldn't actually let him in on the conspiracy. Not quite *one of them*, you see. You can have no idea how badly that rankled. The world is full of men who'd be perfectly content to have been used and exploited if they'd come out of it with billions of euros in their own pockets as well as trillions in the coffers of the APF they were managing, but Ron was never one of them. The chip on his shoulder could have filled in the Thames Estuary, if not the bloody Channel. Don't look at me like that—I'm trying to fill you in on the background here, so that you'll understand the motive for the crime. That *is* relevant, I suppose?"

Stephanie wasn't aware of the fact that her expression was anything but perfectly bland, but she tried hard to simulate the patient sympathy of a saint for the benefit of the invisible cameras. "You haven't yet given me any reason to believe that a crime has been committed," she pointed out.

"I suppose I haven't—yet," he admitted, with a sigh. "After all, everything he did in the wake of the Rump ruling was perfectly legal. He'd always had inoperable myopia, so he had my genes tickled to ensure that I'd have perfect vision. He'd always been a *little* man, so he had my growth hormones tuned up to such efficiency that I'm six feet tall—oh, and the extra inch for good measure. I won't bore you with the amendments to my digestive system—after all, I'm sure that you're as keen as I am to get to the dirty bits. You know what stimulated allometry involves, of course?"

"As I understand it," Stephanie said, carefully, "allometric growth determines the proportions of the developing body before and after birth. One of the key discoveries of applied homeotics is the ability to affect the proportions of an organism—that's why modern chickens have such tiny wings."

"Pretty much," the young man said, although Stephanie knew that he was being generous because she had the layman's habit of cloaking ignorance with vagueness. "And it's why my prick is more than twice the size of my so-called father's. Talk about compensating for one's inadequacies...he'd always wanted to be a ladies' man, you see. Not for breeding purposes, of course—he knew that he was irredeemably infertile by the time that he was in his mid-teens—but because he thought that all his friends, not to mention all his enemies, were getting a lot more sex than he was. If we hadn't consigned psychoanalysis to the dustbin of intellectual history, I'd be forced to wonder whether his insatiable greed for money was ever anything more than the displacement of a sexual avidity that he could never express for lack of willing partners. He always wanted to be a lady-killer, but he never had the looks, the charm, or the stature. Even the money didn't help, because he always knew that the women it bought were whores, no matter how hard they pretended. Well, he's a lady-killer now and no mistake. It wasn't just size, you see. He thought that size mattered more than anything, but he wasn't about to neglect any other enhancements that were going. Are you following me?"

"Perhaps it would be better if you simply tell me what you mean, Mr. Markham-James, instead of beating around the bush," Stephanie suggested. She was trying hard to hide her slightly-painful awareness of his embarrassment, and not just for the cameras' sake.

"My sperms are in tip-top condition, of course," the young man went on, his own voice becoming tautly level, for the first time. "But there's more to semen than sperms. It's a cocktail with all kinds of active ingredients, easily enhanced. The tab-tape revelations have all been disputed, of course, but they're true enough in the main. It *is* possible to engineer the genes that collaborate in the production of semen to produce an addictive effect more powerful than that of heroin. Have you ever been in love, Inspector Greaves?"

"Do you mean the lowered-serotonin thirty-month madness kind of love?" Stephanie parried, expertly.

"Oh, any one of us can do *that*," Randolph Markham-James told her. "In spite of all the remedies girls can buy at Boot's, even the products of somatic engineering can still hook them good and hard. The defense industry has been two steps behind for the last thirty years. Actually, I was thinking of something deeper, something far more meaningful. *True* love."

"I think true implies *faithful* rather than *real* in that particular phrase," Stephanie said, working on the theory that pedantry was probably the safest course to ply in a conversational minefield.

"Really? Well, I'm implying both. Daddy didn't cut any corners when he got his tame Frankensteins to cook up my testicular cocktail. He wanted it all. Not just a thirty-month madness—the whole shebang. Anyone who goes all the way with me more than a couple of times, Inspector Greaves, goes *all the way*. When the hook gets into their soul, they're well and truly hooked, and the odds are that it'll last forever. Even once is a risk, twice is touch and go, and three times is invariably fatal. All those tabloid tales about modern Don Juans don't tell the half of it—or maybe those other guys' daddies simply didn't have inferiority complexes the size of Ron's. I don't believe I'm the only grown-up with the full armory, but I suppose I might be. Either way, though, there must be a couple of hundred more coming up to puberty as I speak. That must be a sobering thought, for a woman."

Stephanie figured that he was probably exaggerating—he was a man, after all. What girls could buy over the counter at Boot's wasn't really an issue, except for the poor ones who couldn't afford to obtain more effective armor from a good somatic engineer. Maybe there was a slight lag phase even in the somatically sophisticated "defense industry," but the logic of the situation suggested that all assertive innovations in seduction technology would be followed in due time by the means to nullify their effects. Nor was there any reason for Randolph Markham-James to suggest that members of the female sex had particular cause for anxiety. So far as Stephanie could tell, unwary males needed just as much protection from *femmes fatales* like Randolph's little sister as unwary females needed from him.

It seemed to be a good time to cut to the chase. "Lynne Wardle seems to have died because she suffered a massive allergic reaction," Stephanie said, having checked the screen to make sure that no new information had come in that could contradict the early indications.

"That's right," the young man said, sourly. "And it's me she was allergic to—my semen, to be specific: the semen whose original design was commissioned by my father, Sir Ronald Markham-James, the pensioners' friend—and whose subsequent reconstruction was carried out by the same engineers. I was the loaded gun that carried out the assassination, but he loaded me and reloaded me. He was the assassin."

"You've given me no reason to think that anyone is culpable, Mr. Markham-James," Stephanie pointed out. "An allergic reaction surely qualifies as an accident—unless you knew that making love to Miss Wardle would have that effect." *In which case*, she didn't add, *you can't reasonably shift the blame to your father.*

"It's not as simple as that," the younger Markham-James told her, unsurprisingly. Stephanie knew that it never was "as simple as that" when one had to deal, even as a policeman, with a man or woman in love.

"How complicated can it be?" she asked, knowing full well that there was nothing on Earth that could stop him explaining, now that he had found a shoulder and had been granted permission to cry on it.

* * * * * * *

"I used to give my father the benefit of the doubt," the young man said, curling his lip contemptuously as he used his tone to indicate that he must have been a fool to do so. "I used to think that he didn't understand what he'd done to me—that he hadn't quite thought it through. After all, he knew how humiliating it was to know that any woman who looked twice at him was only interested in his money. They all look twice at me, of course, but there are so many like me even now that looks are beginning to be taken for granted. My hook is a little further along the line than Ron's money, but it's no better—in fact, it's worse. Greed is an honest emotion by comparison with the grip that psychotropic semen takes."

"They still sell condoms at the chemist's," Stephanie pointed out.

"They still build walls around prisons," Markham-James countered, "even though it takes far more ingenuity nowadays to foil escape attempts. Preventing pregnancy is one thing; preventing all contact with bodily fluids like mine is another. Believe me, Inspector Greaves, anything short of virtual sex over a satellite link qualifies as unsafe where I'm concerned. When I don't really care, of course, even that can be enough, and even when I only care a little bit I can steel myself to issue the rejection slip in good time—but that's not the problem."

Stephanie realized, belatedly, that when Markham-James had asked her if she'd ever been in love he wasn't trying to raise her sympathy for anyone likely to become addicted to him. He'd been trying to raise her sympathy for himself.

"It's when I want to be truly intimate that the problem really kicks in," he went on, without waiting for a prompt. "When I want to be with someone for more than just a little while—really *be* with them—I always know I can make them want to be with me. But I don't want to *make* them want it. I want them to want it for themselves, honestly and spontaneously. When I love someone, I want them to love

104

me for what I am—a person, not a battery of biochemical dirty tricks. I don't want to enslave people I love. I want them to be free."

This time, he waited for a prompt. Stephanie obliged. "Did you love Lynne Wardle?"

"That probably seems unlikely," Markham-James observed, presuming that Stephanie had consulted the open record on the subject of the victim of the alleged crime. "After all, she wasn't *enhanced* like my lovely little sister and all her winsome kind. She had poor parents, and she was natural-born with all her flaws intact. Well, that's what I liked about her. I could never love anyone who wasn't. She was real, and she made me want to be real too."

The man is a walking cliché, Stephanie marveled, without letting the least indication of her cynical wonder show on her face. *This is the pure essence of modern romantic fiction. How could someone like him possibly have fallen for that kind of mush?*

"You probably think that this is the stuff of soap opera," Markham-James said, although all the applied homeotics in the world couldn't have gifted him with telepathy, "but the stuff of soap opera wouldn't be the stuff of soap opera if it didn't reflect the way people actually think and feel. Maybe thinking and feeling that way makes me far more ordinary than Ron would ever have thought possible, but, if it does, I'm not ashamed of it. I'm still human, after all. I have human ambitions, human needs, human standards. Tinkering with my semen didn't make me into some kind of alien, instinctively contemptuous of everything merely human. Maybe Ron thought it would, and maybe that's what he wanted for himself, but if he did he was wrong in more ways than one. I loved Lynne. I fell in love with her, the way you're supposed to do, and I wanted her to fall in love with me, without any kind of push or pull. And I wanted us to be lovers, with all that the word implies. *True* lovers."

"There's no crime in that, Mr. Markham-James," Stephanie pointed out, meaning: *I get the picture—now get to the point.*

"That's not what my father thought," the young man observed. "He had very strong opinions on the suitability of

Miss Wardle as a future daughter-in-law. You'd almost have thought that he'd be required to marry the girl himself."

"What did you do, Mr. Markham-James?" Stephanie asked, very softly. She'd already guessed, of course. It wasn't hard, given that there were only two alternatives, and he was the one with the problem as well as the one with the money—but she needed him to spell it out in order to supply her curiosity with the piquant taste-sensations it required.

"I tried to undo what my father had done to me," he told her. "I went to the men who had made me what I am, and I asked them to unmake me. I asked them to take the juice out of my seminal cocktail."

The safer approach, of course, would have been to equip the girl with proper defenses—but Randolph Markham-James was the chivalrous type. He'd never have sent someone else to the somatic engineers' lab while he could go himself. Stephanie didn't feel able to ask whether he had also asked the engineers to reverse the results of the selective allometric stimulation; there was no way she could have done so without sounding sarcastic, and she knew perfectly well what the answer was.

"They told me at first that they couldn't do it," he went on, "but I wasn't about to take no for an answer. I know all about the crucial difference between the embryonic engineering and somatic engineering, and the extreme difficulty of using the methods of the latter kind to duplicate or reverse the effects of the former, but I also know that necessity is the mother of improvisation. I told them that they didn't have to undo all their Ron-inspired mischief. They just had to make me normal enough to let Lynne remain free of unnatural biochemical authority. Eventually, they agreed that, although they couldn't stop me producing the addictive cocktail without doing undue collateral damage, they could do a further augmentation that would neutralize certain selected effects. They told me that the operation was untried, and couldn't be tested on animals because the mediating function of consciousness was vital to its function, but they said that the computer simulations looked promising. If they'd been as scrupulous as you, Inspector Greaves, all might have been well—but they weren't. Unlike you, they reached for the phone before they even let me into the office."

"They told you that there was a risk," Stephanie said, because it was the most neutral remark she could come up with in the circumstances.

"They didn't tell me that Ron was on the case, and that he wanted them to make damn sure that the risk turned into a certainty."

"Is that anything more than pure conjecture?" she had to ask.

"If you mean *did they leave a trail of recoverable evidence?* I don't know—but I certainly hope so." Randolph Markham-James answered, much as Stephanie had expected, "If you only mean *do I know for sure that it's true?* The answer's a simple yes. It wasn't an accident, Inspector. Even you couldn't get a look at Lynne Wardle's geneprint and developmental record without a warrant, but that's because you're not so far above the law that you can buy your way into any database that exists. If I were giving Ron the benefit of the doubt, I'd have to admit that he might not actually have intended to kill her—in fact, it probably would have tickled his perverse fancy even more if I'd just kept on and on making her sick, until she couldn't stand the sight of me—but I really don't think he cared how far over the top his lackeys went. *Get rid of her*, he must have said. *Make sure you get rid of her, but see to it that all the rest remain vulnerable, and that no harm comes to him.* And that's what they did—the first part, anyhow. They made sure—so sure, in fact, that Lynne went into anaphylactic shock. She was dead within minutes, long before the paramedics could reach her."

The young man didn't bother to add the judgment that getting the first part right had probably made the second part impossible. Stephanie could see the strength of his conviction that real harm had been done to him, and that it was irreparable. Sir Ronald Markham-James, on the other hand, had presumably taken it for granted that he would get over it eventually. Stephanie figured that Sir Ronald was probably right. People lived for a long time nowadays. That was why pension-fund managers had been forced to become so utterly ruthless in playing the world's stock markets. In the long twilight of modern life, what mattered most to the economically advantaged was their annuity-level. As Stephanie's own great-grandmother was still wont to say, far too frequently, love didn't butter any parsnips.

"Do you have any proof that your doctors did anything to you other than what you required of them?" Stephanie had to ask.

"Isn't that what a police investigation is supposed to discover?" he countered, with what would have been awesome naivety if he'd meant it. "Aren't you obliged to launch such an investigation, now that I've made the complaint? I've given you motive and opportunity. What more do you need?"

"I need hard evidence," Stephanie pointed out, dutifully.

"I saw her die. I'm a witness." He must have known how worthless that was, but he wasn't about to let the cameras see that he knew it.

"They told you there was a risk," Stephanie reminded him.

"They were—and are—murdering hypocrites," he insisted, "but they were mere instruments, like me. They were the gunsmiths and I was the gun: the assassination weapon. *His* weapon. That's all I've ever been, and all I ever will be, while he's alive and rich. I'm his way of getting back at the world for all the imagined indignities he was condemned by fate and lousy genes to bear throughout his youth. I'm his gesture of defiance, and he couldn't allow me to throw myself away. He couldn't bear to think that I might want ordinary things, or that I might be able to love an ordinary person. He wasn't prepared to tolerate that."

If psychoanalysis hadn't been consigned to the dustbin of intellectual history, Stephanie thought, borrowing her visitor's sarcastic phrase, *I might be tempted to wonder whether there's a certain amount of projection going on here. I might even be tempted to hypothesize that the one and only reason Randolph Markham-James had for fixating on an unenhanced girl from a poor family was that he knew exactly how far up his father's nose it would get. Fortunately, there isn't the slightest temptation urging me to think anything so ridiculous.*

"The results of the autopsy have just been posted," she informed the young man, having just caught the flash on the screen from the corner of her eye. "The coroner will have to make the final judgment, of course, but the preliminary findings indicate no suspicious circumstances. A freakish accident, it seems—I'm translating the usual jargon into layman's language, of course. Lynne Wardle's death was an unfortunate side-effect of the fashionability of untested devices in somatic engineering, offering no substantial grounds for a prosecution for criminal negligence, let alone anything more serious. You're in the clear, Mr. Markham-James."

"I don't want to be *in the clear*," he retorted.

"Apparently not," Stephanie conceded. "Nevertheless, there are no grounds in the *post-mortem* results for bringing a case against you or anyone else."

"I've just given you grounds," he said, stubbornly.

"I'm afraid that I can't agree," Stephanie told him, coming down off the fence at last. "I can see no evidence of anything but a tragic accident. I understand that you feel badly about it, but I can't take any action on the basis of what you've told me."

"Has it ever occurred to you, Inspector Greaves," the young man said, sneeringly, "that the principal reason why there seem to be so few murders these days might be that the vast majority go unidentified and uninvestigated?"

It would have been extremely unwise to say *of course it has*, so she said "I can understand why you're overwrought, Mr. Markham-James" instead. Then she added: "Perhaps you should go home now, and try to get some sleep. If you still think that there are any suspicious circumstances regarding Miss Wardle's death, when you've had time to think it through, you're at liberty to ask the coroner to hold a formal inquest, and to volunteer to give evidence there. I'll make a report to my superiors, of course, and if they or the coroner decide that an investigation is desirable we shall do our utmost to discover the truth of the matter."

"Or, to put in another way," he said, "you don't want to get involved unless and until you absolutely have to."

109

"I'm a policeman, Mr. Markham-James," she reminded him. "I have to follow the procedures laid down by the law. I can't take any action without proper grounds."

He must have known all along that this was where it would end. Talking had helped him to vent his spleen and calm himself down, but he'd known—even if he hadn't admitted it to himself—that nothing else was achievable. He didn't protest unduly when Stephanie showed him out, and she didn't complain about her time being wasted. It had been a good story, well worth hearing. It had even supplied some food for thought that might turn out to be more than mere confectionery.

* * * * * * *

As soon as Stephanie was back in unmonitored space she phoned Sir Ronald Markham-James. It was still only five-thirty, but he wasn't asleep. He was keeping track of events as they unfolded, and he'd almost certainly been reading the results of the *post-mortem* at the very same time as she had been scanning them herself. He presumably thought that he had a far better understanding of the situation than she did, and he might have been right. Who could possibly know what young Randolph was capable of thinking and doing better than his doting father?

"I'm sorry to trouble you, sir," Stephanie said, after identifying herself, "but there's a possibility that you might be in danger and I'm obliged to notify you of that fact."

"Thank you, Inspector," said the not-quite-Pharaoh of the not-really-New Capitalism. "I appreciate your taking the trouble. I'll make sure that my staff keeps the guns locked up and the kitchen devils safe in their drawers. I can't believe that my son is capable of harming me, but I've always been a careful man and I'm certainly not tired of life yet."

"In my experience, sir," Stephanie said, although she knew that it was a trifle reckless, "people are actually more likely to try to harm their clone-parents than the common-or-garden kind." *If psychoanalysis hadn't been confined to the dustbin of intellectual history,* she thought, *we might be tempted to think that we could understand and sympathize*

110

with a desire to murder one's other selves. After all, it's al-
ways those other selves that are the darker ones, the ones in
need of exorcism.

"Do you have any children of your own, Inspector?"
was the great man's unexpected counter.

"No sir," she said.

"In that case," he informed her, loftily, "I'm afraid that
your experience isn't very relevant. It can hardly be exten-
sive, in any case. There are so few crimes of violence nowadays—and even fewer children of my son's quality."

"That's true, sir," Stephanie said, dutifully. "Monitored
people are careful people, as the saying has it, so it's not entirely surprising that the incidents of violence that continue
to occur—especially those which result in death—are mostly
crimes of unusual passion." She congratulated herself silently on the felicity of that final phrase, but she could only
wonder whether he would catch the full spectrum of its implications and hope that it hit a sensitive spot.

"Unusual passions are the currency of progress," Sir
Ronald informed her, frostily.

"And unfortunate accidents are its cost," Stephanie observed, trying to sound agreeable. Her body might be in unmonitored space but there was no such thing as a private
telephone conversation.

"Genetic engineers do so much good that they can be
forgiven the occasional unforeseeable accident," Sir Ronald
was quick to say.

Stephanie agreed with him—but it was the foreseeable
"accidents" that she didn't like. "Good night sir," she said.
"I'm very sorry to have troubled you at such an unsociable
hour."

"That's perfectly all right," he assured her. "I expect my
son will be home soon. I think I'll wait up for him."

That turned out to be the first unwise thing he had said
to her, because it transpired that his stupid, guilt-stricken and
overwrought son never did get home, in spite of all that
Stephanie had done for him by way of lending him a shoulder.

The verdict returned at the inquest was accidental death,
but in view of all the safety features with which Randolph

Markham-James's car had been fitted, Stephanie couldn't help thinking, when she heard the news, that even misadventure might have been on the generous side. Even in the privacy of her own thoughts, however she scrupulously avoided voicing the thought that if psychoanalysis hadn't been confined to the dustbin of intellectual history one might have been tempted to wonder whether the young man's death might even qualify as a perverse form of murder. Sir Ronald would doubtless live to an extremely ripe old age, worshipped by every annuity-cherishing pensioner in the land, but, even on the basis of a very brief and business-like acquaintance, Stephanie might have felt entitled to suspect that he would never feel entirely complete, no matter what kinds of somatic reconstruction the march of progress might eventually make available to him. That wasn't a can of worms she wanted to open.

Stephanie did feel free to wonder, though, in the months that followed, whether it would have made any difference to Randolph Markham-James's fate if she had agreed to make some sort of investigation of his claims. The DCI would, of course, have squashed any investigation she might have been silly enough to initiate, and it would have been dangerous to utter a false promise in monitored space, but she remained uncomfortably aware of the fact that she could have hazarded slightly more than she had. If she had applied enough ingenuity, she might have given Randolph Markham-James reason enough to hope that he might one day be allowed to testify against his father—and perhaps, therefore, reason enough to look after himself a little better than he had. Then again, if she had refused to listen to him at all until his father had dispatched a team of lawyers to look after him, he might have remained safe in their custody long after he had left the station.

In the end, she decided that she had nothing for which to reproach herself. Randolph Markham-James had, after all, been a guilty man. For all his self-justifying talk about being merely the weapon, he had been the one who had subjected Lynne Wardle to the risk that killed her. He could and should have stuck to his own kind, to partners who had proper defenses against his biochemical arsenal. He could and should have tailored his passions to fit his moral responsibilities, just as everybody else in the imperfect world had to do.

One day, Stephanie thought, when she happened to catch the briefest glimpse of Sir Ronald Markham-James on the TV news, on the day he married for the seventh time, she would have a child of her own—but she would do the job properly. She would allow her daughter to discover idiosyncratic inadequacies and unusual passions of her own, instead of merely inverting those with which heredity might otherwise have equipped her.

And in the meantime, she resolved to make absolutely certain that she never fell in love with anyone who had the means to subject her to a surreptitious push or pull. Everyone had to adapt to the kind of world she lived in, just as everyone always had. It was as simple as that.

BUSY DYING

He couldn't remember whether he'd ever been to that particular spot before, but the open plaza looked vaguely familiar. As he climbed the ugly centerpiece of the fountain, aiming for the pagoda-like roof above the bug-eyed gargoyles, he seemed to be reaching for familiar footholds. They were already shouting his name, but that didn't mean a thing; he supposed that he'd be recognized in any of a hundred cities, in any of four hundred malls. He was quite a celebrity.

By the time he reached his selected coign of vantage a thousand people were converging on the fountain. The design of the atrium was such that the crowds on the second, third and fourth floors had as good a view as the people at ground level, and the escalators were crammed with excited gesticulators hoping that the moving stairways wouldn't carry them too far before the show began.

He checked his watch. *Give it ten*, he thought, beginning to count down.

He knew there were a dozen security cameras on him and that anyone in the crowd with a camcorder would be pointing it at him already, but the CNI were probably all ready to go with an injunction against any mall in this or any other city, and you couldn't trust amateurs to produce A-1 footage even with today's technological aids. He figured that ten seconds ought to be enough to bring down a few news-drones. Even the networks posted drones in malls these days, and not just because of him. Malls were the commercial arteries of the nation, and mallnews was always a big item in the human interest slots.

At five he uncapped the can, and threw the cap into the crowd so that the kids could fight over it. At seven he began to pour, so that he would be ready to drop the can into the rippled pool of the fountain at nine.

Smoothly, with practiced competence, he struck the match with his fingernail. *Is that slick, or is that slick*, he asked himself. He had always cared about matters of style.

His sneakers were still squelching and the legs of his pants were soaked from his dash across the pool, but he knew it wouldn't matter. The rest of him was soaked with something infinitely less inclined to dampen the spirits.

The flames came up about him with an audible *whoosh*, and black smoke billowed forth. For a second or two—-but it might have been an olfactory illusion—he thought that he could smell his own flesh burning.

Wow, he thought.
Wow! Wow! Wow!

* * * * * * *

When her bleeper went off Margaret Percik woke up with a sudden start, surprised and slightly guilty about the fact that she'd nodded off.

She didn't need to check her wristphone; it was Emily signaling that Walter Murray was recovering consciousness. She hurried, intent on arriving before he removed the skimskin sealing his eyelids, but she needn't have bothered. The monitoring devices had blown the whistle on him, but Walter was playing possum. He hadn't moved a muscle; he was probably playing for time while he tried to figure out who and what and where he was. Thanks to him, doctors now knew that death usually caused temporary amnesia, and he had had enough practice in dying to have developed habitual methods of dealing with the condition.

As she checked the instruments she felt sure that he was tracking her movements with avid ears. He flinched, though, when Emily checked his waste-disposal tubes. She carefully peeled the skimskin away from his eyes, and he opened them, blinking against the light. He had to close the lids again for a second or two, but when he could keep them open

115

they focused readily enough on her face: no lasting damage there.

He looked up at her without recognition. Emily moved to the head of the bed so that he could study them both. She and Emily were as handsome as one another but not in the least alike, in spite of the fact that they were wearing severely clinical white coats. Margaret was dark and stern and so comprehensively imaged for authority that she was almost austere; Emily was fairer and softer and decorated. Nobody was supposed to be able to tell a woman's age any more, but that was bullshit. Wrinkles or no wrinkles, Margaret knew, it was obvious to anyone with half an eye that Emily was an absolutely authentic twenty-one, whereas she herself was fifty-five and then some.

Margaret darted a quick glance at Emily, to make sure that she was paying attention. It was important, according to their agreed procedure, that they both looked at him without the slightest trace of sympathy or admiration.

"Can you remember who you are?" Margaret asked.

There was a twenty-second gap before he replied. Finally, he said: "I seem to have temporarily misplaced my name. I'm sorry."

"You were very lucky, Mr. Murray" she said. "If you hadn't fallen into the fountain...."

That drew a slight reaction—as if the horror of it had hit him like a punch in the gut, although he couldn't quite fathom out why the thought was so horrible.

"What fountain?" he said, in a puzzled fashion. "Murray, you say? Is that my name—Murray?"

"You shouldn't play with fire, Mr. Murray," said Margaret, as sternly as she could. "It isn't like the knives and the ropes. We can regenerate burned brain-tissue, but not the field-states that inhabited the neural network before it was burned. Try this one again, Mr. Murray, and you might come back first cousin to a cabbage. I guess you already qualify as a zombie ten times over, but this time you were just a few seconds away from being a hundred-forty pounds of fresh meat with vacant possession. As I said, if you hadn't fallen into the fountain...."

"Do I know you?" he asked.

116

She did her level best to look at him as though he were some kind of insect crawling around the drawer where she kept her underwear.

"Yes, Mr. Murray," she said, sourly. "You know me. And you also know Mr. Stepanova. He's waiting for a call to tell him that you're awake. He has some news for you."

She picked up a remote from the instrument-console beside the bed, and punched out a sequence; the wallscreen at the far end of the room flickered blue, displayed the relevant codes, and then dissolved into a picture.

Stepanova had been waiting to make the call; Emily had bleeped him at the same time she'd bleeped Margaret. He was looking straight into the camera, as purposefully as any man could. He'd been chiseled for it, but it wasn't an overly impressive job. Every man of a certain age went in for that kind of power-dressing of the features, and it rather nullified the effect.

"You're busted, Murray," said Stepanova, with a bitter wrath he did not need to feign. "This is the end. We've got an injunction from the Supreme Court banning you from making any further use whatsoever of any product manufactured by the Confederation which is not on open sale. I have a court order requiring you to hand over all the nanotech equipment that you removed from our laboratories. Your lawyers may have built an effective dam against the possibility of your being certified insane and straitjacketed, but this is nice and simple and utterly unbreakable—and to be quite honest, I think your guys are losing heart now that your bank account is in the doldrums. One more suicide and you are under house arrest for ever and ever *a-men*. You're out of it, Murray—understand? It's *over*."

"I'm sure you mean well," said Murray, mildly. "But I'm afraid I don't know what you're talking about. Do I know you?"

Stepanova frowned, as if he suspected that he was being ribbed and didn't like it—although Margaret had told him exactly what to expect. She keyed the cut-off on the remote, lest Stepanova should start a pointless argument with her patient. Then she handed over the instrument to Murray. He looked at it for a second or two, but then nodded, as though he were glad to find it perfectly familiar. He handed it back. "*That* I recognize," he said.

"But not me?" she countered.

He shook his head. "I'm Dr. Percik," she said, still straining to be as stern and cold as possible. The theory was that she had to avoid providing any comfort that might be construed as approval, and thus as encouragement to repeat the behavior that had brought him to this; apparently it was still standard practice in welcoming attempted suicide victims back from the brink. Personally, she had no faith whatsoever in its efficacy in Walter Murray's case, but she was under some pressure here from her peers and other interested parties, who were far more interested in making him stop than in figuring out why he kept doing it.

"How am I, doctor?" he asked, flatly.

"As well as can be expected," she retorted, bluntly. After a slight pause, during which she nodded an answer to Emily's unspoken question, giving the nurse permission to leave the room, she added: "Stepanova means it, you know. By the time I've collected my fees you'll be as near to flat broke as you can get. The media won't bail you out this time; CNI have them all tied up in red tape. No one wants to talk to you—no one who'll pay you for the privilege, anyhow. Your lawyers aren't even going to try to fight CNI's injunctions. You've finally succeeded in cutting off your nose to spite your face. You may be famous, but you've no job, and if you do anything—and I mean *anything*—that involves the use of prototype nanotech you'll be off the net for a long, long time. Have a little patience, Walter, and you might be able to live happily ever after. Kill yourself one more time, and they'll see to it that you die of old age. I have no axe to grind, you understand—I'm out of it too. That's the last face you'll ever get from me. From now on, you get your Medicaid on credit. Basic treatment, for which you have to stand in line."

"You have a great bedside manner," he remarked. It was impossible to judge how disoriented he was, and how much he understood of what was being said to him. The idea was to get the message across before he recovered his memory and his resistance.

"It's difficult to be polite to a king-sized pain in the ass," she told him. She narrowed her eyes speculatively, and she said: "If you have got any more stolen nanotech squirreled away, you'd better hand it over. However you came by it originally, it's no longer legal for you to have it in your possession. Just tell me where you stashed it, and I'll take it from there."

"I'm sorry," he said, "but I really don't know what you're talking about."

"Everyone's closed ranks, Walter," she said. "We're not going to let you die again. We're not going to let you destroy yourself. This time, you really have to get your head together, okay?"

He just looked at her, meekly, as if he couldn't understand why she was talking to him that way. She couldn't tell whether, or to what extent, he was putting it on. Perhaps, she thought, it might be best if his memory didn't come oozing back; maybe all he needed was a fresh start. She felt slightly ashamed of the thought which came immediately afterwards, which was: *But then we'd never figure out just what the fascination was. Damn Stepanova and his injunctions—there's a mystery here that we ought to be trying to solve.*

She tried to look daggers at him one more time, just for luck, and then stalked out of the room.

* * * * * * *

When the bleeper sounded again she woke up without a start, filled with a dull sense that there as no escape. This time it was the automatic signal that told her that Murray had activated the telescreen in his room. She had arranged a tap, in the interests of scrupulous medical care.

The face that was staring out of her own telescreen inevitably seemed to be looking her in the face, although it wasn't. It wasn't even looking Walter Murray in the face: it couldn't, because it was a recording, doubtless programmed to call him in the early hours of the morning, when no one was supposed to be eavesdropping.

"Hello, Walter" said the caller—who wore, of course, Walter's previous face.

"Who the hell are you?" the real Walter replied, his voice slightly distorted by the bug she had placed to catch it.

"I'm your answerphone AI," replied the caller. "Extensively elaborated and reprogrammed by your good self, for exactly such emergencies as this. Don't worry—you just have a slight touch of amnesia. At least, I hope it's slight. It'll probably all come back to you in a day or two, but I'll give you all the help I can. That's what I'm here for. Mostly I'm just a playback device, but I'm rigged for simple questions and answers. Interrupt me whenever you need to. Your name is Walter K Murray; the K doesn't stand for anything longer, it's a one-letter middle name in its own right. You used to work for CNI—that's the Confederation of Nanotechnological Industries—on the Safety Commission. Your official title was Volunteer Subject, but in everyday parlance you were a guinea-pig or a stunt man. You got fired a year ago for excessive attention to duty—at least, that's your version. Stepanova cooked up a charge sheet that had everything from petty pilfering to reckless endangerment and bringing the good name of the organization into disrepute, but it was mostly false. Are you with me so far?"

"Not quite," said the real Walter, awkwardly. Margaret wished she could see his face, to judge how he was taking it in, but it hadn't seemed worthwhile to plant a spy-eye in a darkened room. The image on the screen flickered slightly as a new subroutine engaged.

"It's okay," said the AI, gently. "Take your time. I guess you really messed up the old brain cells this time. What did you do?"

"I don't know, exactly," he said. "Something about playing with fire and falling into a fountain. My doctor isn't very helpful." He sounded sincere, but Margaret knew that it might be an act.

"You should watch the news," said the AI. "All you need to do is call up the relevant vidclippings. All your suicides are on tape."

"*All* my suicides? How many were there—and why aren't I dead?"

"You've killed yourself ten times to date," reported the AI, dutifully.

"Why would I do that?" said Walter, who should have known better than to confuse an AI with a new question while one still remained unanswered. Anyway, AIs were a lot better with *whats* and *wheres* and *whens* than they were with *whys*—all he was going to get was more data, not expert psychoanalysis.

"Your duties as a volunteer subject," said the AI, painstakingly, "involved prototype medical nanotechnologies whose purpose is to enhance the body's powers of self-repair. Their function is to assist in the rebuilding of damaged tissue, to promote the healing of wounds and the regeneration of lost material. To put it simply, your job was to sustain injuries of gradually-increasing degrees of seriousness, so as to explore the capacities and the limits of the nanomachines that had been injected into your bloodstream. These included anesthetic enems as well as the repair enems. You were good at your work. You liked it better than most—maybe better than anyone. You were part of an élite group, working with the most advanced prototypes.

"When you first began to exceed your brief the guys in charge were enthusiastic—they encouraged you. The back room boys were quite delighted with you, and probably still are. The company men were avid to go with the flow, and the CNI let them; they didn't see any harm in the media attention you got. The first time you came back after being certified dead the euphoria was universal. The CNI brass were as interested as everyone else. It wasn't until the fifth time that Stepanova stepped in, talking about turning the CNI into some kind of circus. He was too late, but he's certainly tried to make up for lost time. Do you need more detail on all of this? I've got two more programmed levels, if you do."

"No," said the man in the bed, faintly. "I think it's coming back now, a little. Testing the limits. That's what it was all about. Testing the limits. Exploring the unknown. Boldly to go where no man...they're trying to stop me, aren't they? They want to stop me."

"Yes they do," answered the AI. "They're trying to stop you, now. But it's okay. You've always been one step ahead of them. Don't worry about a thing. They'll have to send you home in a day or so. Once you're back home, we can sort everything out. Just hang in there, and take it easy. That's all you have to do. Do you want more information?"

There was a long silence before Walter said: "No. Not now. Thanks...I mean...yeah, that's all. Sign off, okay?"

"We'll talk again," promised the AI. "Come home as soon as you can."

The image cut off abruptly.

Margaret pursed her lips as she lay back on the pillow. The AI was right; she had to send Walter Murray home once he was okay physically. Amnesiac or not, he was perfectly lucid. There was no way she could have him put under restraint, as Stepanova had more than once asked her to do, even if she wanted to—and she didn't. That wouldn't be a solution, to Walter's problem or to hers.

She sighed, and lay down in the darkness once again. *What is it about dying*, she asked herself, although the unanswered question had long ago gone stale, *that keeps beckoning him? Why is it that every time he gets his memory back he also recovers all his determination, all his cunning, and all his secretiveness? Just what the hell is going on inside that strangely-twisted mind—and what does it augur for the future, when the products he's been testing come marching triumphantly into the marketplace?*

She wondered if similar questions were going through Walter's still-confused mind—and whether he was finding it as difficult to slip away into sleep as she was.

* * * * * * *

Margaret let Walter Murray have a whole day to himself before she went to see him again. She didn't monitor him continuously, but the tap she'd placed in his house-system gave her a summary of everything he'd been doing, and it had all been recorded in case she needed to take a closer look. It was nearly nine in the evening when she showed up at the house.

"Well, Walter?" she said, when she'd checked his physical condition. "What do you think of your past life?

"What do you mean?" he parried, warily.

"I mean that you're obviously still struggling with the amnesia. One hour watching your vidclippings might be nostalgia, two might be narcissism, but six is definitely honest enquiry. You're trying to figure out just what kind of a specimen you are, aren't you? You can tell me—I'm your doctor, remember."

"You didn't seem that interested yesterday."

"That was tactical," she said. "Refusal to pander to attention-seeking lest the behavior-pattern gets reinforced. Not that *I* think your behavior is mere attention-seeking, you understand, but there is a school of thought which inclines that way."

"Are you allowed to keep me under observation now I'm at home?" he asked, ducking the issue. "Among the memories of general matters that I haven't lost I seem to recall something about invasion of privacy legislation."

"I'm your doctor, Walter, and you've certainly been ill. Dead and back again, for the tenth time. I'm allowed to monitor you for your own good."

"Are you also allowed to block my phone so that I can't call out? Are you allowed to see to it that I can't even get through the door of my own apartment?" She wondered whether it was a good sign that he was letting out his accumulated resentment so easily.

"Yes I am," she told him. "While you're not fully recovered, I'm entitled to protect you from nuisance."

"Well, I'm fully recovered now. My arms are a little weak and my fingers need practice, but I'm fundamentally sound. You can lift the house arrest. In fact, I insist that you do."

"Tomorrow, Walter—maybe the next day. You have amnesia, remember? It wouldn't be right, professionally speaking, to let you loose without addressing your problem."

"I've addressed it. I'm Walter K Murray, known to the tabloid TV vidveg as 'Memento' Murray, although ninety-nine percent of them are too dumb to get the joke. I can recite my entire personal history. No problem. Anyway, I thought you were worried about getting paid. I don't know what you charge per hour, but I'm not sure I can afford house calls."

"You can't afford to be without proper treatment," she told him. "If you want to stop wasting time, why not cut out the hostility and start treating me like the friend I am. I'm your doctor, Walter—I really and truly want you to get well."

She still wasn't speaking softly, but the edge was gone from her voice. She was brisk and frank and she kept eye-contact the whole time. *Trust me*, her eyes were saying. *Confide in me. Just give me a little help, and we can both reach a better understanding.*

When he didn't say anything else, she said: "Did you find out?"

"Find out what?" he countered, warily.

"Why you keep killing yourself. Everyone would like to know—and not just because we want you to stop. We really would like to be able to understand."

"I was rather hoping that *you* could explain that to *me*," he replied, with just a hint of an implied sneer. "You're the doctor, aren't you?"

"The problem with ready-made psychiatric explanations," said Margaret, undismayed, "is that even those who seek counseling—volunteer subjects, I suppose you might call them—very often resist them. It's always better to guide a patient to the point of view from which he can see for himself what his problem is. Recognition is the first step in recovery."

"Try me anyway," he said.

"Volunteer subjects are screened as carefully as the CNI can," she said, blandly. "They don't want people who have a predilection for injuring themselves, or surgery addicts, They want people for whom it can be an ordinary job—sensible, stable people. Occasionally, though, someone a trifle...excep-tional...slips through the net. Someone who likes the work a little too much. In the beginning, no doubt, you represented yourself to yourself as an authentic explorer, impatient with the controls the scientists placed on the experiments. You thought that you were just hungry for knowledge, for understanding. After the first time, though, it very quickly turned into a quest for fame. You'd always resented your own ordinariness, and at last you'd found a way to be extraordinary—a way to make other people take notice of you, even to admire you. You crossed the line the first time you came out of the laboratory and into a mall. When you did that, you blew all your excuses out of the window. From then on, it was showmanship. You've kept on killing yourself because you've convinced yourself that it's the only way available to you to make people see you and take notice of you.

"It's not fame *per se* that you want, although you probably told yourself that when you got that agent to try to fix you up with a fat contract with one of the networks. Yours is a pettier kind of exhibitionism than that. It's far from unique, you know—there's a long history of case studies in public self-mutilation. It's just that nowadays, when medical nanotech can fix almost any superficial injury up to and including self-castration, it's far more difficult to seem to be flirting with death. You're the man who proved that you actually have to go there and back to make a public impact. Fortunately, that impact is on the wane. The religious fraternity and the parapsych fringe lost interest when you couldn't bring back any hard information about the other side, and you must have noticed that the news coverage is getting briefer and more sarcastically dismissive. They're just keeping count now, Walter. The whole business has gone stale, and you can't enliven it just by playing with fire."

It all sounds good, she thought, when she'd finished, *but is it true? Come on, Walter—just give me a clue.*

"You can't tell me I'm insignificant," he said, defensively. "What about that organization out in California—the Thanaticists. They seem to be building quite a little pressure group. LICENSE RESURRECTION NOW. WE DEMAND UNIVERSAL ACCESS TO RECREATIONAL DEATH. GOD BLESS SAINT WALTER THE MARTYR. Some banners."

"They're clowns, Walter. You know what California's like—you still have your general memories, don't you?"

"You're trying to trivialize it," he said, suspiciously. "This is tactical, just like the other stuff. You're trying to belittle what I've done—but I'm not just a trafficker in slit wrists and overdoses, am I? I'm not *playing* with death. I've

been *all the way*, again and again and again. And whatever
the religious people say, I *have* brought back news. They just
want to discount it because it isn't the news they wanted. I
don't remember it just now, but I trust myself enough to believe what I told all those newsmen." He didn't sound entirely certain.

"I believe that too," Margaret assured him. "There's no
Heaven, no miraculous light, no choirs of angels, no judgment. There's *nothing*. Death is death; when the light of consciousness goes out, the darkness is absolute. Death is a
void—a black hole. We always knew that; we didn't need
you to tell us. So why on earth do you keep going back?
What's the attraction?"

He was confused; she felt sure of it. He was in a peculiar
state of mind, wishing to defend himself but not quite knowing how. So far, most of what he knew about his exploits
was information that he'd picked up from the vidclippings.
There was a possibility that he was amenable to argument,
vulnerable to persuasion—maybe more so than he'd ever
been before.

"You say we always knew it," he countered, uneasily.
"But is that really true? Maybe we did always know, deep
down—but how many of us dared to believe it? How many
of us dared to confront that knowledge, while we still had
feeble hopes to cling to? Did you see me on that talk show
with the cardinal and the imam? They didn't know it—but
didn't I show them? Didn't I put a spoke in their wheel?"

"They weren't impressed, Walter," she told him, calmly.
"You must have seen that. They have a dozen ways around
your supposed proof, and they aren't in the least inconven-
ienced by your claims. They can always reason along the
lines that you're just an infidel anyway, or that God knew
that you were coming back here and had no reason to roll out
the red carpet and give you a glimpse of Heaven. Then again,
some people's idea of Hell is eternal darkness, and if ever
there was a man bound for Hell, it's surely you. Suicide is a
sin, Walter, and you're the most successful recidivist suicide
in the history of the world. Maybe you missed your best
chance, Walter. You could have made up a story—a new vision. You could have founded your own little cult based in

your own revelation. It wouldn't have attracted quite as many members as the Thanaticists, but you could probably have managed a dozen disciples."

He pursed his lips in frustration. "I'll remember, you know," he said. "It'll come back to me."

Margaret sighed. "You may be right," she said. "But it might be better for you if you were wrong. You might be saner at this particular moment in time than you've been for much of the last three years. Let me warn you again, Walter—you really have reached the limit of everyone's tolerance. I want you to get well, and even Mr. Stepanova would like nothing better than to see you restored to sense and sanity. You could still do a lot of good by repenting, and maybe get more media attention out of that than you could possibly get out of one more fountain-climb in one more randomly-chosen mall. Think about it, Walter—and if you happen to remember where you stashed the rest of that stuff you ripped off from the labs, turn it in. Please."

He shrugged his shoulders, but she had no way of knowing what he really felt. "Sorry," he said, dully. "I guess I'm a little off-balance. Thanks, Doctor—it really does help."

"I hope so," she said. "I'll unfreeze your door and your phone tomorrow, okay? But take it slowly. Whatever does or doesn't come back, take your time about everything. There really is all the time in the world; according to the CNI, we're on the threshold of immortality. It's yours and mine for the taking, if only we can wait a few more years. This is no time to be trying to kill yourself. Next time, you might not be able to get back."

He thanked her again—but when she got back to the hospital the tap revealed that he'd gone straight back to the AI, plumbing its depths for the most intimate subroutines he'd planted during his previous incarnations.

* * * * * * *

"You have to look at it this way," said the image of Walter's last face but one, delivering a pre-recorded speech that wasn't jigged for interruption. "What we call 'life' is really death. I mean, we begin to die before we're even born.

127

The single cell from which we grow begins to age before it begins to divide, and it's dying all the time while it's growing, changing, developing. Birth isn't the beginning—in terms of the total numbers of cell-divisions that are needed to make us what we finally become, nine-tenths of our lives are spent in the womb. An adult is just a baby grown large, a corpse waiting to keel over. Death isn't what people think it is, and insofar as it's a sham it has to be revealed as a sham—or what the hell is intellectual progress all about?"

Pompous idiot, thought Margaret, as she played back what the tape had recorded.

"The true significance of what you and I have accomplished, Walter," the AI went on, "is to demonstrate how arbitrary that line is which doctors have drawn between life and death. It was always a myth. The body doesn't die all at once, and nor does the brain. All kinds of functions carry on after the stopping of the heart, the scrambling of the brain-waves. We can come back from what used to be thought of as 'beyond'—but all that proves is that it wasn't really beyond at all. And what we come back to isn't life...it's just a different phases of our long, desperate dying.

"What you and I are all about is challenging people's taken-for-granted ideas. The point of it all is to break down the categories of their habitual patterns of thought, to free them from their simplistic either/or calculus of life and death, being and nothingness. That's why we have to keep going, in spite of all they're determined to do to make us stop."

Us, thought Margaret, wondering how significant the choice of pronoun might be. *What kind of man leaves messages for himself that talk about* us? *Is this really for real, or is it just some kind of joke, planted for my benefit, to make fun of* me?

On the other hand, she wondered, might *us* be entirely appropriate. Could the new Walter feel any real mental kinship with the answerphone AI or the earlier incarnation of himself who had programmed it so carefully to relay this rubbish? Maybe it seemed as weird and way out to him as it was to her.

She was interrupted in her monitoring by a call from Stepanova.

"You let him out," he said, accusingly.

"I had to," she told him, slightly awkwardly. "I'm a doctor; my responsibility is to my patient. I can't infringe his civil rights."

"Never mind his civil rights," he said. "You're his doctor—you're supposed to stop the stupid idiot killing himself again. Did you find the stuff? Will he hand it over?"

"I recommended to Mr. Murray that if he had any more CNI materials he should hand then over to me or to you," she said, patiently. "I don't have any authority to search his apartment."

"Nor do I, in theory," said Stepanova, "but I can assure you that the stuff isn't there, unless he's found some hidey-hole that even the best searchers can't locate."

"I'll pretend I didn't hear that, Mr. Stepanova," Margaret said, wearily. Stepanova, she decided, was an even bigger pain in the ass than Murray himself. At least Murray was interesting. Stepanova was just gross.

"Don't be so fucking precious," said the CNI man. "Did you explain to him that next time there'll be no way back—that he can't afford to pay you, and that his medical insurance is worthless? Did you tell him that he'd just be allowed to die?"

"No I didn't, Mr. Stepanova," she said. "I'm not in the business of making crude threats. I want to help him overcome his problem just as much as you do, but I don't think blackmail and bullying would really count as a solution, even if they worked."

"Bullshit," said Stepanova. "Whatever works, *works*, and that's all a solution is. If you don't tell him, I will. One more public performance and he is *dead*. Really dead, for ever and ever. I will personally see to it. It's over. He has to understand that. And he has to give the stuff back; that's not up for negotiation."

"At present, he doesn't seem to understand anything very well," said Margaret. "I don't think he know where the enems are hidden. It might well be best if he stayed that way. If you start pressuring him, you'll probably make things worse. Threats might only serve to rebuild and reinforce his motivation."

"You don't have the first idea what his motivation is," said Stepanova scornfully, the insult hurting her all the more by virtue of its truth. "You haven't even got close—and now your time is running out, along with his. Personally, I don't care what his motives are; I just want to provide him with a bigger and better motive for staying out of view. We have our own ad campaigns for the new-generation enems all planned, and they don't involve malls, fountains or human torches. We don't need rumors to the effect that enems that are actually a great boon to medical science have mentally-unbalancing side-effects. We certainly don't need the kind of delays we'd get if some boneheaded congressman from the backwoods manages to push through a demand for an investigation by congressional committee. I need to be able to tell my people in Washington that it's all over, and I want you to do everything you can to make certain that they won't be disappointed. So tell him to hand over the stuff."

She didn't like the implied threat. "Walter Murray is my patient," she said, flatly. "My only responsibility is to him."

"Your responsibility," said Stepanova, grimly, "is to make sure that he stays healthy. That's all I'm asking you to do. Just make certain that it's over. It's as simple as that."

But it isn't as simple as that, she thought, when she'd signed off. *It really isn't.*

* * * * * * *

Once she'd unblocked Walter Murray's systems and set him at liberty the information relayed by her taps became markedly less informative. The AI answerphone had to return to such routine tasks as clocking up various items of junk mail and messages expressing support and solidarity, plus numerous offers of ready cash for any bootleg enems to which Walter might still have access. Walter also took delivery of two imaginatively-couched death-threats and file copies of seven different injunctions taken out by CNI against him and miscellaneous others, and made a few calls himself—none of them in reply to those he had received. He registered available for employment, checked the state of his asset accounts and his uncollected liabilities, and then filed for bankruptcy.

Margaret could only wonder whether he'd remembered where he'd stashed his illicitly-acquired enems, and whether he might be tempted by the black market prices they might command. If he were prepared to sell them—or even to try to sell them—that would presumably mark an end to his great adventure.

But he didn't try to sell them, and, in spite of Stepanova's continued demands, he didn't give them back to their rightful owners. He spent the second and third days of his freedom being intensively interrogated by the police about the stolen enems, without benefit of counsel—as Stepanova had gleefully prophesied, his lawyers were no longer very interested in him now that he was no longer solvent—but he just kept insisting that he didn't know where they were, or even whether they existed.

It wasn't until the fourth day that he went outdoors for the first time, but once he got back into the habit it became more difficult for her to track his progress. She didn't doubt that he would be followed everywhere by Stepanova's agents, but she couldn't bring to ask Stepanova where he went and what he did.

If Walter's memory was coming back he was careful not to show the slightest sign of it. Not that such signs would have been easily evident; after all, he knew enough about himself by courtesy of secondary sources to be able to function efficiently in a world whose general features he had never forgotten. He seemed to be making a fresh start—but he had seemed to do that before, and it had all been illusion.

After a full week had gone by, though, Walter called Stepanova and asked how he might make amends for his former derelictions of duty. He volunteered to do anything that Stepanova wanted him to do by way of formal public recantation—and, when Stepanova proved more than willing to take him up on the offer, he followed through. He spent the next two days confessing his sins to a series of press conferences. He'd never done that before—but he'd never been bankrupt before, either.

Ironically, it transpired—as Margaret had suggested—that there was money in repentance. He was able to sell a few network interviews, and became solvent again. He began hunting through his files and interrogating his answerphone AI, as if trying to find out whether he really did have any enems still tucked away, and—if so—where they might be. Given that he must have known that he was under surveillance by several different agencies, Margaret wasn't surprised that the answerphone AI couldn't or wouldn't impart that information.

She didn't see him again until it was time for a routine check-up, and she had little alternative but to play along with him, whether it was all deceit or not.

"Have you remembered why you did it?" she asked him, conversationally, when she'd checked that he was fully fit in a physical sense.

"I can remember setting myself on fire," he told her. "But it's hazy—as if I were just an observer, watching it happening to someone else. I can only remember the *outside* of the event, not the *inside*. I can't remember what I *felt*."

"Pity," she said. "You can't be sure, then, that your public promise to be a reformed character will stick?"

"I don't see why not," he said. "I'm perfectly sincere. Even if I do remember the reason, I can still keep the promise. I've listened carefully to all my old interviews—I know how ridiculous much of what I said then really is. I wonder, doctor, whether I might actually have cured myself with the fire—whether I might have burned away the sickness that was making me do it. Maybe that's what I was subconsciously trying to do all along. Is that possible, do you think?"

What she thought was *bullshit!* but she had no intention of letting him know that.

"We can always hope," she said.

"What do you think made me do it, doctor?" he said, appealing to her with wide and innocent eyes. "Was I somehow addicted, do you think? Or was there something about the act of self-murder, the sensation of dying, that gave me a perverse thrill?"

"I don't know," she said. "If you knew before, you were careful to keep it a deep, dark secret."

"Not this time," he assured her. "If I remember, I'll tell you everything. Everything I can."

"What about Stepanova's enems?" she asked. "Will you give those back, if and when you remember where they are?"

He seemed genuinely perplexed. "Mr. Stepanova keeps on at me about them," he admitted. "He's really rather angry about them—and I'm not sure that he believes me when I tell him that I really have no idea where they might be.

Margaret wished that she knew whether or not to believe him, annoyed with herself for her inability to be sure. *Oh Walter*, she thought. *What on earth did I do to deserve you?*

* * * * * * *

Later, at the hospital, Emily asked how Walter was getting along. Margaret gave her a full and frank account of the state of play, not knowing or caring whether it would get back to Stepanova.

"Do you believe him?" Emily asked, as she was bound to do.

"I want to," said Margaret, honestly. "If he *is* a different man, I can't claim any credit for it—but if he isn't, I dare say that some of the blame will attach itself to me. I just have to hope that he'll be okay this time—and that one day, he and I will be in a position to work out what the hell it was all about."

"You might be able to have him put under permanent restraint," she said. "For his own good, of course. That way, you'd avoid the possibility that he's just stringing you along."

"This isn't the twentieth century," Margaret pointed out. "Arguing the case in court would probably do more damage to my image and career than another suicide—there's a sense in which I'm damned if I do and damned if I don't, unless he really is done with it."

"Do you think we'll ever know why he did it?" said Emily, wonderingly.

133

"According to his answerphone," said Margaret, "We're all busy dying—he's just been a little bit busier than most. Last time, though, there was another subroutine, which went on and on about death being the one great mystery, the primal source of existential *angst*. If only he could be consistent.... Perhaps it was like climbing Everest; perhaps he did it simply because he could—and now that Stepanova's made it clear to him that he can't, he'll stop."

Her bleeper sounded then, to remind her that she had other patients to see, and she had to run. Not everyone had state-of-the-art enems to defend them against the slings and arrows of outrageous fortune, and even if Stepanova managed to avoid the congressional inquisition he was so anxious about, the vast majority of people would never be able to afford them.

As things turned out, she was busy in the theatre for the next six hours, and it wasn't until she came out that they gave her the news.

Walter Murray was dead: truly, finally, irrecoverably dead. They were calling it an accident. There was no proof—and she had no doubt that none would turn up—that it was anything else.

She got to him as soon as she could, but it really was too late. There as absolutely nothing she could do, except for a *post mortem*.

She called Stepanova immediately afterwards, knowing full well that she had to keep her tongue under a very strict guard.

"It's a tragedy," she said. "If only he really had had some of the stuff still hidden away, maybe he could have walked away."

"He'd have had to remember where it was first," said Stepanova, dryly. "Anyhow, if he'd handed it over, his conscience might have been clear enough to stop him stepping out in front of the autotruck." That, she knew, was the nearest he was going to get to an admission that it might not have been an accident at all. Needless to say, it hadn't been a CNI autotruck; that would have been too cruel a coincidence.

"His memory was coming back," she pointed out. "He might have remembered at any time. He might still have turned it over, the way he promised he would."

"Pigs might fly," said Stepanova. "My guess is that he knew where it was all along. He would have gone for it when he thought he'd lulled us all into a false sense of security. All that recantation crap was just a ploy. It was only a matter of time before he turned up dead again—dead for good."

Margaret couldn't help remembering how eager CNI had been to play along with Murray in the early days, when it had all seemed like good publicity for their technomiracles. They had encouraged him then, and given him all the motivational reinforcement he had needed. All it had taken to change their minds, though, was a change in the direction of the corporate-political wind. Once Stepanova had been brought in, there had been no real question of waiting to see, or hoping that things would ultimately sort themselves out. Men like Stepanova had no compunction about going all the way, just as soon as they felt that the moment was right.

"We'll never know, now," she said, hopelessly. "We'll never understand exactly what happened, why he did it."

"To tell you the truth, doctor," said Stepanova, "I don't give a damn why he did it. That's your business, not mine. My job is to protect the corporate image of CNI, and I don't mind telling you that I can't raise a tear at the thought that Walter K Murray is getting his last little flurry of publicity. After all, he's got what he always wanted, hasn't he? He'll never have to do it again."

"No," she said, wondering why she felt so sick, given that she'd learned nothing from the call that she hadn't already known.

As soon as she'd signed off she went directly to Walter's apartment. She still had a means of access, and once she was inside she still had the means to seal all the systems and block any traffic. When she'd done that, she carefully winkled out the taps that had been planted there, knowing that their removal wouldn't trigger any alarms. Then she summoned the answerphone AI.

"Walter K Murray is dead," she said. "He was comprehensively mangled by an autotruck. A check showed nothing wrong with its programming, so it's assumed that the fault was his—simple carelessness in observing the rules of the road. In all probability, he was murdered."

"This is very bad news," said the answerphone, neutrally. Mourning was way beyond the limits of its programming. It had no imagination to fill it with fear of its own eventual redundancy; no capacity to shed tears or empathize with its maker's fate; no real sense of the great mystery of death.

"It was bound to end this way, sooner or later," she said, as though she were talking to Walter himself instead of to his simulacrum. "Everybody has to die, and Walter sailed closer to the wind than most. But this isn't the way he would have chosen. If his past really was behind him, it's a cruel fate; if it wasn't, he'd far rather have gone out in a very different style."

"True," said the answerphone, which may or may not have understood what she was saying. How cleverly had Walter programmed it to meet the needs of his future selves?

"We'll never know, now, what it was all about," she said. "No one will ever know why he did it. It's a pity."

"It's a pity," echoed the AI, agreeably.

She didn't smile. "And no one will ever know where he hid the remaining enems, if there were any left," she said, and the added: "Unless, of course, you have deeply-hidden subroutines the taps could never reach."

"Of course," said the AI, once again echoing her thought, as AIs were ever wont to do.

* * * * * * *

She couldn't remember whether she'd ever been to this particular mall before, but the open plaza looked familiar. As she climbed the ugly centerpiece of the fountain people began shouting at her, but it was surprise rather than recognition. Nobody knew her; she wasn't a celebrity; she wasn't Walter K Murray.

By the time she reached her selected coign of vantage, though, a couple of hundred people were converging on the fountain. The design of the atrium was such that the crowds on the second, third and fourth floors had as good a view as the people at ground level, and the escalators were crammed.

She checked her watch, and took her courage in both hands. *Give it ten*, she thought, beginning to count down. There was a certain propriety to be maintained. There were bound to be newsdrones on duty; malls were the commercial arteries of the nation, and mallnews was always a big item in the human interest slots.

She grinned faintly at the thought of Stepanova's probable reaction to the newsvids. *It's all your own fault*, she thought. *If you hadn't made certain that this was the only way I could ever find out....*

At five she uncapped the can, and threw the cap into the crowd. At seven she began to pour. At nine she dropped the can into the rippled pool. She struck the match awkwardly on the side of the box. Her pants and sneakers were cold and damp upon her legs and feet, but she knew it wouldn't matter. The rest of her was soaked with something infinitely less inclined to dampen the spirits.

Someone in the crowd was waving a Thanaticist banner, which had materialized as if by magic. SAINT WALTER THE MARTYR, it said. *Saint Margaret the Martyr*, she thought, *and raised a burning hand in salute.*

The flames came up about her with an audible *whoosh*, and black smoke billowed forth. For a second or two—although it might have been an olfactory illusion—she thought that she could smell her own flesh burning.

Wow, she thought.

Just for a single fleeting moment, she felt she understood everything—literally *everything*.

So dear old Sigmund was right, she thought, wonderingly. *It's in us all, repress it as we may—and all it needs is answering, to show us its ultimate reward. What a world you're making, Mr. Stepanova: eternal life and eternal death for everyone...what a wonderful, wonderful world!*

The thought required little more than an instant, and that was all she had to enjoy the magical sensation. Hardly had the connection been made before she was left with nothing but the unbelievable agony of *being ablaze*—and the hope that when she woke up, afterwards, she might be able to recover the infinitely precious memory of the death-wish fulfilled.

It was nothing but hope, but it was something to cling to, something to carry her through.

Wow! she thought, again, before thought itself was finally eclipsed. Wow*! Wow! Wow!*

THE MAN WHO
INVENTED GOOD TASTE

So you're another one who wants to know everything there is to know about Jon Roriston? Hell, the guy's only been dead a week and already there are three biographies in the works. Well, why not? I'd write one myself if I weren't such a confirmed sprinter in the word-spinning business. You have to hype while the product's hot—nobody understands that better than I do, I can assure you.

How do I get paid—by the word or by the minute? Only kidding—the standard fee will be just fine.

Sure, I know the rules. No hearsay, no speculation—just the straight I-said-he-said stuff. I have done this before, you know. I bet this is your first quickietext, right? You really want to write the Great American Vidnovel, but in the meantime you have to find a way to pay the rent? I thought so. Well, a guy like you should have no trouble at all figuring out Jon Roriston. He was a cat of a very similar stripe, if you get my meaning.

So okay, where do I start—our first meeting? Sure, that's fine by me—I admire a man with an orderly mind.

* * * * * **

For me, of course, it was just routine. I was an old hand, and I'd been number one product manager at Ecomech for six or seven years. I used to pep talk all the smart kids they headhunted out of the colleges, acquainting them with the facts of life. They were always full of ideas, those kids, but four in every five thought the market was somewhere his granny used to go to buy groceries. Jon Roriston was a long

139

way from being the odd man out in this pattern, if you get my drift. Whenever I saw stars in their eyes I used to feel a pain in my bum, and little Jon had the brightest stars I ever saw.

I took him out to dinner at a real nice place. He was as nervous as hell, and I think his nervousness boosted his hostility right into orbit—I mean, I was as nice as pie, and there was no reason for the kid to get quite as snotty as he did. He was downright impolite.

"The fact is," he said, "I didn't quite envisage when I took this job that I'd be instructed to work in harness with an adman. I'm not at all sure, Mr. Farante, that I appreciate your being given a virtual power of veto on my projects."

Naturally, I was all sweet reason in return. I didn't get on my high horse about being called an adman, although I knew he meant to imply that, in his estimation, I was only one step up from two-bit copywriter. "What have you got against advertising, Dr. Roriston?" I said, meekly. "It's an honorable profession."

"It's a profession whose sole purpose is to persuade people that they ought to spend money on things they don't need," he told me. "It deals promiscuously in false promises, cynical glamorization and low-key psychological warfare. I joined this company because I thought I'd be given the freedom to work on projects that will answer people's real needs and I don't see that I need a *product manager* to keep tabs on what I do."

The way he said "product manager" made it sound like an expression of disgust, like "maggot" or "dogshit." I just smiled.

"I meet a lot of people who talk that kind of utilitarian guff, Dr. Roriston," I said. "Although I must confess that I never yet met one of them who really *acted* utilitarian. It isn't easy to separate out people's needs from their desires, son, and the whole of history proves that people are very often willing to sacrifice things which you'd say they really needed in order to get things which they wanted for reasons you might not approve of—things which would enhance their images. Admen didn't invent desire, or vanity, or envy,

Dr. Roriston—we just recognize their power as motivating forces.

"If we can sell a man a product that will increase his self-esteem, we've sold him something he desperately wants, whatever the product actually is. When an adman persuades consumers that they'll feel better about themselves by using a particular brand, he's added real value to that brand. People like you think of it as a kind of confidence trick, and maybe it is, but the consumer isn't the dupe of the trick—he's a fully-fledged collaborator, and the adman is providing a real service. If what you call 'glamorization' is cynical, the cynicism is as much the consumer's as the product manager's, because people never have wanted products that only have use-value if they could get products with glamour as well."

He just shook his head, but I'm a patient man as well as a reasonable one. I persevered.

"The hyping of products is important in any line of business," I said to him, "but it's doubly important in ours, because the biotech industry is mostly about drugs and helping people to be healthy—and I'm sure that I don't have to explain to man with your degrees what the placebo effect is. The better people can be encouraged to feel about our products, Dr. Roriston, the better those products work, and the better those products *are*. That's why you were assigned your very own product manager."

He still didn't agree with me, of course. What smartass can ever bring himself to admit that he's been outsmarted? But he perked up again when I asked him very nicely to explain to me in words that a dumb non-scientists could understand, just what it was that he intended to do to improve the lot of suffering mankind.

"I did my doctorate on the physiology of taste," he told me. "It was part of a project to figure out exactly how, when you get down to the biochemical nitty-gritty, things taste different—and why some things taste better than others."

I told him I was on his wavelength, because admen knew all about matters of taste, but he seemed to think I was trying to be funny. So I asked him what he wanted to do for Ecomech.

"I came to Ecomech," he said, "because it's one of the few big biotech firms that has no significant investment in the new techniques for mass-producing food—tissue-culture meat, cereal manna, that kind of thing. You see, Mr. Farante, I think those companies have a big problem with matters of taste."

"They have, and they know it," I agreed. "They have legions of food-scientists working out how to make their stuff taste good. There's a lot of consumer resistance to things like whole-diet flour, because everybody always says that modern food products don't taste as good as the stuff granny used to bake. It's all nostalgic crapola, of course—in tests, nine out of ten people really can't tell the difference."

"The problem's not that the taste engineers aren't doing a good job," said Roriston. "The problem is they're looking at the problem upside-down. We had artificially-produced whole-diet foods long ago, but they looked and tasted like wallpaper paste—so they started adding flavoring. It began with chocolate and strawberry, and expanded as fast as they could come up with more—now, sixty years on, we have literally tens of thousands of organic chemists trying to make various kinds of nutritionally-adequate mush reproduce all the textures and tastes of traditional foods. It's madness!"

"There you go again," I said, "trying to separate out the needs from the desires. People don't just eat food in order to live; they eat it because they like eating. It doesn't matter to them that whole-diet manna supplies their nutritional needs exactly; they won't eat the stuff unless they like the taste—and they don't just want one kind of taste, they want lots. And why the hell shouldn't they?"

"You don't understand yet what I'm getting at," he said, in a kind of martyred tone. "This is the problem: genetic engineers have succeeded in producing crop-plants whose storage proteins supply all our nutritional needs, and which are actually much better for us than traditional foods—but people don't like them. In fact, the vast majority of people are still addicted to foods which *aren't* good for them—at least, not in the quantities that their appetites encourage them to consume.

"Now, the food technologists' idea of a solution to this problem is to reproduce in whole-diet food the same range of taste sensations that traditional foods used to offer. But that's really a pretty silly way to approach it. *My* idea of a solution is to attack the problem from the other end. Instead of trying to fit the food to people's tastes, I want to fit people's tastes to the food. I want to fix people up so that they *like* whole-diet food, and so that their appetites will encourage them to like it is exactly the right amounts. That way, they'd be guided to good health by their own desires, and they wouldn't have to pay through the nose to have perfectly good food adulterated by hundreds of artificial flavorings that don't fully satisfy them anyway."

"You mean," I said, in a mildly flabbergasted way, "you want to use genetic engineering to shape our desires, instead of pandering to them."

"That's exactly what I mean," he said,

* * * * * * *

Well, right away I could see that the kid had something. In his own way, he was a genius. But he was the kind of genius Einstein was—good at figuring out the theory, but not so hot on the profit side. Not that I have anything against Einstein, you understand, but *my* idea of a genius is the guy who invented the kind of Body Odor your best friend wouldn't tell you about, and paved the way for the marketing of all those deodorants that people had to buy *just in case.*

I guess it was then that I realized, for the first time, that Jon Roriston's utilitarian objections to the artistry of advertising weren't just youthful idealism talking through his metaphorical ass. This kid was an *authentic* utilitarian, who reckoned that if our desires laid us open to exploitation by ads, then we should start thinking seriously about re-orchestrating our desires.

You might think that prospect would horrify an old ad-man like me, but it didn't—in fact, it interested the hell out of me. I had the imagination, you see, to figure out that there might be more possibilities in the kid's idea than the kid had yet seen. That was my job, after all. But first I needed more details about what he planned to do, and what he actually could do.

He didn't need much encouragement to tell me more—it was quite some hobby horse he'd taken to riding.

Taste, he explained to me, is a pretty crude sense at the biophysical level—much cruder than hearing or smell, though not quite as crude as pain. We have only four kinds of taste-buds, which record sweet, sour, salty and bitter. In fact, he said, much of what we think of as the taste of food is really its smell.

I naturally raised the objection that, if that were true, messing about with the taste buds wouldn't be enough to make people like food that they didn't like before, because it still wouldn't smell right. He said that wasn't the point, because taste is a more powerful factor in determining whether we like our food than smell is. He explained that he'd become very interested in the way that people could get *cravings* for certain kind of food, which varied a lot from person to person and from time to time.

Roriston explained to me, with his eyes shining in anticipation, that what he wanted to do was to take control of the biochemistry of cravings, insofar as it was mediated by the taste-buds, in such a way as to make people crave exactly what they needed, nutritionally speaking. If evolution by natural selection was more efficient, he told me, it would already have done that for us, but it was too blunt an instrument, and it was up to us to give it a helping hand.

I pointed out that it was people's cravings that got them into trouble by making them overeat, but he said that was just a fault in the system. He told me that a brief stimulation of the tongue by something sweet initially creates a demand for more, but that there comes a point when satiation is reached. Unfortunately, he said, our appetites have been shaped by natural selection during hundreds of thousands of years when the main problem was getting enough to eat, and there just hadn't been enough selective pressure to secure an efficient OFF switch. Nevertheless, he said, the basic apparatus was in place, and it just needed tuning up.

I was still skeptical. I thought he hadn't thought it through properly. I confided that I had trouble envisaging the entire population of the world queuing up to have their taste-buds retuned so that they would stop liking all the things they liked, and start liking a mere handful of things they hadn't liked before. To most people, I suggested, that would seem like a kind of castration. I didn't think people would go for it.

Then he got down to the real nitty-gritty. He said that he wasn't proposing to rejig the taste-buds people already had. What he was proposing to do was design and market a *new* kind of taste-bud—a fifth kind, better than all the others.

I couldn't get my head round the idea immediately. I could only think in terms of a new sensation sweeter than sweet or saltier than salt—but that wasn't what he was getting at. He wanted to create a new *kind* of taste, which wouldn't be like the other four at all. It would, he said, be a pleasant taste, which would stimulate the pleasure areas of the hind-brain in much the same was as the sweet taste-buds did, but it would do that job so much more efficiently that it would make all other pleasant taste sensations irrelevant. In addition, the new buds would be essentially moderate, switching off their craving when the host body had had its ration.

I was beginning to see the product potential in more detail by then, but I had one more worry. How exactly, I asked him, was he going to make this new kind of taste-bud respond to whole-diet foods? Even before he gave me the answer, though, I knew what the answer had to be—not speaking scientifically, you understand, but as an adman.

"It shouldn't be too difficult," he said. "What I want to do is to tie this new sensation very specifically to a particular organic compound that's not found anywhere in nature. That would become the one and only flavoring for whole-diet foods. It would make people crave the foods, and nothing but the foods, and it would make people crave *exactly the right amount* of the foods, so that they wouldn't be tempted to overeat. And because the reward-factor of my artificial taste-bud would be far greater than the reward-factors associated with the natural kinds of bud, my craving would eventually overwhelm and drive out all the others. It's so neat it's brilliant, don't you think?"

"Dr. Roriston," I said, with utter sincerity, "it's the most brilliant thing I ever heard. If you can do this, you're really going to change the world."

"That's what I figure," he said, as proud as only a pompous smartass can be. "I'm going to be the man who gave good health to all mankind."

"That too, kid," I said, with one hell of a smile on my face. "That too."

* * * * * * *

Once the kid got to work it didn't take him long to stop resenting me. After all, I cleared his project and put top priority on all his requests for apparatus and testing-programs. I didn't interfere in the lab. Not that he ever got to like me, you understand, but he did start calling me Eddie, and I started calling him Jon.

For a year or more everything went smoothly. He was a real workaholic and he really went after his target-dates. Half way through year two, though, I began to pick up bad vibes. Gossip said that he's had some sensational results in his trials, and the test-subjects I talked to said that the new taste-sensation he'd incorporated into his engineered buds was pure magic, but his reports didn't reflect that—they even tended to the negative. I figured he was maybe playing the part of perfectionist just a little too hard, so I went to see him.

"Look son," I said, as kindly as anyone could. "I don't want to rush you, but the safety boys have given your new organics an absolute okay, and your guinea pigs are on cloud nine. Isn't it about time we began to think of launch dates?"

"There's one more problem I have to crack, Eddie," he said. "Just one—then we can go."

"What problem?" I asked.

"It's the buds. We can't customize their tissue-type if we want to sell this stuff to everybody and his cousin, and we can't use drugs to prevent rejection. At present, I can easily get the buds to set themselves up on the tongue and the roof of the mouth, and make them function right away, but in a

146

matter of three weeks they're all gone again, killed off by the body's own defenses."

For a few moments, I just couldn't believe what he was telling me. Jesus, if only all problems could be like that! But I knew I had to box clever, because I remembered only too well how easily he could get on his high horse. So I didn't give him a lecture on why the miracle of built-in obsolescence is God's greatest gift to the manufacturer. He didn't care about petty details like repeat sales, and I knew that I had to play to his wacky ideals if I wanted to keep him sweet. So I took a different tack.

"I see what you mean, Jon," I said. "It's a tough one. But it's not insuperable, and I don't think we should let it inhibit our going for an initial batch of patents right now. It wouldn't be right to deprive the world of what you've already got just because it isn't yet perfect. I believe in your project, son, but I have responsibilities to the guys upstairs, and they get worried when they don't see a bit of action from programs this far down the line.

"Look at it this way. If we put out what we have now, it'll be that much easier to put the improved version on the market when you've cracked the problem. On top of that, I reckon people will be a lot keener to try it out if they know they'll be back to square one in three weeks. No matter how familiar bio-industrial augments become, there's still resistance to them. You and I are sophisticated guys, but most of the people you want to help are still living in the twentieth century, you know."

It was the last argument that swung it, I think. He was converted, and we put in for the patents and clearances the next day. The product was on the market within nine months.

I'm proud of that first campaign—the one which ran all the HAVE YOU GOT GOOD TASTE? ads. The slogan was a natural, of course—handed to us on a plate—but it was still a five-star punch line, and I think we used it very cleverly. We made twenty-five million in six weeks during the initial craze-phase, even though we were working on a razor-thin profit margin. Everyone was over the moon, from the boardroom suits and the major shareholders right down to the office cleaners.

Everyone, that is, except Jon Roriston.

* * * * * * *

This time I didn't have to go see him to find out what his problem was. He was knocking on my door the moment he cottoned on to what was going down.

"Jesus, Eddie," he said, "I just saw the half-yearly report which Sales puts out."

"Sensational bottom lines, aren't they?" I said—though I knew that wasn't what he meant.

"It's not the figures for total sales I'm talking about," he said, in a waspish kind of way. "It's the breakdown that shows what sort of volumes each of the flavored products has done. Do you realize that manna accounts for less than five percent of our output? More than eighty percent of our sales are accounted for by candy bars and chewing gum. *Chewing gum*, for Christ's sake! I didn't even know we were going to make chewing gum until I saw the 3-V ads—and even then it didn't really click. But as soon as I saw the sales figures I looked at the ad budgets—and I found out that you're spending ten or twelve times as much advertising *Good Taste* gum and candy as you are on manna. What the hell do you think you're playing at, Eddie?"

"Sit down Jon," I said, in my best genius-soothing voice, "and I'll explain. You're a scientist, and I know you'll understand when you have all the facts."

He wasn't convinced, but he sat down, and I began to teach him his A-B-Cs.

"A corp like Ecomech," I explained, "can't just chuck its products into the marketplace, buy a few ads and hope for the best. We have to plan things very carefully. Geneswitchers aren't the only hotshots we keep around here—we have a legion of top-flight market researchers who have to go out before every product launch to figure out exactly what the public is prepared to buy, and how much they're prepared to pay for it. It isn't an exact science, but it's as exact as we can possibly make it.

"I didn't bother to tell you what the MR boys came back with when they first test-flew *Good Taste* because I knew

148

you had other things on your mind—your own experiments, your own trials, your own headaches—but their results were very clear, and I knew you'd respect them. You see, they found that the majority of the public isn't quite ready for *Good Taste* manna. People can see the logic of it, but they don't take quite the same utilitarian view of eating that you do. The great majority was more interested in the possibility of using *Good Taste* as a fun thing—and that's not so bad, if you think about it carefully. The first automobiles were fun things, and the first microchips were put into electronic games. It's very often the case that the really mould-breaking discoveries have to be marketed first of all in the leisure-and-luxury sector of the market."

He didn't like it. "But you're actively pushing the gum and the candy!" he said. "If you reversed the advertising priorities, sales of the manna would surely go up."

"You're trying to put the cart before the horse, Jon," I told him. "It isn't that more people buy the gum just because we advertise it more heavily; we advertise it more heavily because we know—thanks to the MR report—that more people will try the stuff if we push it in that form. You have to remember that these are early days, and our first task is to get people used to the *idea* of a new kind of taste, and to persuade them to give it a go. While the buds have to be renewed so often, people can hardly be expected to reconstruct their entire gastronomic philosophy, can they? You have to be prepared to give people time to get used to new ideas. How's the long-life version coming along, by the way?"·

"Slowly," he said. He still wasn't happy—in fact, he had an expression like a bloodhound with a hangover—but he was no fool, and he could see the logic of the case. He stood up to go, but he had an afterthought.

"By the way," he said, "I note that there's also a significant minority market which appears in the sales report as "sprays"—but I haven't seen any advertising on 3-V for any kind of spray. I'm a bit worried about it—I mean, chewing gum's bad enough, but if we're marketing the stimulator without any carrier whatsoever, there's surely a danger that people might prefer to take it neat. If that happens, our long-terms objective of using *Good Taste* to regulate and rationalize people's eating habits might fall completely flat."

He still had the wrong end of the stick, but I wasn't about to turn it around for him—motivation is so important when a guy's working at the cutting edge. I decided to be a little economical with the truth in order to preserve his illusions as best I could. I told him a little white lie.

"Don't pay any attention to that," I said. "We've been trying out sprays for installing and renewing the buds, just to see how they fly."

"They can't be very efficient!" he said. "The tongue takes up the buds much better from saturated pads. With a spray, you'd only get a tenth of the buds to take, and they'd need renewing in a matter of days rather than weeks."

"It's MR again, son," I told him. "Some people simply prefer using a spray, because they hate sucking a wet pad for ten minutes. It's all a matter of getting them used to it. But we don't push the sprays on 3-V—we just make them available as a service to those consumers."

He shrugged his shoulders at that, and let the matter rest—for a while.

* * * * * * *

Do you want me to tell you about the personal side of his life, too? Not hearsay, you understand—we did meet in a social setting now and again, in spite of his being such a dyed-in-the-wool backroom boy. You'd rather not? Well, I guess you can get all that straight from the fillies' mouths. That's one good thing about writing about a guy who died so young, I suppose: all the skeletons in his cupboard are still alive and rattling, if you'll forgive the dodgy metaphor. Okay then—business, the whole business and nothing but the business it is.

The first real dispute we had came when I told him he had to introduce some variety into the product.

"I haven't cracked the longevity problem, yet," he complained. "*Good Taste Mark Two* won't be ready for another two years—and that's the minimum."

"Sorry, son," I said. "The boardroom suits can see the market booming outasightwise, and they want to double up the hype. *Good Taste Two* has to be along by Christmas or the market will begin to stagnate and competitors will be queuing up to take us on. The new buds don't have to last any longer—less, if you like—but they have to be subtly different. I know you can do it. If there's one kind of artificial taste better than the natural four then logic says that there must be two, or three, and maybe hundreds. It doesn't have to score more pleasure points; it just has to be as good, and different enough so that people can tell."

"But it isn't *necessary*," he said, with all the whining-power of a tantrum-throwing smartass.

"Can I tell you about something Henry Ford once said?" I asked him, politely.

"History is bunk," he came back.

"Not that," I said, patiently. "The other one."

"The public can have any color it wants, as long as it's black," he said, just so I'd know that he was a real all-round genius.

"Exactly," I said. "Great one-liner, no? Henry was a utilitarian, just like you. He thought that the most important thing about selling cars to the masses was to keep the price as low as possible, which he did by keeping his production line as simple as he could. One spray job, one color. Within five years of taking that policy decision Henry Ford had lost forty percent of his market to the opposition, because General Motors didn't underestimate their customers that way. General Motors knew that their customers wanted *choices*—choices that they could make on purely aesthetic grounds—and that they were willing to pay for the privilege.

"Jon, you've made the world hungry for new taste sensations, and one just isn't enough. We need a new one this year, and anything up to half a dozen more in the course of the next decade. Nobody else could do it half as well as you, and I'm sure that you have enough pride in your work to make sure that no one else can get into the game with an inferior product. That's what I told the boardroom suits, and I'm relying on you to make my promise good."

151

Flattery, as the old saying goes, will get you almost anywhere. Once the kid was sold on the idea he went at it like a shark at a sick fish. He had tunnel vision, but while he was in his tunnel he sure was a real sharp operator.

He had to cotton on eventually, of course—even the most unworldly scientist can't stay completely out of touch forever. By the time *Good Taste Two* was ready he'd finally figured out that the original was being very widely used in ways that the 3-V ads never mentioned. When he saw the first roughs for the ARE YOU THE FLAVOR OF THE MONTH? campaign he knew what the slogan was supposed to imply, and he really blew his top.

"You conned me, didn't you?" he said to me, when his determination to have a first-class row finally got out of hand. "The first time I asked you about those sprays, you handed me a line. They were being used to carry the stimulator, not the buds—and you lied to me to put me off the track."

"Well," I said, carefully, "we did have a spray-can version of the bud implanter, but it never took off. The sprays that carried the stimulator, on the other hand, went like a rocket once people began to experiment with them. We didn't have to push them on the 3-V, because the boom was led by word-of-mouth advertising. Word-of-mouth is the best kind of advertising there is—it's very effective, and it's free."

"And you knew how people were using the sprays, didn't you?"

I have to confess that I put my diplomatic flair on hold for a minute or two. I mean, the kid had to grow up sometime, didn't he?

"Sure," I said, bluntly. They use it wherever they like to be kissed. *Good Taste* was the biggest boost to oral sex the world has ever seen. Market Research isn't exactly reliable in areas like that, but rumor has it that Sixty-Nine knocked the missionary position clean off the top of the hit parade within a year of *Good Taste* going into the market, and if we play our cards right, it'll still be number one in ten years time—maybe forever. You told me your product was going to change the world, Dr. Roriston and I agreed with you, because we were both right."

It was the first time I ever saw the smartass flabbergasted.

"You knew this would happen," he said, again—had a bee in his bonnet, I guess. "The first time I told you my idea, you already intended to market it like this. You never had any intention of using it the way I wanted it to be used."

"I'm a product manager," I reminded him. "It's my job to know, right from the moment someone tells me his idea, exactly what can be done with it."

"Eddie," he said, "you're a real bastard. You may be a clever bastard, but you're still a bastard. You strung me along, just to make sure that Ecomech would get the patents. You let me think that you'd play it my way, because you knew that I'd take the idea elsewhere if you didn't."

"Look, son," I said to him, not quite as kindly as I might have. "You have to face up to the reality of a situation. I always knew that it would be a bad mistake to use *Good Taste* purely and simply as a way of controlling people's diets— not because it wouldn't work, but because there was too much competition on the technical horizon. For the time being, the product is doing okay even in that line, but in four or five years' time everyone will be getting slim using metabolic retuning and somatic sculpture, and eating what the hell they like.

"Sure, there are lots of people in the world who like to use *Good Taste* as a slimming aid—and some of them may stick with it—but I always knew, and MR backed me up, that if we played it that way we'd only be riding a fad.

"Make no mistake, son—there are already millions of people in the world who don't want to eat manna, no matter how good you can make it taste, because they think that, like everything else that's good for people, a healthy diet is mind-numbingly boring. And if those people don't want to use the product in that particular way, they won't. We can't make them, because they're free individuals, making their own choices. However persuasive ads are, they can't tell people to do what they don't want to do. Our job is to find

153

out what people do want, and then to tell them that we have it.

"We have to reach all the people, Jon—not just the people who want to use *Good Taste* the way you think it ought to be used. At the end of the day, you can only make a profit by letting the people choose.

"*Good Taste* is a sensational product. Everybody wants it, everybody likes it—but most of those people are prepared to like it *because it's fun*. Maybe you think people don't need fun—or that if they do, they shouldn't—but that's beside the point. The public *can* have any color it damn well wants to, whatever you may think about the humble virtues of black—and the same goes for flavors. It's my job to figure out all the colors, including the ones the inventors can't see. There's more than one kind of genius in the world, kid."

"And I suppose," he said, "you're the other kind?"

"That's right," I told him. "Absolutely double-damned right."

* * * * * * *

I honestly thought he'd take it like a man, once the initial bitterness wore off. I'd given it to him straight, and I thought he'd appreciate it. In a way, I was right—he didn't throw any more tantrums; he just got down to work again, and Good Taste continued on the up and up. But he carried a grudge. From that moment on he was determined to get me out of his hair and out of Ecomech. It was okay, because it was time for me to make my next career move anyhow, but I was a little hurt, after all I'd done for him.

He never lost his temper with me again, you know—it was all "yes Eddie, certainly Eddie" on the surface, even while he was working out ways to loosen my position. Underneath, though, there was a real vindictive streak. That's life, I guess. You do your best for people, but you don't have any right to expect that they'll thank you for it. Three months later I moved on, and handed on the *Good Taste* cornucopia to Lady Bountiful from Baltimore—who, in my opinion, wouldn't know a gut-grabbing ad from a hole in the wall.

I liked Jon Roriston, and I mean that honestly. I'm glad I worked with him. More than that—I'm proud that I was able to work with him. After all, he put me on top of some really great campaigns, and made me a present of some great opportunities to exercise my imagination and my artistry.

I was really glad that he was doing so well—getting the Nobel Prize and all—and I was as sick as a pig when he got himself gunned down by some psycho taking a short cut to the history books. But in my heart of hearts—and I'm being as honest now as I know how to be—I can't help feeling that all this grief over the assassination has led to his being a trifle overrated. I mean, he might have been the guy who did the messy business with the test-tubes, but if you want to know the name of the man who really made *Good Taste* into what it is today, it's yours very truly, Eddie Farante.

After all, who else but an adman could really have invented *Good Taste*?

THE ROAD TO HELL

He was shorter than I'd expected. You don't get much indication of height from head-and-shoulders shots, which was all the HV had been broadcasting. The waiting newsmen had snatched all kinds of pictures when his plane landed at Heathrow but the editors only wanted to show him in intimate close-up, unsmiling. Villains always look more sinister displayed that way, even when their hair is silver and they wear old-fashioned eye-glasses. He was still a bogey-man, even after all these years; forgiveness didn't come easy for his kind of crime, even when everyone admitted that it had been a tragic error born of good intentions.

He was standing by the window looking out over Brixton. His cell didn't have a view at all; I guess he was trying hard to be grateful for any glimpse of the homeland he could get.

I offered my hand to him before I sat down at the table, but he didn't take it. He didn't exactly ignore me, but he made it obvious that he intended to keep his distance, literally and figuratively. "My name is Alex Prentice," I told him. "I'm the *amicus curiae* attached to your case. Do you understand what my function is? I'm afraid there've been some sweeping changes to the criminal justice system since you were last in England."

"I'd still be entitled to a lawyer if I wanted one," he said, stonily. "I don't."

"I'm not your lawyer," I told him. "I'm the court's. I'm supposed to make an objective survey of the evidence for presentation to the three judges. If you had a lawyer of your own he'd simply be an advisor—he wouldn't actually be able to plead your case in court. The adversarial system has been abolished."

"I'm sure you're a cost-efficient substitute for the cumbersome apparatus of prosecution and defense," he said, mildly. "You'll find this case very straightforward. I've pleaded guilty to all the charges."

I suppose he knew that I couldn't possibly want it to be straightforward. I was obliged to be neutral, but that didn't mean I wasn't human. Even an *amicus curiae* isn't immune to ambition. This was a high-profile case; there was glory to be gained if I could spring a few surprises. The odds weren't good, but I was certainly going to give it a try—which is to say no more, really, than that I was determined to do my job as thoroughly and efficiently as I could.

"I still have to advise the court as to the matter of sentencing," I pointed out to him.

He laughed, briefly and bitterly. "I'm seventy-two years old," he said. "I've refused all longevity treatments. Do you honestly suppose it matters a damn whether I'm sentenced to ten years or ten thousand? If it's just a matter of *where*, that doesn't bother me. I'll presumably be in solitary confinement, if only to protect me from the other inmates. Believe me, Mr. Prentice, one cell is pretty much like another. I know."

"I still have to make my report," I told him. "I hope it won't be too much trouble for you to answer a few questions. You did come back of your own free will, after all. If the matter of punishment is irrelevant to you, you must have some interest in setting the record straight and explaining what went wrong back in 2011."

"I didn't come back in order to participate in a show trial, or to start pointing the finger at other guilty parties. I still consider myself bound by my affirmations and I won't give away any secrets."

So why the hell are you here? I wondered. *Do you, perhaps, expect to serve as a catalyst? Do you think your mere presence will be enough to force others—including me—to root out truths that were allowed to lie buried thirty-five years ago?* I knew it was wishful thinking, but I couldn't help myself.

"If you want to put me in the dock so that the HV audience can indulge in a log-drawn-out ritual hate session you'll have to do it without my help," he said. "I've nothing to say except that I did what I'm accused of doing. The project I masterminded went horribly, tragically wrong. I'm a mass murderer. That's all there is to it"

"You haven't been charged with murder," I pointed out. "Nobody claims that you caused the deaths deliberately. Manslaughter is the most serious charge on the sheet."

"One way or another, the children died," he countered, dully. "I'm here to answer for their deaths."

"You're a little late," I pointed out. "No one wants a show trial, Dr. Fallon, and no one needs any kind of ritual hate session. We only want to know what went wrong, and how, and why. My job is simply to get the fullest explanation possible. I hope you'll help me, but if you won't, I'll do the bet I can without your help."

He condescended to turn around then. "You're a young man, Mr. Prentice," he observed. "I expect that's why they appointed you to this particular case. "You belong to the generation that came after the one on which I unleashed the plague. To you, I'm a legendary figure, just like the one they named me after. You might just as well be here to interview the Pied Piper of Hamelin. People were in no mood for explanations in 2011; they wanted a lynching. I don't blame them—I don't even say that they were wrong. I won't try to tell you that I let myself be smuggled out to the outlaw state that has protected me these last thirty-five years so that I could continue to use my talents in the service of mankind and try to make amends for what I'd done. I got out purely and simply to save my neck."

"Why come back at all?" I asked, bluntly. Ambush is one of the tricks of the trade. "Why not die in harness? If you're so keen to face the music, and don't intend to defend yourself, why not pass your own sentence?"

"Perhaps I was sent back," he suggested, finally condescending to come away from the window and sit down. "Perhaps I had no choice." I was as sure as I could be that his reluctance had been all show—that he'd been away far too long not to relish the prospect of a long conversation with someone like me. I figured that he was only playing games in order to spin the process out. Perhaps he wanted to make my job difficult so that he could get to know me, strike up a proper acquaintance. I considered his answer with due care. Maybe the people who'd kept him under wraps *had* kicked him out, figuring that his usefulness was ended. It was remarkably loyal of him, if so, to remain so stubbornly silent about who they were and where he'd been.

"Have you looked through the files my office decanted into your cell?" I asked him. I was looking right at him but he wouldn't make eye-contact. He had his hands on the table in front of him, fingers interlaced, and he was staring at them as if they were a work of art.

"Yes," he said. "It's all true. I've already told you—I admit everything. I have no defense, and I don't want to enter any plea in mitigation. I am solely responsible for the failure of my plan. I ran away because I was scared for my life and I came back because I'm no longer scared for my life. That's all there is to it."

I was certain that he had more to say, but that he needed to be coaxed, or seduced into letting it out. He'd been incommunicado for thirty-five years. He had to want his say. No matter how hard he protested, he had to be in search of some kind of absolution, some kind of self-justification. He had to want to confess, and I was the man appointed to hear his confession. All it required was patience, and a little judicious encouragement. It was a test—of my competence, of the strength of my ambition.

"But the plan didn't fail, did it?" I said, craftily. "It was a great success. It solved the rat problem in a matter of days. The problem was that it succeeded just a little too well."

"No, Mr. Prentice," he replied. "It didn't *succeed too well*. The larvae weren't supposed to kill the children. The plan was to kill the rats and nothing else. It failed." His voice was colorless, but there was an enormous depth of feeling there, even after all these years. Whether he knew it or not, he wanted me to delve, to pester, to winkle out the truth. I thought I knew what the secret had to be, and I thought it was my duty to bring it into the open. I wasn't the kind of man to be afraid of opening up a can of worms—if I might be excused a truly dreadful pun. I looked at him steadily, wondering what route I ought to take to what I thought was the hellish heart of the matter.

"Why hookworms, Dr. Fallon?" I said. It seemed like a convenient and dainty way to bait the hook. "I mean, I understand the general thinking behind the plan. You'd been asked to produce something that would kill the rats, and you'd been discouraged from using a virus or a bacterium because there'd been other infective mutations, other escapes. You were commissioned to look for other kind of parasite, something that would be easier to control and direct at one specific target. I understand all that—but why hookworms? That, I just don't get."

It was a nice enough question. How could he resist the opportunity to explain? But he was still playing coy, and was not yet ready to be drawn.

Eliot Barrington Fallon, known to the tabloid media as the Pied Piper, looked up momentarily from his rapt contemplation of his hands, met my gaze for the most fleeting of instants, shrugged his shoulders, and simply said: "Why not?"

* * * * * * *

One of the benefits of being an *amicus curiae* is that you can issue *subpoenas* to just about anyone. Your judgments of relevance can be challenged retrospectively, but the people have to talk to you first. If they choose not to answer, the risk they run of being held in contempt of court is far greater than the risk you run of being censured for overstepping the mark. I knew that was going to come in handy while I was investigating the thirty-five-year-old sins of the so-called Pied Piper; his case was one on which working genetic engineers were notoriously reluctant to comment. Most of the people who'd actually worked with him were dead, and the ones that weren't were obsessively keen to distance themselves from what he'd done. It wasn't easy to find someone willing to put together a sensitive and sympathetic account of his misadventure.

The most helpful witness I found, as things turned out, was Lizabeth Froude. She was only a year younger than Fallon, so she'd been working for the same masters during the same period, but she'd been based in the Scillies, about as far away from Durham as it was possible to be. She'd never met Fallon, she'd never had any children, and she knew as much as anyone about the delicate business of DNA-manipulation. For my purposes, she was perfect—but she wouldn't have volunteered her services if I hadn't insisted.

"Why did he use hookworms?" I asked her. "It seems to me to be a bizarre way of tackling the problem."

"Not in the context of the times," she said, warily. "If you consider the precise parameters of the problem against the background of other lines of research that were fashionable at the time it was a perfectly rational choice. It was approved by the ministry and the military, remember. The proposal seemed reasonable enough to them, before it all went horribly awry. Afterwards, everybody started shouting about what a stupid idea it was and how abominably reckless it had been to use something so viciously nasty, but it looked different beforehand. If anyone had told me about the proposal, I wouldn't have thrown up my hands in horror."

"Could you explain it in such a way that a non-scientist who wasn't even born until 2016 can get a grip on it?" I asked, laying on the layman's humility with a trowel. "Start at the very beginning—the beginning as you see it."

"Firstly," she said, patiently, "you have to understand the awful magnitude of the problem. "The rats had been threatening a population explosion for thirty years and more. They thrived on our wastes, you see—I suppose you could say that they were better adapted to our way of living than we were. At first, it seemed that modern technology was easily capable of winning the war. Anti-coagulants like warfarin kept the problem under control throughout the eighties, even though the first colonies of resistant rats were well-established. It wasn't until the mid-nineties that the smarter, warfarin-resistant strains tipped the balance back in their favor. We were still dumping our wastes then, in vast quantities—an open invitation, which the rats greedily accepted. A new generation of poisons cut them back for a while but they became ever more adept at developing resistance. The speed of their adaptation was frightening in itself. 1999 was a very bad year, but there was a marginal improvement thereafter, a lull before the big storm of summer 2005. You can get all this stuff from the history books, you know. Do I really have to lead you every step of the way."

"I'm sorry," I said. "It really will be a help. Please keep going, as fully as you can."

"By '05, of course, the first escapes had taken place. Bacteria that shouldn't have been able to survive outside the lab, because they were attenuated strains, threw up mutants that *could* survive, and they exported all kinds of other stuff for which they'd been used as cookers: plasmids, virus-cores, entire retroviruses. The number of people affected was very small, and there had only been a handful of deaths, but such was the climate of opinion that it was blown up out of all proportion, construed as an awful warning. The tabloids and TV people had been waiting to pounce for years, and they went out of their way to represent every leak as a catastrophe trembling on the brink of apocalypse. The problem could have been contained by using more carefully-attenuated bacteria and better sterile technique, but public hysteria wouldn't accept that. Genetic engineering was brought under such tight regulation that the only sponsor of cutting-edge research left in the field was the Ministry of Defense, which had the duty of preparing for the first plague war—except, of course, that we already had an enemy on our doorstep in the shape of a plague of rats. The men from the Ministry weren't exactly depressed about that, you know. So of them saw it as an opportunity to test the whole theory of plague warfare against an enemy who needn't be shown any quarter."

That was exactly what I wanted to hear about, but the time wasn't ripe for grasping the nettle. I just nodded, to tell her to keep right on under her own steam.

"The Military had always been skeptical about biological weaponry, of course," she continued. "The old guard had grown up with all kinds of fancy hardware, and they had difficult adapting their image of what war was and how it ought to be fought to the possibilities of biotechnology. There was no conflict, you understand, but the Ministry and the generals had differing points of view. When we were asked to tackle the rat problem, as a way of testing our mettle, we knew well enough that there were people looking for us to take a fall, and who wouldn't be at all displeased to see a cock-up—a moderate cock-up, that is; nobody took the least pleasure from what actually happened. Nobody."

"I understand that," I said. She was drifting away from my line of thought again, but she still had to get to the hookworms. There'd be time to bring up dark-edged conspiracy theories later.

"The rats really were, in themselves, a plague, in the strict sense in which biologists had long used the term. Calling them a plague, however, recalled other connections. The media made sure everybody knew that in the past, plagues of rats had been the forerunners of epidemics of *the* plague: bubonic plague. It wasn't enough for the TV people to go on and on about rats in people's houses and rats devastating the fields of Europe; they had to keep on reminding people of what had happened in the fourteenth century, and again in the seventeenth, when the dieback following the explosion of rat populations released hordes of desperate fleas, which carried the plague to human beings. The media never seemed to tire of telling people that the germs and the fleas were still around, and that only the calculus of probability had kept the plague at bay for three centuries. They tended to skate over the fact that we now had treatments for the plague, that it wasn't the unstoppable killer it had been before. Scare-stories pulled in viewers for the advertisers, and that was the bottom line. That was the background against which people like Eliot Fallon and myself were set to work."

"Surely that should have made Dr. Fallon doubly careful? If he was as sensitive as everyone else to the idea of parasites transferring themselves from rats to people, how on earth did he let it happen?"

"He didn't *let* it happen!" she retorted, hotly. "It just happened. The point I'm making is that there was a climate of fear militating against the possibility of using endoparasites rather than ectoparasites. You asked me *why hook-*

worms? Well, I'm telling you why we couldn't even think
about using fleas. The real question you want me to answer, I
think—although you don't know enough to phrase it that
way—is why hookworms and not tapeworms?"

"Tapeworms? Why should he have used tapeworms?" I
had done my background reading. I just wanted to make sure
that I'd got it all strung together right. It needed to be put on
the record by somebody qualified to build the case and state
it clearly. She was doing fine on that account.

"Because they didn't have our techniques of somatic engineering back then. The bioscientists were only beginning
to make progress in metabolic retuning, and nobody knew
that, within a decade, metabolic retuning would have
crowded out every other method of weight-reduction. You
do know what I'm talking about, don't you?"

"Slimming," I said. "Fighting the flab. Another war
that's since been won."

"Right. Absurd as it might seem to you, weight-control
was an industry in those days, and a fiercely competitive
one. In spite of all the hysteria whipped up against genetic
engineers, there several teams working with tapeworms, trying to capture and control a neat little trick of which the
humble tapeworm was a past master. A tapeworm lives inside the long intestine of an animal, secured by a spiny head
wedged into the gut wall like a grappling-iron. It lives on the
food its host eats, but it has to avoid being digested itself. It
does this partly by armor-plating itself with a waxy tegu-
ment, but walls work both ways, and it has to take food in as
well as keeping alien digestive juices at bay, so it also se-
cretes suppressors that inhibit the host's digestive processes.
That's why people infected with tapeworms become emaci-
ated—it's not so much the food that the tapeworm steals as
the fact that the host can no longer digest what the tapeworm
doesn't need.

"It wasn't unknown for fashionable ladies in the eight-
eenth and nineteenth centuries to infect themselves deliberately with various kinds of gut parasites, in the interests of
being able to consume huge amounts of food and liquor
without becoming obese—a cunning strategy, but all too easily overdone. Insane as it seems, back in '05 the genetic en-

gineers who were being impeded every step of the way in the quest to vanquish disease and conquer cancer could still obtain funding to study tapeworms, with a view to finding a safe and easily-controllable method of weight-control. Some of them, inevitably, wanted to use actual tapeworms rather than merely stealing their genes; others—equally inevitably, all things considered—were wondering whether tapeworms could be engineered to perform other neat tricks, like delivering medicines or manufacturing vitamins. Given that research into the use of virus vectors was in such bad odor, it's hardly surprising that the idea of manufacturing ultra-benign tapeworms was being mooted as a possible way of filling the gap."

"Okay," I said. "I see that. So why not tapeworms? Why did Fallon decide to use hookworms instead."

"Because even the most vicious tapeworms are slow. To attack the rats he needed, above all else, to find something quick. Fifty years of intensive selective pressure had bred fast-adapting super-rats. He didn't want to give them any time to react to the next weapon deployed against them. He wanted something very nasty...something that would do what warfarin had done thirty-odd years earlier, but in such a way that there was no possibility of the rats fighting back. Hookworms secrete the same kind of anti-digestive agents that tapeworms use, but they don't live on the food sloshing around in their host's gut. They clamp themselves over the folds in the gut wall through which food is digested, diverting a stream of blood to flow through their bodies. In essence, they're vampires. In the wild, of course, they're prudent vampires—they exercise a modicum of self-control, so as not to use up their hosts too quickly. Normally, you don't get plagues of hookworms—but Eliot Fallon came up with the idea that it might be easy enough to launch a plague of hookworms against the plague of rats, with an effect sufficiently devastating to wipe them out in a matter of weeks.

"He was right, of course, about how easy it would be to cancel out the hookworm's inbuilt prudence by short-circuiting its cumbersome breeding-cycle. But the other problem, waiting in the wings all the while, was how to make sure that the hookworms did exactly what they were

165

supposed to do, and nothing more. He had to figure out a way of making certain that they couldn't attack people once the rats were dead, the way the fleas of old had done. He evidently thought he had done it, although I have no idea what kind of tests he carried out, but he hadn't. The stray larvae weren't tough enough to cause severe problems to adults, but small children could be killed almost as quickly as big rats, and a lot of them died before treatment could be administered. The tabloids and the TV were avid for any new Frankenstein story, of course, and this was the Frankenstein story to end them all. Their headlines were ready-made. It wouldn't have mattered much even if the victims hadn't almost all been children. They'd still have called him the Pied Piper.

"When I was young, Mr. Prentice, we used to have a saying: *Sticks and stones may break my bones but names will never hurt me.* We didn't understand how much the world had changed. We didn't know that two thousand years after Christ, its names and not nails that are used to crucify people."

It was a neat last line, but I didn't want it to end there. It was my turn now. "Dr. Froude," I said, carefully. "Is there, in your opinion, any chance that it might not have been an accident? You've already said that some of your political and military masters regarded the war against the rats as a trial run for a *real* plague war. Is it conceivable, do you think that someone—with or without Dr. Fallon's collaboration—contrived the crossover that killed all those children?"

She looked at me as if I were a scorpion that had just crawled out of one of her carpet slippers. It must have been quite an effort for her to refrain from saying what she thought.

"I believe that one or two of the nastiest tabloids reported rumors to that effect," she said, very carefully indeed. "To the best of my knowledge, the rumors were utterly unfounded—the product of diseased minds. No genetic engineer would ever be party to such a scheme. We have our own sense of duty, and we are extremely rigorous in its pursuit."

I'll bet you are, I thought.

* * * * * * *

"I understand about the hookworms now," I told the Pied Piper. "I see that it made sense."

He was sitting at the table meekly enough, but he hadn't yet made eye-contact. "Well done," he said, with only the faintest trace of irony.

"I think I can follow the intellectual route by which you arrived at the idea," I went on. If a witness won't take a baited hook, you have to try to lead them. Flattery, they say, will get you anywhere; I was about to put the saying to the test. "I've been reading all your papers," I went on. "The early ones are especially fascinating—the ones about the logic of natural selection."

"Armchair stuff," he said, off-handedly. "An active mind in combination with idle hands is capable of many clever follies."

"It was all new to me," I persisted, doggedly. "I never heard of Mertensian mimicry until I read your paper on it. Fascinating notion."

"Congratulate Mertens, not me."

"Can I just check that I've got it straight? There's a whole series of snake species, ranging from the deadly through the not-so-deadly to the utterly harmless, which all have similar markings. At first, it was assumed that the deadly ones were the models and all the others mimics, but Mertens pointed out that that didn't make sense, because predators that encountered the deadly ones didn't have any opportunity to learn avoidance. He argued that the deadly ones were mimics, just like the harmless ones, and that the not-so-deadly ones had to be the models, because they were the ones that could intimidate predators without actually killing them, giving the said predators the opportunity to learn to avoid that particular pattern of protective coloration. Is that right?"

"Yes," he said, staring at his hands as if he couldn't quite figure out how the fingers came to be interlaced that way.

"It's a neat idea—the deadly mimicking the not-so-deadly, the imprudent mimicking the prudent. I think I see how it led on to the papers on the life-cycles of parasites. It seems like a puzzling thing, at first glance, that something like the malarial parasite should have such a weirdly complicated life-cycle: mosquito to man and back again. How could such a clumsily chancy thing evolve by natural selection? Why hasn't the parasite been refined by natural selection so as to cut out the mosquito, completing its life-cycle within the human host? Because if it did, it'd be too deadly, wouldn't it? The parasite that survives and thrives in the long term is the one that can't do too much damage to its hosts. Parasites cut out for long evolutionary careers need built-in prudence...the force of natural selection actually incorporates handicaps, so that parasites can remain quietly endemic without ever becoming a plague, and one of the time-tested methods of handicapping is the use of alternate hosts. The nastier the parasite, the more convoluted its life-cycle has to be."

"It's a wonderful world, Mr. Prentice," he said, with what sounded suspiciously like a sigh. He was studying the ceiling now, but he was listening. He was following my every move along the fatal line of reasoning that had tempted him, and caused his spectacular fall from grace.

"Hookworms are nasty too," I said. "Tapeworms are mild by comparison, but even they need alternate hosts. Hookworms are real bastards, though...and what an odyssey they have to undertake! The larvae climb grass-stalks so that they can transfer to the skin of passers-by, then it's through the sweat-glands and hair-follicles, into the blood or the lymph-vessels, all the way to the lungs—then up the bronchia to the mouth, so that they can get back to the small intestine again. Very cumbersome...and very necessary, because a more efficient cycle would wreak havoc among the host population. I can see how the ideas came together—how you got caught up with the notion of making a deadly mimic out of the clumsy model. I can see why it appealed to you so much, and why it was so simple in genetic engineering terms. All you had to do was snip out the handicapping genes, so that the hookworms could produce eggs that mostly hatched inside the primary host, producing a hookworm population explosion in the gut. It wasn't to the long-term advantage of the worms, of course, even though the population explosion would also flood the rats' feces with more eggs and larvae. As the rat population dropped sharply, so did the probability of rats picking up the excreted larvae. From epidemic to low-level endemic in one fell swoop. Magic. The real Pied Piper would have been proud of you."

"The one you're thinking of wasn't real," Fallon pointed out. "He's a character in a story."

"I thought it was a poem by Browning," I said, happy enough to trade corrections.

"Before the poem there was a story," he said, "and before the story a legend. The legend probably had some truth in it, referring to the exploits of a real fourteenth century rat-catcher, whose campaign against the rats was effective enough to release the plague on the human inhabitants of the town where he worked. The plague would have killed the children first, of course. It's even conceivable that the flea-bites might have made them so restless before the plague-symptoms developed that they seemed to be dancing to inaudible music."

"You knew that all along, didn't you?" I said, quietly. "It was lurking at the back of your mind, with the notion of Mertensian mimicry and all the rest. Hookworm infestation causes itching too, doesn't it? Itching and fever. You had the Pied Piper legend in mind from the very beginning."

I won the round. He looked at me. He looked deep into my placid eyes.

"What if I did?" he said. He knew *what if*. He had to know. He just wanted me to voice it.

"Is it possible," I said, "that what you did *wasn't a mistake*? Is it possible that it was just the intellectual climate of the day that made people see it as another horrible foul-up, another case of scientists trying to play God and letting loose the Devil? Did you *know* that the larvae would be capable of infecting humans as well as rats? Did you kill those children on purpose, Dr. Fallon?"

"Am I to be charged with that?" he said, in a tone so level as to be almost macabre. "There was some slanderous gossip at the time, I know—talk of new weapons of biological warfare—but it was just nasty-minded speculation. No such accusation is formally made in those files you kindly sent me."

"No such accusation is made in the files," I conceded, silkily, "but when I spoke to you last, you accused yourself of mass murder. I pointed out to you, if you recall, that you'd only been charged with manslaughter, but you seemed oddly reluctant to accept the correction. Did you mean it literally, Dr. Fallon? *Was* it murder? Did you really intend to kill people as well as rats?"

"Why would I do that?" he inquired, as mild as milk. He was still looking at me, still confronting all that I stood for. "Even if my military masters had wanted me to, why on earth would I have gone along with them, knowing what the consequences would be?"

"Maybe you thought the human population explosion was getting out of hand," I said. "Maybe you thought the plague of people needed to be dealt with as urgently as the plague of rats. Maybe you believed, along with your military masters, that the capabilities of plague warfare had to be *displayed*, in accordance with the logic of deterrence."

"You have a nasty mind, Mr. Prentice," he informed me, before he turned away.

"I have a neutral mind," I retorted. "My duty is to consider all the possibilities, including the possibility that you might be innocent in spite of your admission of guilt, and the possibility that you might be guilty of worse crimes than those with which you have so far been charged."

"The parents still want my blood, don't they?" he said, wryly. "I suppose you figure that you might as well hang me for a sheep as a lamb. But I'm too old, and too tired, to be hurt by anything you say or anything you do. If you want to charge me with murder, Mr. Prentice, do so. I can't and won't complain."

"I can only make it murder if I convince myself that it was murder, Dr. Fallon," I told him, mimicking his mildness with Mertensian guile.

"I don't believe that your masters would let you do it even if you did," he replied, with an accuracy which told me that I was getting through at last. "If I went down for premeditated murder, I couldn't go down alone."

170

THE CURE FOR LOVE, BY BRIAN STABLEFORD

* * * * * * *

Fallon was right, of course. If he testified that the parasites' crossover from rats to humans hadn't been accidental, he'd have been pointing a finger at the people who'd funded and monitored his work. Officially, they'd washed their hands of him thirty years before, appointing him sole scapegoat; unofficially, they'd almost certainly connived at his escape, and might well have continued to fund his research in some far-flung corner of what had once been the British Empire.

I knew how unlikely it was that I'd get anything self-incriminating out of the civil servants or the generals, but I still had to take testimony from those who were still alive, so there was no harm in trying. Brigadier-General Sir Allen Waterfield (retired) seemed to be my best bet; although far from senile, he'd acquired a reputation for tactlessness in the course of trying to defending his particular rural backyard against the continuing urbanization of the land around the high-speed railway linking London to the Channel Tunnel. Garden-of-England-ism wasn't exactly a true-green political movement, but he certainly wasn't as solidly steel-grey as he had been when he was in Military Intelligence. I was pleased when he received me out of doors, in his own sweet-smelling garden, where the hum of busy insects provided an altogether appropriate background to our conversation.

"I've never shirked my share of the responsibility for what happened," he told me. "I was OIC of the military end of the operation and I had to carry the can. Matter of duty. Simple fact is, though, that I was just a layman. Scientist produces a plan like that, rubber-stamped by the Scientific Civil Service, you have to trust his judgment. Man like Fallon says the bloody worms can't possibly infect human beings, you're inclined to believe him. Said he'd exposed himself to infection, you know, before he asked for volunteers—probably had, silly bugger. We did call for volunteers, and sure enough, the worms couldn't get a grip on 'em. Didn't try it on kids, though—how could we?"

171

"Even if the original worms were incapable of affecting children," I pointed out, "the disaster might still have happened. Genetically-engineered organisms do tend to be unstable—even complex metazoans."

"Didn't know that at the time," he said, firmly.

"No, of course not. Were there any other projects involving hookworms under way at the time?"

"What do you mean, *projects*?"

He knew exactly what I meant. I was asking whether anyone was interested in using hookworms for any purpose other than solving the rat problem.

"I mean that if Fallon produced the idea out of nowhere it must have seemed utterly bizarre. I wondered if there was other research going on."

"Does Fallon say there was?"

"No, he doesn't. To tell you the truth, General, he doesn't say very much about anything. He seems to feel that he's still bound by all the oaths of secrecy he took."

"He is. So am I. What are you getting at, Mr. Prentice?"

"I wondered whether you might in be a better position than he is to judge what might now be safely revealed," I said, tactfully. "If there's information that might help us to understand the background to Fallon's mistake, which he feels duty bound to conceal, it's conceivable that someone possessed of higher authority might feel free to release it on his behalf."

"I'm retired," Sir Allen pointed out. "I don't have any authority now. Have to talk to my successors. Their decision. Tell you this much, though—the only man working with hookworms was Fallon. Tapeworms were fashionable, lots of people were taking an interest in various other nematodes, but hookworms were Fallon's thing. Any other projects apart from the rat problem were his—and I mean *his*. Nobody ordered him to work with hookworms, nobody told him what he ought to do with them. Does that answer your question?"

Nearly, I thought, *but not quite nearly enough.*

"Do you have any idea why Fallon has come back?" I asked him.

"How could I?" he countered. "Haven't seen or spoken to the man in thirty-five years."

"But you saw and spoke to him frequently when the crisis was blowing up and getting out of hand. You can judge his state of mind *then* better than anyone else who's still alive, perhaps better than the man himself."

"You're asking me why he ran rather than why he came back?"

No I'm not, I thought. "If you'd rather look at it from that angle," I said, graciously.

"Don't know. Man wasn't a coward, I know that. Didn't panic—probably never have got away if he had. He was cool. Not dispassionate, mind—he understood the magnitude of the tragedy, and the horror of what he'd unleashed—but he was methodical to the end, working to stop the thing in its tracks. Didn't duck out till they actually went to arrest him. Had it planned."

"Did he have help?" I was quick to ask.

"Who from?" he snapped back. The over-sensitivity was suspicious, but it wasn't evidence.

"Sympathetic colleagues—maybe bioscientists who thought, *there but for the grace of God go I?*"

"Maybe."

"Perhaps he always intended to face up to his responsibilities, just as you did," I suggested. "Perhaps he thought it a matter of duty too. Perhaps some higher duty intervened to take him away, and has only now released him. Was he that kind of man, in your estimation? Is he that kind of man?"

"Maybe," he repeated, obstinately.

"How long were specimens of Fallon's hookworms kept in store once the epidemic was over?" I asked, switching tack abruptly.

"As long as I was on active service," he told me, equably. "Probably still locked away. Have to keep the buggers, just in case they still exist *out there*. Might have to fight the war all over again. Who can tell?"

"So they're still the subject of active research?"

"Didn't say that. Still around, that's all."

"With some potential utility as a weapon of war."

"Can't say. Haven't had any plague wars yet, thank God. Till we do, no way of knowing what kind of weapons might be deployed and what kind of defenses we'd have to muster."

He'd been ready for the question. He'd expected it. What did that imply? Did it matter what it implied, given that it didn't prove anything?

"Do you know what Mertensian mimicry is, general?" I asked him. "Did Fallon ever explain it to you?"

He hadn't expected that one. His eyes narrowed as he tried to reason out my motives for asking.

"I think I heard him use the term," he admitted, cautiously. "I forget what it means."

"It refers to a situation where something very nasty masquerades as something rather less nasty," I told him, blandly, "the true measure of its venomousness unappreciated because those who encounter it are conditioned to see and respond to the moderate nastiness whose guise it wears."

"Too complicated for me, son," he said. "I'm just a soldier."

"All kinds of people wear uniforms," I pointed out. "At the end of the day, all battle-dress is a kind of protective coloration."

"Has Fallon or anyone else you've talked to accused me of using him to disguise a weapons-test as an unfortunate accident?" he asked, bluntly, at last justifying his reputation for impetuousness.

"No," I said. "Dr. Fallon hasn't accused anyone but himself of anything, and none of the witnesses I've spoken to have made any such claim. Is it conceivable, do you think, that anyone could have persuaded a man like Fallon to go along with something like that?"

"No," he said, "it's not."

"Is it conceivable that anyone—without his or your knowledge—could have sabotaged his project?"

"Barely—but if someone did, it wasn't for the purpose you just hinted at. If anyone sabotaged that project it can only have been green zealots out to poison the reputation of genetic engineering. It definitely wasn't the military, nor the government of the day."

At least I had his firm and specific denial on record; that was better than a string of maybes. I didn't suppose I'd get any more, and I certainly didn't expect any more—but I wasn't the only one able to spring a surprise or two. As we shook hands before I got into my car, he produced a bolt from the blue.

"It might be worth remembering," he said, with carefully calculated negligence, "what the lame child saw—the one who couldn't follow where the piper led. That might help you get off the dead-end road your thoughts are presently following."

It took me quite a while to work out what he meant, and why he'd taken the trouble to throw me the scrap, but I did it—and I began to think that perhaps the concept of *Military Intelligence* wasn't such an oxymoron after all.

* * * * * * *

"The road to hell," I quoted at Eliot Fallon, "is paved with good intentions."

"So they say," he said. He was able to look me in the face, now. He'd settled into his new routines. He was as nearly at ease with himself as he ever would be.

"I think I understand what happened," I told him. "I also think I understand why you can't admit it. I think I know why you let the Military spirit you away instead of facing up to things back in 2011, and why you felt that you had still to come back and face the music, in the end."

"That's very clever of you," he said, tolerantly.

"I really thought it might have been planned the way it happened," I confessed. "I suppose I wanted it to be that way, so there'd be something spectacular for me to find out and show to the world. I apologize for that."

"There's no need," he said. "A lot of people out there would be only too happy to find out that I killed their children deliberately. That would fit in with their scheme of things. It would make me out to be *evil*. They can deal with evil, you see. It's something that merely has to be stamped out, with no holds barred. Incompetence is rather more ambiguous; it leaves them uncertain, not sure how much vengeance they're entitled to exact. It left me uncertain too—I didn't know how much vengeance they were entitled to exact either. The last thirty-five years haven't been easy."

"More people are on your side than you might imagine," I told him, elliptically.

"I'm not one of them," he answered, bleakly. I'd realized that, of course.

"Neither am I," I said. "I'm strictly neutral, and my duty is to assess, carefully and conscientiously, all the evidence placed before me, and any further evidence that I can discover by assiduous search. I've done that, to the best of my ability. According to the evidence, you caused a genetically-engineered organism to be released into the environment on a massive scale, in order to kill the rats which were over-running the country. The measures you took in order to ensure that the organisms were incapable of infecting human beings were inadequate, and in spite of the availability of effective treatments, many of the human beings who were infected—almost all of them children—died. You've pleaded guilty to the various charges arising from that sequence of events, the most serious of which is manslaughter."

"That's exactly where we started from," he pointed out.

"Sometimes," I said, "it takes a lot of work to establish that the obvious is, in fact, obvious. That's the nature of evidence. Suspicion is a different matter altogether. Officially, of course, I'm not allowed to elaborate patterns of suspicion—but I'm only human. So is Brigadier-General Sir Allen Waterfield, whose evidence served only to confirm the obvious. May I remind you of a story, Dr. Fallon?"

"Is it relevant to our business?"

"Not to our business, no. That's concluded."

"In that case, you may."

"When the Pied Piper of Hamelin led the children away into the land beyond the mountain, one lame boy couldn't keep up. He was still outside when the magic doorway closed again—but he saw into the land beyond it. It was a beautiful place, like the mythical land of Cokaygne or the Fortunate Isles, or...well, you probably know lots of other names. The faithless parents of Hamelin, who'd refused the piper his due, knew only that they'd lost their children—but the lame boy knew that he'd led them to a better place."

176

"But that's not what the real rat-catcher did," Eliot Fallon pointed out. "The man who spawned the legend, if there was one, delivered the children up to agonizing death, and the adults too."

"Not by design. The rat-catchers of 2011, of course, were the genetic engineers. They too were faced with faithless paymasters, who forced them to work on projects they'd rather not have been involved with, and projects they couldn't consider worthy—but they did their best within the restrictions, and took what opportunities they could. If it was permissible, and fashionable, to work on tapeworms, they were content to do it, and to do their level best to design *benign* tapeworms: symbiotes rather than parasites. Tapeworms to control weight...and to deliver other rewards. Tapeworms whose infestations would actually improve and empower their hosts."

"I believe some people were working on projects like that," Fallon said.

"And others were working on hookworms," I said. "One other, anyway. Hookworms that could kill rats and...well, and do other things, I guess. A sword that was capable of beating itself into a ploughshare. Exceedingly prudent hookworms, which would not only alternate between different hosts but would treat those hosts very differently. A wild idea, perhaps, but not a crazy one. After all, malarial parasites get along pretty well with mosquitoes, don't they? To a man who understood the niceties of Mertensian mimicry and the life-cycles of prudent parasites, it probably wouldn't seem crazy at all. But the plan went wrong. Maybe it was overcomplicated, maybe it was badly thought out; hindsight certainly assures us that it was too ambitious."

"That's all pure fantasy," Fallon said, equably.

"Yes, I know. It would be an even purer fantasy, wouldn't it, to imagine that the prudent worms are still out there, being prudent, while their recklessly deadly kin have long since eliminated themselves from the scene. I mean, if anyone even suspected that, there'd be another tabloid storm, wouldn't there? Not the sort of thing any responsible adult would encourage or condone. The professional scaremongers would probably start wondering whether there might be labs somewhere in the distant corners of the globe where a whole flock of new hookworm species is being brought to maturity. God alone knows where all the speculation would end."

"It shouldn't even start," Fallon said, staring at me. His eyes suddenly seemed to be filled with an intense and eerie light. "There's no need. The simple facts of the case are that a man made a new kind of hookworm to make war on a plague of rats. He made a mistake, and the worms that killed he rats went on to kill thousands of children. It was his fault, and his alone, and he ought to answer for the consequences of his mistake. That's all there is to it."

"I know," I said. "That's exactly what the evidence says."

* * * * * * *

That was the end of the matter, so far as I was concerned. Involvement with such a high-profile case certainly didn't do my career any harm, but it didn't give it the kind of meteoric boost I'd dared to hope for when I took it on. I had to find other ways of becoming a high-flyer.

They do say that the road to hell is paved with good intentions. Sometimes, I wonder if any of them are mine. I suppose we all do—all those of us, at least, whose work involves us in important matters of right and wrong, good and evil, innocence and guilt.

THE SCREAM

Paul Scrivener moved his knight to imperil Jim Alvey's rook, and then sat back in his chair so that he could watch the frown of concentration deepen on the sheriff's face. For half an hour now he had been patiently building a king's side attack, drawing a ligature around the beleaguered black pieces and squeezing the potential out of them. Alvey had defended as stoutly and as patiently as he usually did, but he could see that the writing was on the wall unless he could identify some cunning ploy that might free his pieces and turn the tide.

They had been playing regularly for more than four years now; Scrivener won three games out of five, and was glad that it wasn't more. All the pleasure went out of the game when it was too one-sided. There wasn't that much pleasure left in life these days, and he was anxious to conserve all that he could.

While he studied Alvey's clouded expression, further confused by the yellow lamplight that shone down at an angle, Scrivener fanned his own face with a palm-leaf. It was a hot night, and the humidity always seemed worse in the evenings than it did it in the blaze of noon. Every year the swamp-line crept closer; every year the river-floods were worse. When he had moved into the house nine years before it had seemed high enough on the hill to be safe for half a century, but now it no longer seemed such a secure haven. There was little or no chance of his being flooded out, but the spreading jungle-weed and the insects it brought with it weren't just a threat to the gardens and the vegetable-patches of the neighborhood; they were a threat to its whole way of life. Had the county not been devastated by the plague war,

179

and its population reduced from thirty thousand to six-and-a-half, a mass migration of the population would already have begun, but the war had changed the attitude of the survivors very dramatically. A social solidarity and a stubborn determination had been created, which must have been far closer to the spirit of the pioneers of five centuries before than to the competitive individualism of their twentieth-century grandparents.

To the people who remained, the runaway Greenhouse Effect was just one more aspect of the ongoing crisis, one more weapon of the war between Dixie and the Devil, against which all possible material and spiritual resistance must be mounted.

Alvey looked up without having played, taking a rest from the effort of concentration.

"Hot as Hell tonight, Doc," he remarked, watching the rhythmic movement of Scrivener's makeshift fan.

"It's not so bad," said Scrivener, laconically. "It's just the sweat of the swamp makes it seem so. It'll get better. Competition and natural selection will make the weed grow taller, pushing the canopy higher and higher. Eventually, the foliage will make a screen, under which the likes of you and I can walk in relative comfort. It's already happening down-river. That's the whole idea of induced tachytely—it's evolution while you wait. You and I won't see the climax community of the weedkin, but Roy and his kids will."

Roy was Alvey's son. In time, Roy would probably become sheriff, following in Jim's footsteps just as Jim had followed in Joe's. The Alveys had always had the kind of stubborn regard for tradition that the whole community had recently recovered. The Alveys were a much-respected family nowadays.

"They will if'n the skeeters don't get 'em," Alvey agreed. "Pity you guys couldn't just make the trees, without all the vermin comes with 'em."

Alvey's "you guys" meant scientists in general, not even genetic engineers in particular. Alvey would have said the same if Scrivener had been a physicist or a geologist, and there was no point Scrivener pointing out that he had only ever worked with human beings. These days, in Romilly and a thousand small towns like it, all scientists were culpable, and all were expected to take responsibility for one another.

"We didn't make the weedkin," Scrivener said, mildly. "We just made it easier for the weedkin and the other green redeemers to remake themselves. We gave them increased plasticity and increased capacity to cope with mutation; they have to find their own ways to thrive in adverse circumstance—just as we do."

Scrivener's "we" meant "people," not just "you and me." Alvey understood that. He was an intelligent man, in spite of the hick act he sometimes put on for Scrivener's benefit.

The sheriff was just about to drop his gaze to the chessboard again when the scream split the night. The nodding head snapped upright and Alvey looked straight into Scrivener's eyes for one painful instant before he jerked to his feet and looked wildly out into the night, trying to figure out the exact direction from which the sound had come.

It was that kind of scream: the kind of sound which made a puppet of a man, jerking him around by his reflexes. The night was far too hot for the blood to run cold, but Scrivener felt a numbing terror clutch at his heart, as though it were trying to tear him in two. There was only one scream, then nothing. It lasted for maybe two seconds, and died abruptly, without fading to a sob or a sigh. It was a scream like a stroke of lightning, or a bullet in the back: an explosion of agony which expended all its energy in an instant.

Scrivener watched the sheriff reach for his holstered gun, then hesitate and twitch his fingers impotently. Beyond the lamp-lit verandah the night was black; there was nothing to be seen. The scream had sounded less than a quarter-mile away, but not so close as to be on Scrivener's property.

"What the fuck was that?" whispered Alvey.

He's hoping it was an animal, Scrivener thought, surprised by his capacity for clinical analysis. *He knows that it wasn't, but he won't admit to himself that he knows. He doesn't want it to be human. He'd far rather think that nothing on earth could wring that sound from a human throat. That's what the other people will decide—that it was just some animal hollering, nothing to be scared of.*

Aloud, he said: "I don't know." It was a very easy lie to tell. It wouldn't have been any easier to say the words if they'd been true. Scrivener wished that he didn't know, wished that he dared doubt, but he didn't. He'd always known, deep down, that he'd hear the sound again. He'd always known that there was no hiding place, that retirement and flight to the Deep South weren't enough to hide him from the consequences of his error. A weird temporal echo allowed him to hear himself speak the words that he'd said only a few moments before to Jim Alvey: "We didn't make the weedkin; we just made it easier for the weedkin and the other green redeemers to remake themselves." He hadn't made the cause of the scream, but he'd made it possible for the cause of the scream to remake herself.

"Whatever it was," said Alvey, "it's likely to be my business. Sorry, Doc—I can't finish the game. Leastways, not right now."

"That's okay, Jim," said Scrivener, wishing that he didn't sound quite so calm. "We'll call it a draw. We'll start over, some other night."

Alvey looked down at the table, at the paralyzed black pieces which he couldn't have freed, barring some miracle of inspiration, but he didn't protest.

"You could set it up on your machine," he said, picking up his hat and straightening his pants. "Play it out against the program. It'd be a real tough test for the silicon grandmaster." He didn't mean it. Neither he nor Scrivener ever played against computer programs; they both thought chess, like all games, ought to be a matter of man against man.

"Best of luck, Jim," said Scrivener, wishing that he dared mean it. "I hope it turns out to be nothing."

"Yeah," said the sheriff, as he jumped down from the verandah and strode away into the darkness, "Maybe it's nothing." He gave the strong impression that he wished he dared mean it too.

* * * * * * *

Scrivener checked the water-meter, and figured that he could take a brief cold shower. Afterwards, he dressed for bed. He thought that it was best to wear light pajamas in spite of the heat, to keep the flesh of his thighs from sweating too much when his legs rested together. He kept a single sheet on the bed, just in case something got inside the mosquito-netting. There was no way you could keep the insects entirely at bay, but you had to minimize the problem. The rapidly-proliferating new insect species weren't carrying anything particularly nasty—induced tachytely hadn't yet succeeded in generating Son of Malaria—but their bites itched and there was always the possibility of an allergic reaction.

He tried to go to sleep, but he couldn't. The scream didn't echo in his mind—not, at any rate, as the ghost of a sound—but the possibilities awakened by the memory wouldn't lie quietly. He had found it increasingly difficult to sleep for eight hours a night, or even for five, since he had turned sixty. It didn't require much disturbance of his mental equilibrium to deliver him into the untender care of Morpheus' dark sister, Insomnia.

He tried to tell himself that he wasn't at fault. The fact that the road to Hell was paved with good intentions couldn't allow people to give up on their good intentions. In an era when desperation licensed such wild cards as the tachytelic weedkin, his project had seemed like something carefully planned, something wholly controllable, something cleverly virtuous. It hadn't seemed like a crazy gamble. But Scrivener had seen the shock in Jim Alvey's startled eyes when the scream had lanced through the sheriff's train of thought, and he knew what kind of horror would overcome those same oddly mild and gentle eyes if Alvey ever found out what had caused it. Not that Alvey ever would, of course. When—probably by dawn's early light—one of Alvey's men eventually found the body, there would be nothing at all to provide a causal link between the death and the scream. It would be a conundrum as unyielding as the problematic position which the sheriff had gratefully abandoned in order to go about his business.

Even so, it was impossible for Scrivener to convince himself that he wasn't responsible, that it wasn't his fault.

In the long run, he thought, *it'll all be okay. People will come through. The ecosphere will pull through. Because of us—the scientists. We provide the means by which society and wilderness alike may heal themselves. Without us, the world would be damned. In the long run, it'll all be okay, and the pain in which the whole bloody world is screaming will go away. In the meantime, there's nothing much that can be added or taken away from the world's pain by one man's endeavors or one man's mistakes. It's just a drop in the....*

The phone rang. Without being quite aware of the fact, Scrivener had been waiting for it to ring. The scream hadn't just been a scream; it was a message, a threat, a promise.

He picked up the phone, and said "Hello," as non-committally as he could.

"Did you hear?" she said, rhetorically. She had made certain that he would hear. How long had she been out there in the darkness, lying in wait? "Did you understand?"

"Martha," he said, awkwardly. "Don't do this, Martha." It wasn't clear enough, he knew. He wasn't able to say precisely what he meant by 'this', and that would allow her to misunderstand.

"It's in the nature of a scorpion to sting," she said. "There's no use in asking it to show civilized restraint of its own accord. You have to handle it right. You have to give it a reason to live and not to sting."

"You're not a scorpion, Martha. You're a human being. You're not a prisoner of some blind, unreasoning instinct. You don't have to do this!"

"You don't understand, Paul," she said, softly but quite distinctly. "You don't understand your own creation. You don't understand what an incredible thing you've done."

"Who was it?" he asked, not so sure that his voice would sound as distinct as hers. "Who was it, Martha?"

"A young one," she told him. He could hear the contrived relish in her voice—or was it contrived? "Succulent and tender. You've no idea how fresh they are when they're in that condition—like a breath of cool wind in your soul. It's hot down here, isn't it, Paul? Did you think you needed the heat to soothe your poor arthritic bones? Can't you stand the chill of winter any more?"

184

"The sheriff was here," he told her. "He's a good man. One incident won't mean anything, but if you don't move on he'll know that something's crazily wrong. He'll come after you, Martha. You don't know what it's like down here—how fiercely they resist the things that are done to them, day by day, by cruel circumstance."

"Did you tell him?" she jeered. "Did you tell him what the scream was? Did you tell him who I am?"

He couldn't reply immediately. He couldn't say no. She waited for him, probably knowing exactly how he was going to cop out.

"I will," he said. "I'll tell him everything. Tomorrow, I'll tell him everything."

"It's too late for that," she said. "You should have done it thirteen years ago, if you were ever going to do it. Instead, you chose to hide. You chose to hide me, and you chose to hide *from* me. Will you tell them now to shoot me down like a mad dog? Will you tell them now that I can't be taken into custody, can't be tried, can't be jailed? Will you tell them to crush me underfoot like some poisonous insect? You've had thirteen years to do that, *Doctor*, and you've held your tongue."

"I won't let you come here," he said. "This is my home, and I won't have you violate it. This is where it stops, Martha. This is where I draw the line. I'm going to tell him, Martha. Go now, and don't ever come back this way again."

"I don't believe you," she said. "If you're so concerned about this precious little community, pack your things. We'll go on together—any place you fancy. I'm tired of being alone, Paul. I need you. I want you. And if you don't want to come with me, I might just have to kill you. It's the nature of the beast, Dr. Scrivener—the nature of the beast that *you* made. I'm your creation, Paul; I'm the only thing you have to leave to posterity. You shouldn't have run away. You shouldn't have run from the project, and you shouldn't have run from me. I never ran away. I never ran away from what I am."

The moment she put the phone down he began to wish that he'd hung up on her. He'd let her run the whole conversation. He'd let her decide its beginning and its end. He'd

displayed his impotence yet again, and in so doing had conceded that everything she said of him was true.

He knew that he ought to tell Jim Alvey everything. He
knew that he'd always known that—that the true reason he'd
courted the man's acquaintance and made a friend of him
had nothing to do with love of a stupid game and everything
to do with the knowledge that he would one day need a confessor. And yet, in all the years he'd known the sheriff,
through all the long sweltering evenings when they'd sat outside, he'd never said a word about his reasons for coming
way down south, or about the project he'd left behind. Time
after time he'd hesitated over it, and left it all unsaid. Maybe
he'd left it too long. He'd certainly left it long enough to let
death into his adopted community, just as he'd let it into the
community where he'd lived most of his working life.

He wished that he could just pick up the phone, and call
Jim, or Roy, or the station-house, or anyone at all—but he
couldn't. He was still a coward, still a runaway, still a man
who couldn't draw the line and stick to it. He was impotent,
in more ways than one.

He wouldn't believe me, he thought, and knew that it
was true. Alvey wouldn't—couldn't—believe him right
away. Alvey would check back, and make sure, and weigh
things up and down and sideways. In the end, he would
probably believe, but not until there'd been more deaths—
maybe many more. By the time Alvey could be convinced,
Hell would have broken loose and he, Paul Scrivener, would
be well and truly in it, burning in the fires of universal hatred.

But there was only one alternative to picking up the
phone, and that required a different kind of bravery, which
he wasn't sure he had.

* * * * * *

The next evening, as dusk was fading, Alvey mounted
the steps to the verandah where Scrivener sat, dispirited to
the point of exhaustion. The lamp was already lit, in anticipation of another long and sweaty evening.

"Long day?" Scrivener asked, when the ritual exchange of greetings was complete. He couldn't bring himself to ask outright about the body.

"Yeah," said Alvey pausing before lowering himself into the chair that was permanently set out for him. "Look, Doc—I need some advice. You're the only person I can come to."

Alarm made Scrivener tense up inside, but he was sure that he wasn't showing any signs.

"Why me?" he asked.

"It's about what we heard last night," said Alvey, finally settling his lean frame into the chair. "Half a dozen other people down the hill say they heard it, but they were maybe twice as far away from it as we were. I talked to the Riddicks and Old Man Johnson, and they all said that it sounded like some animal hollerin'. I'm probably the only person in town that thinks somethin's not right—even the kid's ma closed up about it. She lost her husband and one of her daughters in the war; she's learned too well how to take it. There's no rage left in her, no sense of atrocity."

"Atrocity?" Scrivener repeated, uneasily.

"Sorry, Doc—not *that* kind of atrocity. Fact is, the boy didn't have a mark on him. No sign of violence whatsoever. The medical examiner went over him with a fine-toothed comb, and couldn't find a thing. Only thing he could put on the register was 'Heart Failure'. He told me it wasn't really a cause, just a statement. He didn't have any explanation at all. No suspicious circumstances, no evidence of any crime. It's like he just dropped dead—except that you and I, Doc, know that he didn't just *drop* dead. You and I heard him scream."

"What kind of advice do you want, Jim?" asked Scrivener, carefully.

Alvey paused for a moment before replying, and his gaze wandered over the jungle-weed that was spilling over Scrivener's fences, springing up all over the place. Then he looked back at his companion, and his sheriff's gaze was steady and penetrating.

"If I'd been on my own when I heard it," he said, "I guess I'd be doubting my memory by now. You can't really remember a sound, can you Doc? Not if you only hear it

187

once, for a short space. It's not as if a scream were music, is it? You have no clues to help you reconstruct it. But when I heard that scream, Doc, I looked up—and what I looked at was you. I saw you hear it, and I knew that what you heard was just as shocking to you as it was to me. I can't make the scream sound again in my head, but I can picture your face, and I know that what we heard was something real, some- thing awful. I read it in your eyes, and that's what keeps me from doubting myself. So I know that you'll understand me when I say that only you and I know that there's something here that has to be figured out. I know that you'll understand me when I say that you're the one person I can trust to take my question seriously. The M.E. couldn't, you see. He just shrugged it off."

"What question?" Scrivener asked, forcing the words out of a mouth that had suddenly gone dry.

"The question that's nagging me. You see, I know that what you and I heard last night was a cry of pain—the cry of a man in absolute agony. And yet, the body my men found this morning hasn't a mark on it. Hell, there isn't even a bruise from where the poor kid fell over. It's like he was just *switched off.* So what I want to know, Doc—and what I'd like to ask your advice about—is this: what kind of pain can a boy have, to make him scream like that and to kill him stone dead, without leaving any sign at all on his body? I know you don't *know*, Doc, so don't bother to tell me that— but I also know that you're a scientist who's worked in hu- man biology, and a pretty smart guy all around. Give me some ideas, Doc—some possibilities."

The sheriff's eyes were frank and friendly; he really was asking for help from the one man who might understand him. He didn't suspect a thing. Scrivener was ashamed to find the anxiety easing out of him. There was no proof of any crime, no shadow of suspicion to darken his doorstep; Jim Alvey just wanted to talk, to express his unease. In that, he was ex- ceptional. Ninety-five million people had died within the borders of the USA during these last thirty years, and that was in a nation which had escaped relatively lightly. The boy's mother was the one who had the right attitude; people surrounded for such a long period by so much death couldn't afford to let grief prick them into demanding explanations and excuses. Death simply was; it was everywhere. Martha didn't leave any trail of horror where she went, or any pattern that would show up on a police computer. All the death certificates said "Heart Failure." What else could they say?

"Take your time, Doc," Alvey added, calling Scrivener's attention to the fact that he had made no attempt to reply. The scientist looked into the sheriff's eyes, and saw nothing there but patience. Alvey thought that he was thinking about it, and wasn't trying to rush him.

I could tell him now, Scrivener thought. *I could offer him the whole thing on a plate, couched as a hypothesis. Without accusing myself, without even implicating myself, I could lay it out for him. But what good would it do? The only way I can give him enough to justify shooting her down on sight would be to tell him everything, and even then...he's too decent a man. If he goes after her, she'll surely kill him. I can handle it myself. I can make her go away. That's all that's needed, and all that can be done without more lives being lost. I just have to make her go away.*

"Maybe the boy suffered some kind of fit," he said, although the hypocrisy tasted like ashes in his mouth. "Maybe the internal spasm which stopped his heart caused him great pain—something like angina but worse. Even after your heart stops, you still have oxygen in your brain for a little while—enough to let you feel, maybe enough to let you scream."

"People with heart attacks gasp," said Alvey. "They don't scream. They get short of breath, as if their lungs won't pump—in my experience, that is. Do you know different?"

"Not all attacks are alike," said Scrivener, weakly. "Maybe not the heart—maybe the brain. I know he didn't have a stroke, or the M.E. would have found a clot or evidence of the hemorrhage, but maybe something more like an epileptic fit—an electrical event, that left his motor nerves free to operate long enough to produce the scream." Silently, though, he said: *You already know the answers, Jim. You spoke the words yourself. Absolute agony. Pure pain and nothing else. No further cause in the poor kid's body.*

189

"Could it be somethin' we haven't seen before?" asked Alvey, not pushily, but as if he were groping for support. "Somethin' the M.E. didn't know to look for. Could it be somethin' left over from the last war—or the first shot in the next? Could it be somethin' cooked up in a lab, Doc? I know you've been out of the work for a while, but you'd know if somethin' like that were possible, wouldn't you?"

"Everything's possible, Jim," said Scrivener, softly. "Anything and everything that could kill or maim a man can come out of today's labs. Maybe the plague war isn't over. But if that's what it is, what can you or I do about it?"

Alvey didn't answer that for a moment or two. Then he stood up, replaced his hat, brushed his pants, and said: "I just wanted you to think about it, Doc. I still do. I want you to turn it over in your mind, and see if anything strikes you. I really would appreciate your advice, if you can think of any to offer. I don't know what we can do, but I wouldn't feel right if I just let this thing pass without tryin' to figure it out, even if it ain't really my business because there ain't really any crime. I'm not that kind of guy."

"I know," said Scrivener, softly, wishing that he weren't that kind of guy himself. He watched the sheriff walk away, and then he settled back in his own chair, waiting for the phone to ring.

* * * * * * *

The phone never did ring, and the sleepless night finally caught up with Scrivener. He nodded off in the chair, and when he finally caught himself up with a start and opened his eyes she was there, sitting in the sheriff's chair. He knew that she had taken up that position so that the table could be between them. She still had some talking to do.

"You didn't tell him, did you?" she said.

"No," he admitted.

"I knew you wouldn't. He'd never understand, would he? The best you could hope for is that he'd act without understanding—and that's not what you want, deep down. You don't want them to shoot me down. Not because you love me—you're not man enough for that. Not even because you

190

made me, because I'm your one and only Eve. It's just that you'd have to face them, then. You'd have to stand before them, and face the force of their uncomprehending hatred, the malice born of their stupid incapacity to understand. You can't stand the idea that they'd think of you as a fool, one more of the reckless madmen who brought the human race to the edge of annihilation."

"What do you want, Martha?" he demanded. "Why did you come here? Not, surely, because you love me? You must have given that up a long time ago."

"You underestimate the durability of female love," she said, mockingly. "It's only natural that those who allow doctors to exercise godlike powers over them should fall in love with their re-creators, isn't it? The sexual success of cosmetic engineers is legendary. And what you tried to do, you tried to do for the sake of love, didn't you? For the enhancement of human understanding? You wanted to move beyond good and evil—and you succeeded."

She was deliberately twisting words he had used. She knew exactly what he had meant when he had spoken of moving beyond good and evil. That had always been his aim. In the past, men had decided what was evil—hunger, thirst, pain, fear, sickness, misery—and had formed their notion of good negatively, as the relief or repair of evils. Almost all of the non-military applications of biotechnology had been directed towards that kind of good: the relief of hunger; the healing of disease; the alleviation of peril. He had wanted to go beyond that kind of corrective philosophy, in search of some notion of positive, creative good. His ambition had been to improve the quality of human life, to transcend the legacy of the natural, to add to human powers of communication, understanding and love. Everything she said was true, even though she was mocking him. Her very existence—and the killing habit which she claimed as her "nature"—was the greatest mockery of all.

"What do you want, Martha?" he said, again.

"I want you to be with me," she said, simply. "I'm lonely. You have no idea how lonely I am. I need you, Paul. That's all there is to it."

He looked into her eyes, as he had earlier looked into Alvey's. The lamp above the table cast its light at the familiar angle, throwing unkind shadows across her lined face. She was still handsome, after a fashion, but age had made its indelible mark. Why couldn't fate have decided that she be counted among the casualties of the long war? Why had *she* survived, when so many innocents had perished? Why had he?

"How many people have you killed, Martha?" he asked.

"I didn't keep count," she said, flatly.

"You don't have to do it. You're a human being—a *moral* being. You have a choice."

"What the fuck do you know about it?" she demanded. "You don't know. You can't know. Do you think a junkie has any real choice about grabbing his next fix? Do you think a torture-victim has any real choice about answering questions? And that's just crude conditioning—answer or else. That's just pain as blunt instrument. What happens inside me is right inside the fucking brain, Paul. It's the addiction circuit itself that's activated by direct stimulation. Even those rats with electrodes pouring shocks into their pleasure centers were just beating themselves over the head with rough-hewn bricks compared to the precision and purity of what you gave me. You have no idea what *good* really means, Dr. Scrivener, for all your talk about accentuating the positive and eliminating the negative. You have no idea what pleasure is: pure, unadulterated, perfect pleasure. Sure I have a choice, Dr. Scrivener. It's the fact that I have a choice which makes me choose pleasure, because I'm the only fucking human being on the surface of the planet who *can* choose pleasure. Nobody who had the choice could ever choose anything different, because that's what choice is: the chance to go for the best, the chance to grab what's really worth having."

"And even then," he said, when it was clear that she had finished, "it's not enough. Even though you have what you have, you want something more."

"Yes," she answered, flatly. "I want more. I want... sympathy. I want love. Ordinary, everyday companionship. Even though I have the other thing, I still have to live in the world.

I'm not a monster, Paul—I'm a human being. As you keep reminding me, I'm a human being."

"Why me?" he asked, hollowly. It was a stupid question.

"Because you're the only one who understands," she said, her voice half-way between innocence and bleakness. "You're the only one who understands who I am. Nobody else ever has, or ever could. When I tried to explain, even to the special ones...I had to kill them, Paul. I had to."

"And if I won't be understanding," he said, "you've decided to kill me too, haven't you?"

"I wouldn't really do that," she told him, although the lie was quite transparent. "I'd never harm you. But you have to come with me. You have to. I can't go on without you."

And I can't go on at all, he thought, miserably. *I don't know why I ever thought I could. Even if you'd disappeared, the way I wanted you to. Even if you'd died, the way you ought to have done. How could I just...go on?*

He reached across the table with both arms, palms forward and fingers splayed.

"All right, Martha," he said, quietly. "Let's see how much choice you have."

She rose to the challenge nobly. She folded her fingers around his, and their palms touched, face to face. They looked into one another's lamp-lit eyes, and she really wasn't going to make a move. She really was opening out to him, offering her heart. She really was as lonely as that.

Her scream echoed in his ears for a little longer than the couple of seconds it lasted, but it died away. As Jim Alvey had observed, it wasn't easy to remember sounds of that outlandish character. The human mind simply wasn't equipped for imaging such things—but the sight of her astonished eyes lingered much, much longer. The visual imagination is so much more apt than the auditory, so much more responsive to facial expression.

He tried to figure out what he felt, but it wasn't easy. It was all so unexpected. For the moment, it was pure sensation, which might be negotiated into joy, or exultation, or horror—maybe even terror.

He could still see her face when he finally realized that he was not alone, and that Sheriff Alvey had already drawn his gun.

* * * * * * *

"Where were you?" Scrivener asked.

"Right out there in the jungle-weed," said Alvey. "I saw the woman headed up this way and followed her."

"You had a hunch," said Scrivener, wondering why he was being sarcastic.

"I had a little more than a hunch," said Alvey. "But not enough. I wish I'd had more. I wish she'd stayed away, until you'd thought it over. Tomorrow, you'd have told me everything I wanted to know, wouldn't you?"

"There isn't a mark on her," Scrivener pointed out. "Even though you saw us, even though you heard her scream, you have no evidence that any crime has been committed. All that happened was that we held hands for a few moments, and then she dropped dead. Even if everyone were to accept that she screamed in pain, that wouldn't prove a thing. As I suggested to you earlier, the only explanation anybody could accept is that she had some kind of electrical storm in her brain—some kind of fit. There's nothing suspicious about my being on the scene, given that I have the perfect alibi for the moment of the other death. Anyway, what do you have that's more than a hunch?"

"I looked at you right after we heard the other scream," said the sheriff. "What I saw in your face then...it wasn't just shock. It was recognition. You weren't puzzled, Doc. The moment you heard that sound, even though it was like nothing on earth, you knew what it was. You'd heard it before."

"That's not evidence," said Scrivener, dismissively. "If you took that into any court of law in the land you'd be laughed right out of it."

"I know that," said Alvey, whose own expression still looked strangely amiable. His big dark eyes seemed as frank and guileless as they always had. "That's why I figured I had to take it slowly, step by step. I kinda figured on worming it out of you by stealthy persuasion. I think you'd have been ready to trust me with the story, given time. Pity the lady was in such a hurry. She did kill the boy, I suppose?"

Scrivener nodded mechanically. Alvey still had his gun in his hand, and he was still standing up—not that there was anywhere for him to sit down, given that there was a body in his chair.

"Did you hear what we were saying?" asked the doctor.

"Most of it," said Alvey, "but I have to say that I couldn't make much sense out of what I heard. I already knew she'd done it a lot more times, even though none of it showed up on the police computer."

"What did you check out? Medical records?"

Alvey shook his head. "Too much ordinary heart failure to show up the pattern. I had to check with the State University. Did you know that the Archivist there has programs that sort and store data from every newspaper in the world? Helluva thing—awesome amounts of information, and all cross-correlated, if you only know what to ask. Nobody had ever asked before, but it was in there right enough. Screams in the night usually get reported somewhere around the bottom of page five even in local papers, and they only get promoted to page two if someone links them to a mysterious death, just so long as there's no evidence of a crime—but they do get reported. Enough, anyhow. I was able to confirm that our little incident was by no means the only one—and that the first ones on record happened up in Canada, in Toronto. You worked up in Toronto, didn't you, Doc? You were there when the whole thing started, weren't you?"

"You knew this when you came to see me this evening?" asked Scrivener.

Alvey nodded.

"Stealthy persuasion," the doctor quoted. "You surely have a flair for the key phrase, Jim. Stealthy persuasion. Absolute agony."

"I'm not sure we have time for stealthy persuasion any longer," said the sheriff. "I'm asking you right out, Doc—what the fuck is going on here? I know I just saw you commit a murder, but I still can't figure out how or why."

"Aren't you supposed to read me my rights, so that whatever I say can be used against me? Don't you get into procedural difficulties when you come to court if you don't do that?"

"I'm askin' you as one friend to another, Doc. I just want to know what's happenin' here. Just now, I'm not thinking about makin' a case."

For thirteen years Scrivener had found himself unable to speak. Now, with Martha lying there, stone dead, he found at last that it was impossible to remain silent.

"It was an experiment," he said. "Have you ever wondered what it might be like really to get in contact with someone else? To be able to share your feelings, maybe even your thoughts?"

"I guess," said Alvey. "You mean telepathy—something like that?"

"Telepathy's just a plausible impossibility," said Scrivener. "Because we 'hear' our own thoughts, as if they were words spoken in the private spaces of our mind, it seems plausible that someone else might be able to listen in—but it isn't like that really. Without an actual connection of some kind—a physical connection—there's no way the information can get across. Even radio waves need a transmitter and a receiver adapted to their task. But we have technologies now that seemed to me to offer the chance of making such a connection. We have ways of persuading damaged nerve-tissue to regenerate, and it only requires a change of perspective to turn those techniques to the further purpose of making our nervous systems more elaborate. I operated on Martha's left hand, restructuring the superficial tissues so that her nerve-cells could extend filaments through the epidermis— and then through the epidermis of any hand that was touching hers, to link up with the nerves in the other hand. I gave her the ability to form an actual multi-synaptic interface between her nervous system and that of another person.

"I didn't expect miracles to follow the formation of such a bridge, of course. But once it was in place, I thought there was a chance that the two people so linked might be able to train themselves up, to find some way of exchanging information. I thought that there must be a possibility of making the bridge functional, of actually transferring experience of some kind directly from one system to the other. I assumed that in the beginning it would only be very primitive sensations, but that in the fullness of time Martha and the passive volunteers might cultivate new facilities and new aptitudes. I asked them to try hard for any possible effect, just to make sure the cross-stimulation was possible.

"Maybe I should have stopped when the early results were all to do with pain, but I didn't. I thought—hoped, at least—that the pain was just a matter of teething troubles, that we'd get past it. Instead...well, maybe the trick that Martha learned wasn't the only one that was there to be learned. Maybe it was just a fluke of ill-fortune. On the other hand, maybe there's a very good reason why natural selection didn't give us nerves that could extend themselves to that kind of communication. All that Martha learned was how to increase the pain sensations, and restrict them to the passive partner. While she learned it, she was also hooking her new skills up to certain circuits in her hind brain—the circuits that generate the physical rewards we construe as pleasure. By the time I cut off the experiments in the lab it was already too late—she was conducting experiments of her own. When she rang me to report her 'results' I knew how badly it had all gone wrong.

"I was scared, and bitterly disappointed. I should have stayed, revealed my hideous failure to the world, faced the music...but I didn't. I quit. I retired. I came down here. Martha had already disappeared...having discovered that the greatest pleasure of all, the purest pleasure that life has to offer—her life, at any rate—is that to be obtained by linking up one nervous system to another, and flooding the passive system with pure pain.

"'Absolute agony' is absolutely right, Jim. That's what does it. What it must feel like to the victim you can't possibly imagine. All the pain you've ever felt is a localized response to injury. What Martha could do went way beyond that. Way beyond. They died of it—shock, followed by brain death. The heart failure is secondary, I think—an effect rather than a cause. The only symptom is the scream. For Martha, that self-same shock of connection was pure pleasure. Again, you can't really imagine that, Jim, because all the pleasure you've ever felt is moderated, muffled, half-hearted, no matter how intense it seemed. Martha was the ultimate sadist, Jim. Her infinite pleasure was the infinite pain of her victims. Maybe it could have been different...maybe some-one else, using exactly the same physiological apparatus, could have become something infinitely better. But how could we possibly dare to try, knowing that the risk was there of creating another Martha...perhaps hundreds of Mar-thas? How could we ever dare to make connections, knowing what they might lead to?"

"How did she come to be the volunteer, Dr. Scrivener?" asked Alvey, quietly. "How did you choose her?"

"She was my wife," said Scrivener. "She'd been my lab assistant for years, but by the time I performed the operation, she was my wife."

"Who operated on *you*, Doc?" he asked. "Who gave you the power?"

Scrivener was mildly surprised by that one. "When I say 'operation'," he said, "I'm not talking about scalpels. It was all quite bloodless—and painless. I didn't need anybody else. I did the operation myself, after Martha walked out but be-fore I found out to what extremes she'd gone on her own be-half. I had to stop my own investigations after that, you see. Because of everything I said just now. How could I carry on, knowing what a risk there was? I daren't use what I'd given myself, in case I became like her."

"But you were strong enough to kill her," Alvey pointed out. "When it came to a contest, you won."

"That wasn't a contest," Scrivener told him. "I took her by surprise. She wasn't expecting it. She only wanted to hold my hand. I wasn't even sure that I could do it—I only knew I had to try."

Alvey's gaze flicked back to the dead woman. Scrivener followed the direction of the sheriff's stare. Martha looked so very peaceful, not at all the way someone who had died of absolute agony ought to look.

"What now, Jim?" said Scrivener. "Are you going to shoot me down like a rabid dog? Maybe you want me to write it all down first, so you can show it to the tribunal when you have to explain it."

"I don't think that'll be necessary," said the sheriff. "All I want is that you should tell your story. It isn't up to me whether you're charged with murder, or anything else. I just want the facts on record so that the proper authorities can make up their minds."

"That's very big of you, Jim," said Scrivener. "But I'll bet you're not willing to put that gun back in its holster and shake me by the hand. Now that you know I'm a monster, you'll never trust me again—and nor will anyone else. From now on, I've lost my place—not just in Romilly but in the whole human world."

"No, Doc," said Alvey, calmly. "It ain't like that. I spent a lot of time sitting here with you, talkin' an' playin' chess an' all. The folk down the hill still call you an outsider, but you're the best friend I got. I pride myself on bein' a good judge of character, an' I still believe you'd have told me everythin', given a little stealthy coaxin'. I'll put my gun away now, an' we can walk down the hill together, just like we have a dozen times before."

"Thanks, Jim," said the doctor, sincerely. "You're right, of course. I'm still a human being. I can make my own choices."

* * * * * * *

A full twenty minutes had passed before the sheriff's scream rent the air. He was a big man, and he had big lungs. He could be heard half way across the county, but even the people who were pretty close eventually persuaded themselves that it was just some kind of animal hollering. These days, they told themselves—what with the damn scientists throwing evolution into a higher gear in the desperate attempt to stop the world going to hell in a hand basket—you never could tell what would turn up next. When they found Jim Alvey's body the next morning they naturally fell to wondering all over again, but when they'd talked it out between themselves there was nothing much to be done.

After all, the guy hadn't a mark on him—and even though he was the sheriff, he hadn't an enemy in the world.

www.ingramcontent.com/pod-product-compliance
Lightning Source LLC
Chambersburg PA
CBHW032007240626
47153CB00003B/1158